Not If I Kill You First

Lucky Goldman

Dedication

This book is dedicated to the fight against corruption worldwide.

Acknowledgments

I wish to acknowledge my wife-Yetunde Mary, who was the first to read through the original manuscript and offered constructive criticisms every now and then.

To my children: Obehioya, Adesua, Ann Marie, Elinor and Julia, who were always pushing me to write the next page.

And Sir Shamson Lisa, for his many positive insights after going through the manuscript.

About the Author

Lucky Goldman is an economist who divides his time between reading and researching world economies. A dedicated family man with five children, Goldman has investigated corruption and corrupt practices in Nigeria and has gone ahead to write academic papers on the subject. His free time is invested in analyzing Western economic policies and their impact on third-world economies. Such free time also affords him the opportunity to spend time with his lovely wife and children.

Chapter One

It was a cold Monday morning in the city of Lagos, but Banji Smith couldn't care less. He had plans for the day, starting with making a long-distance call to a friend in Stockholm. Just as he was about to dial his friend's number, his mobile phone buzzed. He was startled. He wasn't expecting an early morning call. He stared at his phone to see who the caller was, but the caller ID was hidden. He frowned. This was not strange in his line of duty, as callers may opt to hide their identities, for whatever reason.

Smith stared at the phone for a couple of seconds before hitting the answer button.

"Is this Mr. Banji Smith?" A tense voice asked.

"This is Banji Smith," Smith replied calmly. "And who's this?" The caller hesitated. Smith waited.

It was important for Smith to know or at least have an idea of the person he was dealing with.

"My name is not important for now, but we could meet, if it's okay by you."

"I have no problem meeting you, but I must be sure it's worth my time. Why do you want to meet me?

There was no immediate response. Smith listened and could hear the man breathing evenly over the phone. It was obvious that the man was trying to make up his mind as to whether to continue the conversation or not.

"I have a dossier I want you to take a look at." The man said slowly.

"A dossier? What dossier?" Smith queried.

"It's the Halliburton Dossier. It holds a lot of vital information, which I believe will help nail some of the guys involved in the Halliburton bribery scandal.

Smith felt a wave of excitement run through his spine. He managed to remain calm. Is this caller who is refusing to give his name, for real? Or is he just playing him for a sucker?

Realizing quickly that he had nothing to lose by playing along, Smith asked, calmly. "Where can I meet you?"

"I would appreciate it if you could make it to the Marina area of Lagos by nine-thirty this morning. Find your way to Madam Tinubu Square. I will give you another call at around that time to state the actual meeting location."

"I will be at Madam Tinubu Square by nine-thirty," Smith said without hesitation. "And I will be expecting your call."

The call ended with Smith staring at the phone one last time, thinking. This nameless and faceless individual he had just had an interaction with, claimed to have a dossier, containing information on the Halliburton bribery scandal. Who is this man, and is he making a bogus claim?

Smith was trying hard not to think of the catastrophic fallouts that could result from opening a dossier on the Halliburton bribery scandal. It could only be likened to opening a can of worms. The worms, in this case, would be powerful individuals and their corrupt deeds. Individuals with the wherewithal to fight back and often choosing to fight dirty. Smith took a deep breath, then tucked the phone away in his pocket. He got to his feet, and yeaned noisily before strolling to the kitchen, to prepare himself a quick breakfast.

Finishing a cup of coffee after breakfast, Smith, not one to be late for an appointment, hurried out of his apartment. He was not to realize that he had completely forgotten the phone call he had planned to make to his friend, in far-away Stockholm.

*****

The operational office of the Department of State Services (DSS) was located in the Ikoyi district of the city of Lagos. It was a three-storey building that is often mistaken for a residential building because of its exterior, which was designed with a view to diverting attention from the building. It was here that security operatives gathered daily to identify, analyze, and prevent any security threat to the Nigerian State. Threats ranging from terrorism, espionage, economic crimes of national dimension and many more are first referred to the DSS, which may then co-opt other security agencies if it deems it necessary. It was also here, that certain functions, not specified in the "book," are assigned to operatives under the guise of "the national interests."

When Victor Edobor, head of the national financial fraud unit walked into his office on this Monday morning, he wasn't expecting anything out of the ordinary. It was expected to be a quiet morning with the normal Monday meetings. So, he allowed himself the leisure of thinking about the burden of family life. The thought of the one person he disliked the most popped up instantly- his father-in-law. It was a thought he would rather hide away, deep down the bottom of his heart, if he could help it, but he just couldn't.

He started to think of his wife's father and how much he disliked the man and, for good reasons, too. He hated the fact that he often pretended to his wife that all was well between him and her father, when, in fact, the hatred between the two men was mutual. He selected a black pen from the four pens on his desk and in front of him, holding it tightly between his fingers. He thought of his wife, then his father-in-law whom he believed was constantly trying to come between him and his wife. His hand moved towards his mouth until the tail end of the pen was in his mouth. He bit down hard.

Why won't this man simply let them be, after many years of marriage? And to make matters worse, the man was constantly trying to impress their four children with his "overly good" grandfather attitude.

"Grandfather, indeed!" Edobor said out loud.

Grandchildren rarely give a damn about their grandparents, if not for the flow of gift items from grandparents, which Edobor considers as bribes meant to buy the attention of the grandkids.

Edobor wondered as to why it was so difficult for grandparents to see that their grandchildren's love for them, in many cases, was superficial and defined along a narrow scope of selfishness. One day, he too was going to be a grandpa, but he was certain that he wasn't going to allow any grandchild to play him for a fool, ever. He was too smart and too knowledgeable for that crap.

He gazed at the picture of his wife, which he had placed at the right-hand angle of his desk, and grimaced. Why can't his wife just accept the fact that he wasn't ever going to be truly able to love her father, the way she wanted him to? He hated the old man's guts and vice versa. Fair enough. He looked away as the thought hit him that his wife, an only child, was super close to her father, the first man in her life. Edobor almost felt sorry for his wife-Bolanle, at the realization of the precarious situation she finds herself in. She was a brave woman, who was doing her best to manage the relationship between the two men in her life. Two men who hate each other's gut, two men she loves dearly.

The phone began to ring. Edobor reached for the phone, as a smile crossed his face. He was somehow glad that the phone rang at that exact moment, to force him back to the present.

He picked up the phone. "Victor,"

It was a female voice and one Edobor will never fail to react to. It was the voice of Jessica Olaniyi, Secretary to the deputy director of the DSS Shola Davies. This could only mean one thing. Something was bothering the deputy director. When this happens,

Jessica makes a call, and agents run around, to fix that "something".

"Yes." There was no need for compliments.

"The deputy director wants to see you today after lunch. Shall we say twelve-fifty?"

It was not a question, and Edobor was no fool to assume it was. The meeting time was scheduled for twelve-fifty, and there was absolutely nothing Edobor could do to change the time.

"I will be there for the meeting."

"A car will be waiting to pick you up from there by twelve o'clock,"

"I can drive over myself…."

"You don't have to." The call ended abruptly.

Edobor held the phone to his ears for a couple of seconds, before dropping it. Thereafter, he picked up the black pen once more and wrote down the meeting time. This call could only mean that his day was about to get very busy.

He dropped the pen, and his mind drifted to Deputy Director Shola Davies, a tough man who is well respected for his ability to plan and organize men to execute even the most daring operations. Even the director of the DSS respects him as his trusted right-hand man. The deputy director was reputed to have the ability to read through men and know, almost with certainty, what such men were thinking. On the contrary, it was almost impossible to guess what Davies was thinking, not when his face was almost, always emotionless.

What could possibly be troubling the deputy director? Edobor wondered. He decided not to brainstorm on the matter since it would only end up being an exercise in futility. Well, a meeting has been scheduled, and the answers to his questions will be provided at the meeting. He was conscious of the fact that the deputy director only gives out information on a need-to-know basis. If you don't need such information to properly execute your mission, he wasn't obliged to share such information. It would amount to a waste of time to do that. He was far too busy for that. And far too secretive. This creates a kind of myth about him that makes even the hardest agent play the catch-up game, during meetings with the deputy director. He was a man of high integrity and a no-nonsense character, driven only by the love of his country, as far as everyone in the agency was concerned.

*****

Banji Smith drove his Toyota Camry slowly through the ever-busy Lagos Broad Street. It was five minutes past nine in the morning, and the street was beginning to get busy, with both human and vehicular traffic. He took a right turn, drove a few minutes, and then turned left onto a road that would take him straight to Madam Tinubu Square.

He arrived at Madam Tinubu Square and began scanning the place, looking for a place to park. Unable to find a parking space, Smith continued to drive ahead, away from the big shopping mall in the center of the square. He spotted a parking space some hundred meters from the shopping mall and quickly maneuvered his car, into the space. He cut off the engine, then glanced at his wristwatch. The time was twenty-five minutes past nine. He waited in his car for the call that was to come.

At exactly nine-thirty, Smith's phone started to ring. The phone rang for a couple of seconds before he stabbed the green button with his index finger.

"Banji Smith on the line…"

"I am around the shopping mall. Where are you?"

"I couldn't find a parking spot, so I drove off, to park some hundred meters from the shopping mall. I am sitting in the car, a grey colored Toyota Camry. Just walk straight ahead. I am parked just before the State Library."

"I am walking down. I will be with you shortly."

Smith looked around his surroundings as if to reassure himself. The State Library was right across from him, and people were beginning to file in, as a security man stepped forward to open the gate. Smith observed a heavily pregnant woman, walking tiredly towards the library's gate. As he looked, the woman suddenly turned towards him. Their eyes locked. He bowed his head slowly towards the woman, a smile on his face. The woman smiled back before walking slowly through the gate.

He looked at the rear-view mirror, then the two side mirrors. His eyes, as if by its own volition, drifted back to the rearview. It was then that he saw a man in his late fifties, hurrying towards his car. The man was of average height and wearing a brown suit. He was carrying a briefcase in his right hand. As the man approached the car, Smith noticed that the man was looking over his shoulder as if someone or something was after him. He looked agitated. The man reached the passenger side of the car and stopped. He bent over to look at Smith, who turned his face towards him. They stared at each other for a couple of seconds before the man reached forward to open the passenger door. He entered the car quickly, then dropped the briefcase between his legs before closing the car door.

"Do you want me to drive, or do you want us to talk here?" Smith asked.

"You may as well drive around while we talk." The man replied.

Smith drove away from Madam Tinubu Square and headed towards Broad Street. He was alert, his eyes partially fixed on the rear-view mirror, trying to detect any tail. He drove around aimlessly for some ten minutes, before he was satisfied that no one was following them. Then he drove the car into the parking lot, opposite the Western House. He stopped the car, and turned off the engine, after which he turned towards the man sitting in the passenger's seat of his car and looking straight ahead.

"You wanted to see me, and you mentioned a dossier on Halliburton," Smith said calmly.

"That is correct and thanks for agreeing to meet with me."

"Can we start by you telling me who you are? Then, about the dossier and how you got access to it?"

The man shifted in his seat as if trying to shield himself from the questions. Then he turned his face away, looking out the car window. After a moment, he adjusted himself once more, then turned to face Smith.

"My name is Anthony Osaro," he hesitated. "I worked as a financial manager for Halliburton for ten years."

He looked around eagerly for no apparent reason. Smith waited patiently, allowing him to take his time.

"Ten years is a long time to work in any organization. In ten years, you get to see everything. You become an integral part of the organization, if you know what I mean."

Smith nodded but said nothing. He rested his back in a relaxed posture. His job, for now, was to encourage the man sitting next to him to keep talking.

Mr. Osaro looked Smith over, trying to reassure himself that he could trust him completely with his secret.

"In ten years, I saw the good, the bad, and the very ugly sides of the Halliburton empire. While the good and the bad may be taken for granted as with many other organizations, the ugly side is something that is truly ugly."

Smith perceived that the man sitting next to him was in deep emotional pains, evidenced when he mentioned the word "ugly."

He decided he needed to say something, to try and lessen the burden of guilt that the individual sitting across from him was carrying.

"Frankly speaking, ugly is a terrible word. I guess you found yourself entangled in the whole "shitty stuff" Halliburton was doing back then. You somehow blame yourself for not having the courage to do something about it, then."

"Not having the courage to do something about it back then, is a right way to put it. Again, if I had acted back then, the dossier I now have in my possession, may not have been created."

"Now, about the dossier? What's in it?" Smith asked. His face hardened.

"It contains most, if not all, the bribe monies that Halliburton paid out to Nigerian government officials as bribes. It also contains the names of who was paying what and who was receiving what, including dates of payments. The dossier was created from my dairy."

Smith couldn't help but notice that Anthony Osaro seemed a bit more relaxed, after naming the content of the dossier. It was like lifting a heavy load off his chest.

"Nigerian government officials are claiming that there was no bribe money paid to any officials…."

"They should tell that to the birds. I was there at Halliburton, and I can tell you categorically that millions of dollars were paid to government officials as bribes. Our corrupt system is what is preventing people from coming forward with the truth."

"You said you have the dossier, and we are here discussing it. What exactly do you want from me?" Smith asked.

Mr. Osaro looked at Smith, a sadistic smile on his face.

"I don't have the dossier here with me. It's in a safe place." The sadistic smile widened, then quickly disappeared. He continued, "I wanted to be sure that I could trust you absolutely, before handing it over to you,"

Smith understood. Osaro was right in keeping the file hidden, until he was sure that he was handing it over to someone worthy of it. The dossier was potentially a big deal.

"What do I want from you? He continued. "I want all those bastards responsible for milking this country, using Halliburton, to be punished. That should include those in the United States as well."

Smith took a deep breath, then looked Osaro straight in the eyes, trying to decipher if he was a patriot of some sort or simply an insane man, seeking vengeance. He couldn't be certain. One thing he was certain of, however, was that a dossier does exist, and if he gets his hand on it, he is going to do all within his power to fulfill Osaro's wish.

"Anthony, you are aware that some former officials of Halliburton have already pleaded guilty to bribery and corruption charges in the United States of America…”

“I am aware of that,” Osaro conceded. “These were small and middle-class officials. The big fishes are swimming free and enjoying their ill-gotten wealth. They are shielded from prosecution by both Republicans and Democrats alike.”

“Here in Nigeria, the officials are insisting that there was no bribe money of any sort paid by Halliburton.”

“This is the reason why my dossier is important. It will expose them all and their evil deeds.” Osaro said, pains written all over his face.

Smith watched as Osaro adjusted his tie, then took from his pocket a handkerchief with which he wiped his sweating face. Smith was now certain that he wasn’t dealing with an insane man. He was dealing with an intelligent man, a patriot, who was determined to bring all those who had hurt his country to reckoning.

“I suggest we meet again on Thursday,” Osaro continued. “You will get the dossier by then, I assure you.”

“Then we meet again on Thursday,” Smith said, indifferently.

Osaro adjusted his sitting position, he was now facing away from Smith. He cleared his throat, then took a deep breath.

“The ball will be in your court after you get the dossier. I trust that you are patriotic enough to follow the investigation to a logical conclusion. These people must be made to atone for their crimes.”

Smith said nothing but glanced at the rear-view mirror. His

mission this morning was to put a face to the mysterious caller and to establish that Anthony Osaro was not insane. These he had accomplished. His mind took the liberty of wandering off to Thursday when the dossier would be handed over to him.

"It will be your duty to go after them as soon as you receive the dossier," Osaro said, turning to face Smith once more. "I have done my part by compiling the dossier. Make them pay for what they did to your country- our country."

Anthony Osaro opened the car door abruptly, then reached for his briefcase.

"What time do we meet on Thursday and where?" Smith asked, startled at the sudden action of Osaro.

"The time will be four-thirty in the afternoon," Osaro replied as he wangled himself out of the car. "Everything will be ready by then, in a USB memory stick. The meeting will be at my office. The address will be communicated to you some forty-five minutes before the meeting."

This said, Osaro closed the car door. He turned around, moving his head slowly from left to right as he observed the surrounding areas. Satisfied that he had no immediate security concerns, he began to walk away from the car and from Smith, mingling quickly with the crowd.

It dawned on Smith that he was on to something big. If the dossier Osaro was promising to hand over to him on Thursday, contains the kind of information Osaro said it contained, then a scandal was inevitable. It was sure to be a scandal like never before seen in the history of Nigeria, meaning that heads will roll.

Smith sat in his car for a long time, playing out the different scenarios in his mind. He was jolted back to reality when a lady, pulling a huge dog, an Alsatian, shouted an obedient command to the dog. The dog ignored the command and began to pull the lady in the opposite direction, in pursuit of a cat. Smith wondered why such a beautiful but fragile-looking lady should own such a huge dog. He shook his head sadly, started his car, then looked closely to make sure the dog wasn't dragging the lady towards his exit route, before slowly driving out of the parking lot.

Chapter Two

Victor Edobor walked into the immaculately furnished office of deputy director Shola Davies at exactly twelve forty-eight. He was ushered in by an unsmiling Jessica Olaniyi who promptly stood aside, to let Edobor proceed towards the deputy director's desk. Although Edobor had his eyes zoomed on the deputy director, he couldn't help but notice how beautiful Jessica looked, in her beautifully colored red dress. Then his eyes roamed quickly around the office, taking in the décor that was as intimidating as the man occupying the office. The desk, the bookshelf, the Persian rug, and the sheer vastness of the office, were all designed to convey the message that the one occupying the office was truly important.

"Victor's here, Sir," Jessica announced.

Deputy Director Shola Davies straightened up, as if he just became aware of the intrusion of the two standing in front of him. He nodded his head, then glared at Edobor, who took a bow. His gaze shifted back to Jessica, then another nod. Jessica turned and walked out of the office, closing the door gently behind her.

"Have a seat." The deputy director said, his eyes locked on Edobor.

Edobor took the seat directly facing the deputy director. He knew from experience that the deputy director didn't expect any form of pleasantries, so none was volunteered. He also knew as a rule of thumb that agents meeting with the deputy director, were not at liberty to say a word until the deputy director started talking. So, he kept his peace and waited for his superior to begin.

"I want to take the liberty of assuming that you are familiar with the Halliburton scandal?" Davies began.

"I am, sir." Direct question, direct answer. Nothing more, nothing less.

"Your department worked the case and came up with all kinds of deductions. Inconclusive, in my opinion."

Edobor stared expressionlessly at the deputy director, not sure where he was heading with his line of reasoning.

"It saddens me that your effort led to no arrest, not even one." The deputy director said, looking genuinely pained.

"The Economic and Financial Crimes Commission (EFCC) took over the case following a directive from the Presidency. We were in the middle of the investigation when that happened, sir."

"That I know. Now tell me what I don't know." Davies said, looking menacingly at Edobor. "Would you've been able to make some arrest if you had pursued the case further?"

"I think so, sir."

"Don't fence with me, Victor. I asked you a direct question."

"There was enough evidence to point to that, sir. We were beginning to track the money paid into individual accounts." Edobor said calmly. "The jigsaw puzzle was beginning to fall into place, when the rug was pulled from under our feet by the president."

Deputy Director Davies turned his gaze away from Edobor momentarily. He reflected on Edobor's statement, briefly. When his gaze returned, his face appeared a lot more subtle.

"In my position, I hear a lot of things, you know," Davies said, almost in a whisper. "Sometimes, very valuable things and at other times, pure nonsense. It's part of my job, to decide what is valuable and what isn't from all that I hear."

Edobor stayed calm, waiting for what was to come. He knew that the deputy director was just now doing a preamble, the substance would come soon enough.

"I heard recently that a dossier is out there on the Halliburton scandal," Davies said, his unwavering eyes pinned on Edobor. "I heard also that a certain man who once worked with the company, compiled the dossier."

Edobor looked away, shifting unconsciously in his seat. He felt a surge of excitement run through his spine for no apparent reason. He had worked on this case before. He felt betrayed back then, when the case was closed abruptly and without any good reason. His team was on the verge of a breakthrough, when they were ordered to close the case. He recalled vividly that he had personally interviewed most of the suspects involved but none of them ever mentioned anything about a dossier.

"The man I heard, may be willing to come in with the dossier, if he can get past his trust issues. Like I said earlier, maybe this one information is valuable, and maybe, it's just pure nonsense."

"I am sure you have a plan to find this man, sir? Assuming this is valuable information."

"Of course, I do. You are the plan, Victor." Davies replied.

Edobor tried without success to shift his gaze away from the deputy director's hypnotizing gaze. He could feel Davies's eyes burning down on him.

"I want you to find this man and retrieve the dossier," Davies said, stabbing his index finger on the desk. "Put together a team for this assignment. Jessica will hand a file over to you containing all the information I have managed to gather, on how to find the man with the dossier."

"Do I have a choice?" Edobor asked.

"About what?"

"As to accepting this assignment or not."

"Absolutely not. I want you in on this job." Davies said.

The deputy director turned his head slightly to look at the wall clock. He raised an eyebrow.

"That will be all for now, Victor."

Edobor nodded his head. He got to his feet, took a bow, and started walking towards the door. He was halfway to the door, when the deputy director's voice reached him.

"Keep in mind, Victor, that failure is never an option."

Edobor turned to face the deputy director. It was not the first time he had heard these exact same words. Then, he addressed Davies.

"From my experience, sir, when the premise is right, the conclusion is often right." He paused, then continued. "The premise here is that you heard something. You said, sir, that some of the things you hear turn out to be valuable while others are not so valuable."

Deputy Director Davies gazed at Edobor, the way a predator would a prey. He was wondering where Edobor was going with his sermon.

"If your premise about the existence of a man and his dossier falls within the valuable things you hear, then the conclusion will be valuable as well. The conclusion in this case, sir, is that I will find the man and his dossier."

The deputy director lost his predatory instinct. He nodded his head slightly.

"That's fair enough."

Edobor bowed, then turned and started walking towards the door once more. The door opened, almost automatically as Edobor reached it.

Jessica was holding the door wide open as Edobor walked through. She closed the door behind her, to lead Edobor to her office, to hand the file over to him.

*****

During the drive back to his office, Victor Edobor sat in the back seat of the black Honda Accord car, his mind busy replaying all that transpired during the meeting with the deputy director. It occurred to him that the deputy director could, at this very moment, be on call with the Director of the DSS-Hamzat Abubakar, briefing him about the outcome of their meeting. That would automatically mean that the countdown to finding the mysterious man and his dossier has begun. He was so engrossed in his thoughts that he failed to notice the car had reached its destination. It was only when he noticed that the car was stationary, that he bothered to look out through the window. He got out of the car, nodded to the driver, and watched as the car sped off, disappearing around a bend.

Back in his office, Edobor immediately walked to his desk. He sat on the edge of the desk and then grabbed the intercom.

"Get agent Banji Smith to see me, ASAP."

"Immediately, sir." Adesua Jerome said.

"I will appreciate that," Edobor said, a sudden softening in his voice.

Adesua Jerome, the receptionist per excellence, had been with the agency for as long as Edobor could remember, preferring to remain a receptionist even when she could very easily have changed her job designation. She prizes herself in the knowledge that she has personally tutored virtually every other receptionist and front desk employee in the agency for as long as anyone could remember. This had earned her the nickname "Madam Secretary" and a lot of respect."

Edobor replaced the phone and then took the file Jessica had handed over to him. He glanced at the caption- "The Halliburton's web." He opened the file and began to read.

It wasn't until forty-five minutes later, when the intercom buzzed, that Edobor was forced to reluctantly drop the file. He reached forward and grabbed the phone.

"Banji Smith will be here to see you by five o'clock, sir." Adesua announced.

"Noted, thanks."

Edobor dropped the phone and glancing quickly at his wristwatch; he noted that he had about two hours to burn before the meeting. He took a deep breath, then turned his attention once more to the file, to continue reading.

*****

Chapter Three

The United States Embassy in Lagos was a beehive of activity on any given day. It wasn't uncommon to see people gathered in front of the embassy as early as five in the morning, waiting for visa interview appointments. The crowd usually arrived long before most of the embassy staff. To an independent observer, watching the crowd in front of the embassy and the seemingly relaxed postures of the security personnel standing behind the iron gates, security at the embassy appeared relaxed and could easily be taken for granted. However, this was the kind of conclusion that could get someone into serious trouble.

The strategic location of the embassy made it possible to position many surveillance cameras around the perimeter of the building. In addition, every security personnel wore a bodycam that continuously recorded activities around designated areas. Footages are then sent to a central office where they are screened continuously. It was here that any potential security breach is detected. An alert is then sent to security personnel stationed at the exact location, providing information on the nature of the "possible" security breach. The area is then processed immediately with utmost efficiency by a team of CIA-trained counter-terrorism experts.

Among the team of CIA-trained security experts was a man named Raymond Westland. At forty-five, Westland was still muscular and stood a little under six feet in height. He was the head of special operations at the U.S. embassy in Nigeria. Handsome in his own way, Westland sported a mustache and a well-kept beard that gave him a look of respectability. He seldom had more than a few things to say, preferring instead to listen. When he did speak, however, his few words carried unmatched authority and power. Deep inside though, Westland was cold, ruthless but rational. He was aware of the enormous power his position conferred on him, but he was equally aware that power was transient by its very nature.

Westland's handler back in the U.S. was a powerful businessman-turned-politician with enormous wealth and connections to get anything done. His present position as head of special operations overseeing covert operations in the sub-Saharan Africa region was made possible because his handler presented him as the best choice for the job. The job was as intriguing as it was challenging, often involving long meetings with U.S. security chiefs. Then, it was left to Westland to direct the affairs of men, as he often referred to it. He would make a phone call and then receive feedback shortly afterward to say, "cleared." This was a term used to notify him that a certain "enemy" or "troublemaker" for the United States was now lying dead somewhere. On a few occasions, Westland had calmly sat at his desk, with the computer in front of him, to watch the actual takedown of the so-called troublemakers. It was all in a day's job as head of special operations.

There was only one man capable of making Westland feel uneasy. That man was his handler, whom he privately referred to as

Mr. Red. His choice of the codename was necessitated by the fact that his handler was so powerful and so high up the political ladder that even the President of the United States would think twice before making a move against him, no matter the circumstances.

As Westland stepped into his office that morning, he was instantly overwhelmed by a sense of uneasiness for no apparent reason. He tried to shake it off, but the strange feeling persisted. Though it was just a feeling, experience told him that such feelings were not to be ignored, especially in his line of duty. As he closed the door behind him, a phone started to buzz somewhere in the office. It was a unique and customized ringtone, meaning that the call was from one of his many spies scattered all over. The uniqueness of the tone and the fact that "hello Nigeria!" was intertwined with it indicated it was a call from one of his spies in Nigeria. He closed the door behind him and walked over to a shelf to retrieve the phone.

He pressed the green button with his index finger and then pressed the phone to his ear. He knew that the person on the other end would wait for him to say something, a kind of reassurance before any information could be exchanged.

"Does the lion sleep tonight?" Westland asked.

This was one of the many codes Westland had perfected when communicating with his spies. If the lion sleeps tonight, it was an instant indication that all was well; otherwise, trouble was on the horizon.

He felt the person on the other end of the phone hesitate, deciding how best to respond to the question.

"No," replied the voice. "The lion does not sleep tonight."

"What troubles the lion?" Westland asked.

"The Halliburton bribery scandal." The voice was clear and assertive.

Westland felt a muscle twitch on his cheek. Odd, he thought. This matter was long dead, at least on the Nigerian side.

"I am listening."

"The President wants the case revisited." The informant paused.

"Go on."

"The DG has assigned Deputy Director Shola Davies to assemble a crack team for the investigation."

Westland took a deep breath as he realized that the information he had just received was a big deal. He had traveled this road before. That was four years ago when Halliburton was being investigated for corrupt practices, both in the United States and in Nigeria, simultaneously. He had had to pull all the strings at his disposal before he was able to "convince" the then President of Nigeria to abandon the investigation. He had managed to convince the President that the outcome of the investigation was likely to embarrass some very powerful individuals, both in Nigeria and in the United States. It had worked.

"Who is leading the investigation?"

"Victor Edobor. I think you are familiar with him from about four years ago."

"I remember him," Westland said. "I want every single detail on the case as it unfolds."

"Got it. I will keep you abreast of developments."

"Good." Westland disconnected the call.

*****

Westland stood still long after the call ended, the edge of the phone pressed against his lower lip. He was trying to figure out what his next course of action should be. Then, he reached a decision. He must notify Mr. Red of this development at once. It would be counterproductive not to consider the possibility that extra "muscle power" might be needed this time around. It was no secret to him that Mr. Red was one to always tuck away an ace card, which he could draw upon later as leverage, should the need arise.

His eyes drifted to the wall clock. It was four forty-five in the evening, Washington time. He had to make the call; a call he would most certainly have postponed if he had a choice, but he didn't have a choice. He felt his hands start to sweat. This was always the buildup to the inevitable call to Mr. Red. He walked over to a white cabinet, fetched a bottle of whiskey, and poured himself a generous quantity. Then, he replayed the information he had just received from his informant in his mind.

Mr. Red was a businessman and a political top dog back in the U.S. His real name was obviously not Mr. Red, but Westland couldn't care less about this. The nomenclature Westland had assigned to him serves as a reminder of who the "real" boss was. This had certain advantages as far as Westland was concerned. It served to remind him that Mr. Red had handpicked him as head of special operations and that he wasn't a man to be messed with. His unquestionable loyalty to Mr. Red allowed him to step on powerful toes—politicians and bureaucrats alike—without fear of backlash.

A one-time director of Halliburton, Mr. Red was the head of the organization when it was entangled in the multi-million-dollar bribery scandal in Nigeria in a bid to gain access to lucrative oil wells. The subsequent scandal and investigation that followed was an embarrassment that threatened Mr. Red's reputation. He pulled his weight, and his reputation survived. He was amazingly clever at covering his tracks with the help of people like Westland, who acted as his front man and helped clean up his many dirty tracks. In this case, Westland was instrumental in making sure that others took the fall on behalf of Mr. Red.

Westland finished the glass of whiskey. His hands had stopped sweating; the whiskey saw to it. He pulled open a desk drawer and retrieved another phone. This phone was secured—so secured it was nearly impossible to track, let alone bug. It was a phone used only in matters of utmost urgency. It gave him direct access to Mr. Red.

He dialed a number and waited.

Two rings and no pickup. Maybe Mr. Red was engaged with some state matters or something. He tried again, but no luck. He would wait for about an hour and then try again. He dropped the phone back into its holding place.

He was about to close the drawer when the phone buzzed, almost startling him.

Westland hurriedly picked up the phone. He quickly outlined the reason for the call, just as he had done for many years as a spy when reporting to a superior. Then he waited.

He could hear Mr. Red breathing evenly over the secured line, one that even the best spy agency in the world would find hard to track.

Silence.

It wasn't his place to break the silence. He knew Mr. Red was rapidly processing the information he had just received. His response would certainly come when he chose. When it did come, it would most likely be in the form of a cross-examination, followed by directives. He prepared himself.

"Is your informant trustworthy? If they're re-opening the case, are they doing it covertly? Do you have anything on the President that we can arm-twist him with?" Mr. Red asked in rapid succession.

"My informant is very credible, sir," Westland replied. He was relieved at the tone of Mr. Red. It would appear as if reason would prevail because of the obvious nature of the case.

"For now, the matter is being treated covertly. It's only a matter of time before one of the officials leaks it to the press." Westland added quickly.

"If they're treating it covertly for now, I suggest you ensure it stays that way for as long as it takes. Wouldn't be too difficult to do that in Nigeria, would it?"

"Not at all, sir."

"Do you have men ready in case we have to take action?"

"I could assemble men at a moment's notice, sir. I have men on ground."

"It could be a mess. This must be prevented at all costs."

"I agree, sir." Westland concurred.

"I didn't ask for your agreement!" Mr. Red snapped.

"Certainly not, sir."

"You are to create as many obstacles as you possibly can for them. The aim being to derail the investigation. No expense spared."

"Understood."

"The new President's anti-corruption posture and the re-opening of this case. A cause for urgent concern."

Westland didn't know if Mr. Red was asking a question or merely thinking aloud, so he said nothing, preferring instead to listen.

"Is there a cause for concern?" It was unmistakably a question this time.

"I would not underestimate the president or the new director general of the DSS, sir." Westland replied.

"A reason why you must be proactive in your countermeasures."

"I am on top of it, sir. I will do everything possible to derail the investigation."

"Yes, you will!"

The line went dead.

Westland put the phone away. The heat was on. He was sure that Mr. Red was, at this very moment, making phone calls to his many contacts, trying to dig up dirt on the new President of Nigeria.

Westland's sharp mind began to function again. There was no doubt in his mind that the investigation would turn into a major storm if he couldn't come up with a solid countermeasure. He was familiar with the man his informant had mentioned as leading the investigation, having dealt with him in the past. Westland had succeeded in frustrating the investigation the last time, and he intended to do so again. This was his goal. However, his sixth sense was telling him that it was going to be a different ball game this time around. Well, he had time on his side and could afford to wait for his opponents to make the next move. Their next move would kickstart things from his end.

*****

Shola Davies was excited, albeit cautiously, when Edobor walked into his office accompanied by Smith for a hurriedly arranged meeting. Jessica had earlier informed him that Edobor was requesting an urgent meeting regarding the newly assigned Halliburton case.

"There is an update on the Halliburton case. I would like to see the deputy director as soon as possible." Edobor had informed Jessica on the phone.

The meeting was fixed for the earliest time Jessica could squeeze into the deputy director's schedule — 4:30 p.m. The deputy director was supposed to be having his lunch around this time, but the urgency of the meeting made it impossible to think of food. A cup of warm coffee with some biscuits should suffice until the meeting was over. Afterward, the deputy director planned to go to his favorite restaurant for a late lunch. That is, assuming the meeting ended on a positive note.

When Jessica opened the door to usher Edobor in, the deputy director's eyes immediately fell on the younger man tagging behind Edobor. He was wearing blue jeans and a white T-shirt. He looked athletic and in good shape. He was careful enough to stand a shade behind Edobor, an indication, as far as the deputy director was concerned, that the younger man understood and respected authority.

Davies nodded at Jessica when their eyes locked. She took a few steps backward and then shut the door with the finality of an undertaker closing a coffin lid.

"Have a seat, gentlemen." Davies said, pointing to the seats in front of him.

"Banji Smith, sir," Edobor said, pointing at Smith. "He's familiar with the Halliburton case as a former member of the investigative team. He's the reason we are here today."

Davies glanced inquisitively at Smith. For all its worth, he was trying to figure out how the man sitting in front of him could possibly be the reason for the hurriedly scheduled meeting. He shifted his gaze back to Edobor.

"I am all ears." He said in a priestly manner.

Edobor rotated the office chair so that he was slightly facing Smith. He nodded his encouragement.

"I got a call on Monday from a man claiming to have a dossier on the Halliburton bribery case…" Smith began calmly.

"Make me understand it," Davies interjected. "This man called you out of the blue to inform you about his dossier on Halliburton?"

"That's correct, sir. According to him, he has everything on record and is willing to make it available to me."

"What a huge coincidence," Davies said, raising an eyebrow. Then he gazed intensely at Edobor before shifting his attention back to Smith. "A man called to inform you about a dossier just as we got the matching order to begin an investigation?"

Smith said nothing.

"Who is this man and what does he want?"

"His name is Anthony Osaro, and he was the financial manager at Halliburton during the period in question." Smith answered. "He wants nothing but to see the culprits brought to book."

"Good. Why is he trying to get his little secret across to us now, after all these years?"

"I believe he was waiting for the right moment, sir. I deduced this during my meeting with him." Smith replied.

Davies nodded slowly, a frown on his face.

"Do you believe this Anthony has in his possession the dossier he talked about?" Davies asked, a frown on his face.

"I would not confirm or deny its existence, sir." Smith replied, unwilling to commit himself.

Davies impatiently shifted his attention back to Edobor. He needed reassurance that Smith understood he was in the presence of the deputy director. Edobor quickly turned his head to glare at Smith.

"I spoke with Mr. Osaro on the phone, after which we met," Smith said calmly. "There were all indications that he was dead serious about the dossier, sir."

"Banji is to meet Anthony again on Thursday, sir," Edobor added quickly. "Anthony promised to hand over the dossier to Banji by then."

Davies grimaced.

"Where's the meeting point? Do you suppose we could pick him up during the meeting and make him talk?"

"That's not a very good idea, sir," Smith protested. "We can't force him to give us anything or make him cooperate with us at this stage until we are certain, that he has the dossier in his possession. Then we can make him an offer that will make his cooperation worthwhile."

"Banji is right, sir." Edobor said softly.

Davies turned his head towards Edobor once more. His fingers laced on top of his desk.

"Arresting Anthony under any guise would be tantamount to inviting the press to a feast. This could hamper our investigation and endanger Anthony as well." Edobor explained.

"Good. Go ahead and hold the meeting, Banji," Davies instructed. "We meet here on Friday morning for an update. Understood?"

"Absolutely, sir." Edobor replied.

The deputy director reached for a writing pad and flipped it open. He brought out a pen from his breast pocket and wrote something. Then he read what he had written, after which he carefully dropped the pen on top of the pad. He glared at the two men in front of him.

"That will be all for now, gentlemen."

"May I ask you a question, sir?" Smith asked.

"Go ahead." Davies muttered.

"Does the president have the political will to pursue the investigation to a logical conclusion?"

Edobor shifted uncomfortably in his seat. The question was totally unexpected. He kept his eyes focused on the deputy director, trying to read his body language. Smith, realizing that his question was causing some discomfort in the room, quickly added,

"Sir, the president is going to come under a great deal of pressure both from within and outside Nigeria to abandon this case."

"At this point in time, and for the record, I dare say without fear of contradiction that your question is neither significant nor relevant." Davies replied patiently.

Davies picked up his pen, examined it carefully, and then returned it to his breast pocket. He slowly pushed away the writing pad. Then he looked up.

"You have work to do, gentlemen. And I have work to do."

As if by automation, the door swung open. Jessica held the door open wide enough for Edobor, followed closely by Smith, to walk through. The time was 5:45, and the evening traffic was just beginning to build up.

Chapter Four

Shola Davies sat alone in his office long after the meeting had ended. He read through the notes he had made during the meeting and then added some footnotes. His source was dead right after all, as usual. As deputy director, Davies made sure he had men scattered all around, acting as a great pool of information for him. He preferred to refer to these men as sources rather than informants. As far as he was concerned, the term "informant" connotes some level of disdain and negativity, hence his preference for the term "source." The deputy director saw nothing wrong in arm-twisting some of these men to get the needed information out of them should the need arise.

Davies, as a matter of principle, was not one to threaten anybody directly. His body language was usually the culprit in this. His method was simply to ask for a favor in such a subtle manner that it gave the impression that the "source" had a choice in the matter. Each one of his sources, however, was wise enough to give him what he wanted. His style was usually cordial and civilized. A phone call would be made to arrange a lunch meeting, with a time frame provided for the meeting. Afterward, the source was allowed to pick the exact time for the meeting.

"A time that's convenient for you." Davies would always say.

He was deliberately throwing a lifeline, aiming to arouse a sense of importance in the source's psyche. The source then picked the exact time for the meeting without giving a second thought, to the fact that the time chosen was within the time frame created by the deputy director.

These sources were wise enough to appreciate the fact that Davies' seemingly polite demeanor was not a sign of weakness but rather a sign of strength. Even more so, his request for information, though made politely, was often done in such a way that the only possible outcome was to grant Davies his request. Davies' body language during such meetings was often a direct contrast to his sympathetic voice.

When the DG summoned Davies to his office to notify him that the President wanted the Halliburton case revisited, Davies knew right away that he needed to act fast. He had gone back to his office after the meeting and made several phone calls. The result of one of the calls was positive and pointed him to Steven Eze, a former senior official at Halliburton, who was said to be in the know.

His meeting with Steven Eze was as cordial as it could be. Davies explained to him that he needed information on the Halliburton bribery allegation. He spelled out how much he would appreciate any help Steven Eze could provide. Thereafter, he sympathetically explained the consequences of non-compliance, with all the consequences seemingly outside his realm of control.

Two days later, he received a call from Steven Eze informing him of the possible existence of a man with a dossier.

"It's all hearsay," Steven had said. "I'll talk to a couple of other guys and get back to you."

It was on the basis of this sketchy information from Steven Eze that Davies had summoned Edobor to kick-start the whole process. The virtue of patience, as far as Davies was concerned, was a hallmark of the vulture, not for people like him. Patience was nothing but a sheer waste of precious time, in Davies' own dictionary.

Davies was optimistic after learning that Smith was contacted by Anthony Osaro around the same time, he had commissioned Edobor to commence the investigation. This was a good sign, and all things being equal, this should be over fast enough, Davies thought. But things are not usually "equal" in most real-life situations, as Davies had come to realize. His thoughts were cut short when the office door opened abruptly.

Jessica let herself in, a seductive smile on her face. Davies stared, grinning from ear to ear.

Jessica locked the door behind her, then moved seductively towards Davies. She stopped halfway to where Davies was sitting. Their eyes locked. Her smile widened. She put her right thumb into her mouth and started sucking it while moving slowly towards Davies. She reached his table, then lifted her left leg to rest it on the table. She wasn't wearing any underwear. Davies gulped, staring wide eyes at the clean-shaven virginal.

Jessica removed the thumb from her mouth. She inserted her middle finger inside her virginal, letting out a gentle cry as she thrust even deeper. When she brought out her finger, she slowly put the wet finger into Davies' mouth. He loved it and sucked away eagerly. Then, Davies lifted himself halfway from his seat to reach for Jessica's virginal. He touched the clitoris, rubbing it tenderly. He could feel the virginal wet and slippery. This was the way he liked it.

Jessica slowly dropped her leg, stepping back teasingly. She waited a couple of seconds, gently rubbing her breast. Then she turned around and lifted her clothes to reveal her roundly shaped bottom. She bent over as if picking something from the floor. Davies gazed at the virginal from behind, trying hard to control the urge to dash towards Jessica.

When Davies couldn't control himself any longer, he got up and rushed towards the still bent over Jessica.

The command was soft but instructive.

"Eat my honey pot, baby!"

This was all Davies needed to pounce. He eats away at Jessica's wet virginal like he had never eaten before. As Jessica gently cried out from pleasure, Davies pushed his tongue deeper and deeper, making Jessica reach orgasm multiple times.

"Take me now!" Jessica pleaded eagerly. "I need your hard dick in my wet pussy, please!"

Davies was ready to go long before Jessica's plea. He hastily removed his clothes and then positioned Jessica properly. He penetrated her as deeply and as hard as he could.

Jessica's soft scream was music to Davies' ears. She began to slowly move her waist to the rhythm of Davies' pounding. Jessica screamed louder, but there was no stopping Davies. He held Jessica by the shoulders, forcing her backward and allowing him to penetrate ever deeper. He continues to pound Jessica relentlessly, stopping only when the two of them reached climax.

Davies was breathing heavily as he released his grip on Jessica. They both dropped to the floor, exhausted. Davies, a smile on his face, looked over at Jessica, who lay down beside him with her eyes closed. He could hear her breathing evenly. He reached over and kissed her on her forehead. She opened her eyes and smiled.

Jessica then turned sideward and grabbed Davies' soft penis. She started to massage it. Her smile widened as she tried to imagine how the now "relaxed" penis could have been the giver of so much pleasure. She adjusted herself to rest her head on Davies' chest. She felt herself dozing off, still holding on to Davies' penis.

*****

Davies lay on the floor beside Jessica, who had by then fallen asleep. He gently pulled her closer as his mind drifted down memory lane. He recalled the very first time he had sex with Jessica. It was a little over two years ago. He remembered it as vividly as if it were yesterday. They had both attended a five-day security summit in Johannesburg, South Africa. The summit, which kicked off on a Monday, ended on a Friday. A gala night immediately followed, as was customary with such summits, with plenty of food and wine to go around.

Davies had stayed until three o'clock in the morning before calling it a day. He had ordered a taxi to take him back to the Hilton Hotel, where he was a guest. As he waited outside for the taxi to arrive, Jessica suddenly emerged. The two of them subsequently boarded the taxi back to the hotel. Arriving at the hotel twenty-five minutes later, the pair staggered to the second floor, where they each had their own rooms. While Davies fumbled with the lock to Room 201, Jessica had no such problem with Room 203, which was directly facing Room 201. The two of them somehow ended up in Room 203. They woke up at 9:35 on that Saturday morning to find themselves together in bed in Room 203.

Jessica was the first to wake up and sleep-walked into the bathroom for a quick shower. She came out of the bathroom naked and was stunned to find Davies sitting on her bed, staring at her with wide eyes. The sight of Jessica standing in front of him; naked, was too much for Davies to resist. He stood up, walked rapidly to where Jessica stood still trying to process what was happening, and pulled her over to whisper something into her ear. Then, he picked her up and carried her to the bed. As soon as he started kissing her, Jessica responded passionately. They made love like wild animals.

Thoroughly exhausted afterward, they spent the rest of the day together in the hotel room, naked.

They left South Africa the next day on a Kenyan Airways flight back to Lagos, Nigeria. Jessica sat by the window and did everything possible to avoid talking with Davies, who sat one seat away from her. She was glad when another passenger appeared, brandishing her ticket and claiming the middle seat as her own. The flight was quiet and uneventful, with Jessica sleeping almost throughout the flight and Davies opting to read.

Arriving in Nigeria, two DSS official cars were already stationed, waiting to drive the pair to their respective destinations. While Davies boarded one of the cars, Jessica declined the offer to board the other, preferring instead to ride home with her husband, who was at the airport to pick her up.

"See you in the office on Wednesday." Davies murmured as he handed his bag to his aide.

"Absolutely. I should have a report ready by then." Jessica responded without making eye contact.

"Take your time. It's not too late if you hand in the report by Friday." Davies said, trying desperately to make eye contact with Jessica.

"I will keep that in mind, sir." Jessica said. She then looked Davies over and smiled.

Jessica picked up her bag and turned around. Her husband should be out there somewhere.

"You look astonishingly beautiful. Don't ever forget that." Davies whispered to her.

These were the exact same words Davies had whispered to her back in the hotel in far-away South Africa as she stood naked. She felt her nipples harden. It dawned on her then that she wouldn't object to a repeat of their sexual escapade. She smiled and walked quickly towards her husband, who was slowly jogging towards her.

Davies watched Jessica walk into her husband's embrace. He was quick to observe that Jessica's husband was tending towards the fat side, with a stomach that was becoming a bit heavy. It occurred to him that Jessica might not be getting the sexual satisfaction she needed from such a man. He turned and walked towards the waiting car. As he got into the car, he realized, for no apparent reason, that he was having an erection. He smiled a devilish smile as he realized that the sexual escapade with Jessica was not going to be a one-time thing.

Chapter Five

Banji Smith got out of bed at six forty-five with a slight headache. He didn't sleep much during the night. He recalled waking up at least three times to use the bathroom. This was unusual and unprecedented. He couldn't recall ever waking up that many times in a single night to use the bathroom. The Halliburton case and the forthcoming meeting with Anthony Osaro must be responsible for it, he reasoned.

He rubbed his chin steadily, then walked over to the window. He looked out at the street and observed that traffic was beginning to build up. He pulled the curtains apart to allow the early morning sunlight to find its way into the bedroom. Moments later, he opened the window and allowed himself the leisure of filling his lungs with fresh air. This helped to clear his head. After a couple of minutes of inhaling the fresh air, he took a deep breath, then shook his head twice, trying to ascertain whether the headache was still there. It wasn't. He shut the window and headed for the bathroom to take a quick shower.

Once out of the bathroom, he grabbed his clothes and hurriedly dressed. He checked himself in the standing mirror and was pleased with what he saw. Then, he walked to the reading table and pulled out a chair. He sat down and started going through his mobile phone to see if any voice messages had been left for him. None. Next, he went to his Facebook page to try and catch up on trends. There was nothing interesting to him. He gently dropped the phone. His mind shifted to Osaro and his phone call, then to Edobor and his phone call, and finally, to the meeting with Deputy Director Davies. Things were moving very fast, he thought to himself.

His meeting with Osaro was scheduled to take place much later in the day. By the end of the meeting, he should be in possession of the dossier, which could potentially burst open a can of worms that could hurt a lot of powerful people. And powerful people don't like getting hurt, not if they can do something about it.

Smith stared across the table at the TV stand, where his car key was dangling from a key holder. He stood up and walked over to retrieve the key. He checked himself once more in the mirror. He nodded at the image that stared back at him. He felt confident and optimistic.

He took a quick glance at his wristwatch and realized it was time for him to get going. He walked out, full of optimism. He had no way of knowing that this was going to be the longest day of his life.

*****

Smith got down to work the moment he arrived at the office. He started with a search through the database of the Halliburton file. The computer he was using was unusually slow, he noted. He wondered why. Then, he remembered. He was using a completely different model from the one he had back in his office. Edobor had requested that he move back to the operational headquarters of the

DSS temporarily due to the reopening of Halliburton's case. The office was small but well-ventilated, with posters of most-wanted persons hung on the four walls of the office.

Smith turned his attention to the computer, trying to figure out why it was so slow. It dawned on him that the file he was trying to access was much larger and that the computer was accessing it from a central system, which required a lot of screening. This realization helped a great deal in calming his nerves.

It wasn't until midday that Smith was satisfied, he had gotten all the vital information he needed from the database. He folded his hands behind his head and stared absent-mindedly at the computer. Something was not adding up in the database. What could that possibly be, he wondered. Then, it flashed through his mind. The names of many of the top executives of Halliburton, who were in a position to know something, were missing. Only a few names were mentioned—fewer names than his team had previously questioned. Was this an error of omission or commission? He was still pondering it when he heard a knock on the door.

Edobor opened the door and walked in. Smith nodded his head in salutation.

"I noticed that the names of many of the top officials who were on ground at the time are missing from this database. Is this an error or a deliberate act?" Smith asked as Edobor pulled a chair to sit in front of him.

"Your observation is correct. Many of the names were not included in the database."

"And why is that sir?" Smith asked calmly.

"Some of the names were those of foreign businessmen and some top U.S. politicians who happened to be stakeholders at Halliburton," Edobor said sadly. "Also missing are those of some Nigerian businessmen and their politician friends."

"These people pulled some strings, and we danced?" Smith asked, bewildered.

"The former Attorney General issued a directive to that effect with the approval of the President. We were to avoid a diplomatic row with the U.S. at all costs." Edobor said, a cynical smile on his face.

Smith noticed the smile and knew full well what it meant. It was a smile that spoke volumes.

"I understand, sir."

"I am assuming that your meeting with Anthony is risk-free?" Edobor said patiently. "A quick meeting at his office or whatever location he decides, he hands over the dossier, and that's it."

"It should be that easy, except if he develops a sudden heart attack and dies during the meeting." Smith said jokingly.

"We don't want that to happen. Today is not a good day to die."

Smith smiled. He looked Edobor over.

"Is anything bothering you, sir?"

"Not really. Just glad that fate has given us another opportunity to finish what we started."

"True, sir. It's an honor to be back working on this same case with you." Smith said proudly.

Edobor stood up from his seat. He was a busy man and took no delight in wasting precious time.

"Let me know as soon as you get a call from Anthony."

"Okay, sir. I will keep you posted."

Edobor turned and started walking towards the door. When he reached it, he stopped abruptly. He cleared his throat.

"This meeting with Anthony sounds all too easy if you ask me. I personally don't like it when things are this easy. My advice to you is simple: be on the alert. Don't take anything for granted during the meeting."

Edobor cleared his throat once more, then turned around to face Smith.

"Banji, Providence has given us a second shot at this case. We simply cannot afford to fail."

He gave Smith one last penetrating look before turning to the door. He pulled it open and stepped into the long corridor to walk back to his office.

*****

Lunch time came and went without anything out of the ordinary happening. Smith tried to busy himself with other issues as he waited for Osaro's call. Smith hated the waiting game. In his line of

49

duty, the waiting period was usually the longest and most difficult. He picked up a pen and paper and tried to write something. He knew what he wanted to write, but surprisingly, his mind couldn't focus enough for him to do it. The forthcoming meeting was clouding his thoughts. He picked up a copy of *The Guardian* newspaper from his desk and began to flip through the pages. He wasn't looking to read anything special; he just wanted something to keep his mind busy.

He flipped to the editorial page and saw an article on the withdrawal of U.S. troops from Iraq. Just as he started to read, the phone rang, startling him.

He hurriedly picked up the phone.

"Banji Smith."

"My office is on the fifth floor, Western House building. Office number 506." The unmistakable voice of Anthony Osaro announced.

"And the meeting's billed for four-thirty." Smith added.

"That's right, Banji. Please, come alone. Four-thirty on the dot. Is that clear?"

"I get it." Smith said dryly.

"Good." Osaro said before ending the call.

Smith glanced at his wristwatch. The time was 3:20. The drive to Western House should take about half an hour. This gave him enough time for a quick meeting with Edobor.

*****

Banji Smith sat in the driver's seat of his Toyota Camry, ready to go. He reached forward and adjusted the rearview mirror, then adjusted the side mirrors to the right angles. If there was one thing Smith enjoyed doing when driving, it was being able to observe other road users without the occupants of any of the cars detecting that they were being watched. It was something he had perfected over the years as a security measure.

Satisfied with the angles of the mirrors, Smith started the car and drove out of the parking lot. He made a left turn and navigated a narrow road before taking a right turn that would connect him to the main road leading to Broad Street. He drove for roughly eight minutes, then decided to turn right at the intersection. As the car began to slowly swerve to the right at the intersection, Smith suddenly changed his mind and decided to drive straight ahead instead. That was when he noticed a man on a motorbike, seemingly appearing from nowhere, driving rapidly towards him. He hated bike riders, especially the commercial ones in the city of Lagos, for their recklessness.

Smith kept driving at the pace of traffic. The bike rider drove through the intersection as if asking to be knocked down. Smith glanced quickly at the left-side mirror and noticed that the bike rider was beginning to reduce speed.

A relief.

The two cars between Smith and the bike rider took a left turn out of the main road. Smith continued to drive straight ahead. He glanced at the rearview mirror and noticed that the bike rider was once again speeding rapidly towards him. He reached a juncture and decided to make a right turn to connect to the road that would lead him to Western House. As he started to turn, he heard a skidding noise and then a crash. He quickly stepped on his brake as he felt the impact of the crash. He looked through the rearview mirror and caught a glimpse of the bike rider as he tried desperately to steady his bike after ramming it into Smith's car.

Smith switched off the car engine, slowly got out of the car, and walked to inspect the damage. The bespectacled bike rider lifted his head to stare at Smith, who was walking nonchalantly towards him.

"Mister man!" the bike rider roared in anger. "You should watch more carefully next time before making a turn."

Smith ignored him, choosing instead to inspect the extent of the damage done to his car. The right rear light was shattered. The bike rider continued to protest that the accident was Smith's fault, not his. After inspecting his car, Smith turned and stared at the bike for what seemed like an eternity. Then, he shifted his attention to the bike. He could see no major damage to it. Anger began to build up inside of him.

"I noticed how dangerously careless you were riding before the intersection," Smith said calmly, despite the anger that he felt towards the bike rider.

"You can't say that mister. I wasn't riding dangerously."

"I believe something is wrong with you upstairs," Smith interrupted. "You are obviously on some kind of drugs or something."

"Mister man, I no dey on drugs. Na you no look before you begin turn!" the bike rider protested in pidgin English.

Smith's anger reached a boiling point.

"Do you know what I am capable of doing to you?" he asked, his eyes red with fury.

The bike rider gasped at Smith in horror. He tried to speak but couldn't. Realizing that words had failed him, he banged his hand angrily on his bike several times in protest.

"I am going to arrest you and send you to jail where you belong. You will not regain your freedom until my car is fixed," Smith said angrily. "Also, I will notify the traffic authority to withdraw your permit. You are as reckless as they come."

This apparent threat drove the bike rider to near insanity. He suddenly started screaming and running around in a circle, hands raised above his head.

True to the nature of bike riders in the city of Lagos, other bike riders started to gather in droves at the scene of the accident in solidarity with one of their own. Seeing the owner of a Toyota Camry standing menacingly at the accident scene, the mass of bike riders reached one conclusion — the rich guy was out to intimidate one of their own. They weren't going to stand aside and do nothing. They gathered around the bike rider like chicks around a mother hen. In anguish, the bike rider went ahead and narrated to them how Smith had threatened to send him to jail and to have his driver's license withdrawn. The mob went completely crazy on hearing this and began using their bikes to block the road. They started singing and dancing all around in protest and solidarity with their colleague. The traffic build-up had begun.

It wasn't until a police patrol team arrived at the scene that some semblance of order was restored. The policemen disembarked from their van; guns drawn. As the policemen approached, the crowd of bike riders quickly rode away in different directions, leaving their lone colleague behind. Traffic began to flow steadily again.

The policemen went directly to Smith to check on his welfare. Smith introduced himself and explained what had transpired. The bike rider, seeing that the policemen were focusing their attention on Smith, decided to make a break for it. He got on his bike and was about to drive off when one of the policemen spotted him and instantly shouted a stop order. The bike rider, together with his bike, was subsequently bundled into the police patrol van to be driven to the police station.

It wasn't until Smith got back into his car that he remembered Anthony Osaro and his dossier. He glanced quickly at his wristwatch. The time was 5:00. He was thirty minutes late for the rendezvous.

"Shit," he screamed as he started the engine, engaged gear, and drove off rapidly. This time though, he wasn't minding the pace of the traffic.

Chapter Six

A lonely figure wandered upstairs towards the fifth floor of the Western House complex at twenty minutes past four. He was wearing a hat, positioned in such a way as to conceal part of his face. He had a mustache that only a keen observer would detect as fake. His left arm was paralyzed, slowing down his movement. He had difficulty climbing the stairs, but he continued to ascend.

When he reached the fifth floor, a lady held the entrance door open for him to pass through. He bowed and then lifted his hat slightly as a sign of gratitude. He continued down the corridor, moving slowly and occasionally lifting his head to check the office room numbers. Finally, he located office number 506. He stopped in front of the office and then turned to look down the long corridor for any sign of human traffic. The corridor was as silent as a graveyard. This did not, however, dissuade the lonely figure from bending down to tie his shoelaces and, using the opportunity, to listen and scan the corridor further.

Satisfied that he had the corridor all to himself, the lonely figure sprang up. He braced himself, then checked his wristwatch. It was two minutes before four-thirty. He waited, silently counting to twenty. By the time he glanced at his watch again, it was four-thirty on the dot. He took a deep breath, then knocked on the door to office number 506.

Anthony Osaro opened the door and almost had a heart attack. Standing in front of him was a ghostly figure, pointing a gun fitted with a silencer at his forehead. The figure took two quick steps forward, practically forcing Osaro to jump back despite being paralyzed with fear. The figure then closed the door softly behind him.

"You will do exactly as I say. Hesitate once, and I will kill you without hesitation." the figure said, almost in a whisper.

There was a moment of silence. The ghostly figure waited long enough for Osaro to fully grasp the consequence of even the slightest hesitation.

"I am here to collect the dossier. Please, hand it over." He sounded polite.

Osaro heard the word "dossier" and was still trying to understand what it meant when the figure in front of him reacted.

"The dossier, now!" The menacing voice had a tone of finality about it.

Osaro staggered to a desk to retrieve an envelope, which he waved with shaking hands towards the ghostly figure.

"Open the envelope and show me the contents."

Osaro obeyed without hesitation. It was all a bad dream, his mind kept telling him. It had to be. How else could he explain the fact that everything seemed to be moving so fast? It was unlike him not to have something to say, even in a very challenging situation.

Today, however, words just wouldn't flow. Fear had subdued that part of his attributes.

The figure took the USB stick from the envelope. He examined it cautiously.

"What's this?"

"This is the dossier. Saved in the USB," Osaro managed to mumble.

"Not in paper form?"

"No, please, I have it only in the USB."

The ghostly figure dragged Osaro to the computer.

"Put in your password, now!" he whispered.

Osaro took a small notepad from his desk, glanced quickly at the password he had written down, and typed it in. The computer came alive.

The ghostly figure violently pushed Osaro away from the computer.

"Empty everything in your pocket on the table," he ordered.

Osaro obeyed. It dawned on him that his hands were supposed to be up in the air. He hurriedly lifted both hands. This nightmare was starting to look real. He could feel himself and clearly hear the startup sound from his computer as it booted. And he could see the man in front of him, gun in hand.

Without warning, the ghostly figure stepped forward towards Osaro — left foot, right foot, halt. He lifted his gun and shot

Anthony Osaro in the head twice. Osaro collapsed to the ground. He was dead before he hit the floor.

The ghostly figure walked calmly to the computer. He inserted what looked like a disk into the computer and waited a couple of seconds before retrieving it. The computer went blank immediately, its memory completely wiped clean. Satisfied, the figure went through the items Osaro had emptied from his pockets. Nothing of importance. He quickly ransacked the drawers but found nothing of significance. He scanned the room for any hidden cameras; there were none.

He glanced at his wristwatch and noted that he had spent exactly twenty minutes, since walking into the building. Fair enough, he thought to himself. He walked to the door and listened. Silence.

He took one last look at Anthony Osaro's lifeless body before opening the door. Then he stepped into the corridor and into oblivion.

*****

Banji Smith arrived at the Western House complex at a quarter past five. He opted to use the stairs instead of the elevator and ran all the way up to the fifth floor. Once on the fifth floor, he quickly located room 506. He knocked on the door and waited. No one opened the door. He knocked again, this time a little harder. Still no response. He placed his ear against the door to listen but heard no movement from the inside.

Smith shook his head in anger and frustration. He had arrived too late for the meeting, and Osaro, who had obviously been disappointed, had left the office. This was not good.

"Damn it!" he screamed, banging his right fist against his palm.

He took a deep breath and tried to think. He had to get hold of Osaro one way or another and as soon as possible too. This was the only way to rectify the whole damn situation.

"Goddamn it to hell," he murmured.

He turned around to rest his full weight against the door. As he did, his elbow banged against the door handle. He turned around slowly and almost punched himself in the gut. Why didn't he try the door handle after knocking? He reached for the handle and turned it. To his surprise, the door opened. He stepped cautiously into the office, groped for the light switch, and turned it on. The first thing Smith noticed as soon as he switched on the light was that the office had been ransacked.

He pulled his gun and stood motionless, listening. It was total silence. He moved further into the office, his eyes quickly taking in everything. It wasn't until he looked down that he saw the lifeless body of Anthony Osaro. He was lying face-up, with blood gushing from his head. His eyes were wide open, staring emptily at the ceiling. The blood flowing from the wound had clotted on one side of his face, making it look like one of those gawky, ghostly figures from a horror movie.

Smith turned away in horror. He fumbled for his cell phone and called Edobor.

"Anthony has been shot dead, sir." Smith said without mincing words.

"What do you mean 'shot dead'?" Edobor asked, a note of urgency in his voice.

"I arrived at his office to find him dead, shot in the head." Smith answered.

"What are you talking about? Dead? How?" Edobor asked in frustration.

"Someone got here before me and shot him in the head."

"This is not looking good!" Edobor screamed.

Smith could almost feel the frustration in Edobor's voice. He remained silent and waited. It seemed like an eternity before he heard Edobor clear his throat.

"Today's not a good day to die, especially not for Anthony," Edobor said. "An ambulance is on the way. I'm on my way too, with the squad."

"Okay, sir." Smith said in a rather subdued voice.

Smith understood that the squad referred to the forensic team, whose job it was to comb the crime scene for any evidence. They were quite good at it, even though they sometimes overreached their boundaries. Combing a crime scene, as far as the squad was concerned, involved taking complete control of the scene and barring investigators from accessing it until the process was complete. Their painstaking work, though time-consuming, would often pay good dividends.

"The police will have to be informed, as murder falls within their jurisdiction," Edobor said calmly. "In the meantime, scan the scene for whatever pieces of evidence you can find before the squad and the police arrive to tear the place apart."

The moment the call ended; Smith walked backward to rest his back against the door. From his vantage point, he looked over the office, taking in as many details as he could. He was trying hard not to miss anything, no matter how trivial. His attention then turned to where Osaro's lifeless body lay.

He tried to imagine the exact spot the killer had been standing when the fatal shot was fired. It didn't take him long to figure it out. Walking over to the spot, Smith stood there with his eyes closed.

When he opened his eyes, he was almost certain he knew how the events leading to Osaro's death had been orchestrated. From where he was standing, he calculated that the killer would've had to raise his gun to take the head shot. Using his hands as an imaginary weapon, he pictured the exact position where Osaro must have been standing. Then he lifted his imaginary weapon and fired. The killer, he figured, would have been slightly shorter than his victim. He guessed correctly where the shell casing would have landed following the shot. His eyes locked onto the shell casing. The squad would have to process the scene further.

He returned once more to his motionless posture. As he was about to move towards the computer, his eyes quickly took in the items on the table. He figured that the killer had forced Osaro to empty his pockets before killing him. Ignoring the items, he walked over to the computer and bent forward to examine it closely. When he lifted his head from the computer, his eyes fell on a small notebook by the edge of the table. He hadn't noticed it before. He picked up the notebook and started checking each page. On the last page, Osaro had written "pw" in tiny letters in the top right-hand corner. Smith immediately saw it as an inscription that was likely a password of some sort. He quickly pressed the start button on the computer. He wanted to try the password.

The computer came up, displaying the name Anthony Osaro. No other features. Smith was taken aback. He tried again. Still nothing. He stood there thinking for a while, and then it occurred to him that whoever killed Osaro had tampered with the computer's memory. He didn't bother to turn off the computer; there was no need. The computer went blank on its own accord.

Smith turned his attention towards the door and listened. Loud voices and the sound of rapidly approaching footsteps told him that the office was about to be invaded by either the squad, the police, or both. Smith took a deep breath and waited for the invasion.

*****

Edobor was the first to walk through the door, followed by a team of forensic experts. The three ambulance nurses rushed towards the corpse as if their instincts had automatically directed them to it. Six policemen, led by a superintendent of police, forced their way in shortly after. The police superintendent stared at Smith suspiciously as he entered. He had been briefed and knew that Smith was the one who was supposed to meet with the deceased man before he was killed. His eyes shifted from Smith to the corpse and the nurses crowding around it. He walked over and spoke briefly with the nurses. The nurses then stepped aside, allowing two of the forensic team members to examine the body.

Edobor walked over to Smith, who had stepped aside as the men rushed into the office.

"This is how I found him, sir." Smith said.

Edobor nodded.

The police superintendent suddenly turned around and looked over at Smith, who was standing and talking with Edobor. He walked over to stand in front of Smith, staring him down and longing to place him under arrest. However, he knew this was never going to happen. The DSS would not stand for it.

"I am Police Superintendent Lekan Ayeni. I will be leading the investigation from the police side," Ayeni said. He was forty-two years old, slimly built, with dark hair that was beginning to recede at the front. His eyes were small but alive and penetrating; his mouth was full, and his nose short and blunt. He looked every bit the tough cop he was. He joined the police when he was only nineteen and had worked his way up to become a police superintendent.

He looked momentarily at Edobor as if seeking assurance that he could go ahead and question Smith. Edobor nodded his approval.

"I have a few preliminary questions for you, Mr…?"

"Banji Smith. I'm with the agency." Smith replied.

"You found the dead man, right?"

"Yes, I did."

"May I ask what time you arrived here to find him?"

"I got here at a quarter past five." Smith answered.

Edobor turned his head towards Smith. There was a discrepancy between the time Smith was supposed to meet Anthony Osaro and the time he claimed to have arrived to find him dead. Edobor realized then that Smith was yet to furnish him with details of what had happened. He hadn't expected the police to rush their team over to the crime scene so quickly. He had tried to convince the police to stay away until the DSS had combed the place but had been stonewalled by them.

"I want to assume that you booked a meeting with the deceased. Was the meeting booked for the time you said you arrived here…?"

"Superintendent Ayeni, that will be all for now," Edobor interrupted. "Let the forensic people do their job. We'll take it from there in our next meeting."

As if the scene had been rehearsed, the head of the forensic team stepped forward and asked everyone to exit the office except for the ambulance nurses.

Superintendent Ayeni's small eyes moved from Smith to Edobor, then back to Smith, who met his penetrating gaze. Ayeni nodded slowly before turning and storming out of the room.

"We need to talk." Edobor said to Smith as soon as the superintendent was out of earshot. He signaled for Smith to follow him as he headed for the exit door.

*****

Sometime around seven o'clock that Thursday evening, a lonely figure walked slowly towards a parked silver Mercedes-Benz. He was wearing a cowboy hat and dragging his left leg. He dragged himself to the car, opened the back door, and entered. He then reached for the seatbelt and fastened it without saying a word. The driver of the car looked straight ahead as if unaware that a passenger had entered his car. The lonely figure moved his head slowly from left to right, wanting to ascertain that no one had tailed him. Satisfied that he had covered his tracks, he took a deep breath and assumed a relaxed posture. The driver started the car and drove off into the night.

The driver was aware that the passenger seated in the back seat was no ordinary passenger. He had to be some special agent or a spy for the CIA. It wasn't as if it was any of his concern; after all, he too, was an employee of the U.S. intelligence community in Nigeria. His assignment that evening was simple enough. He was to pick up an individual and drive him from one location to another. He was under specific instruction not to attempt to engage the individual in any form of communication. As he drove the ghostly figure through the streets, he occasionally looked through his rearview mirror. This was not because he was interested in his passenger but because he was looking to make sure that he wasn't being followed. He couldn't, however, help noticing that the figure behind him had adjusted his hat in such a way as to make it impossible for him to get a glimpse of his face.

Half an hour later, the car came to a stop in front of an old cinema house in the Apapa area of Lagos. The figure opened the car door, slowly climbed out, then closed the door and waited. It wasn't until the car had driven off that the figure began to slowly walk towards the entrance of the cinema hall. He could see the beautifully lit entrance gate to the cinema ahead of him. Some moviegoers were busy buying tickets, while others were checking posters and trying to decide on which movie to watch. No one paid him any attention as he walked through the gate and into the cinema house.

Twenty minutes later, the same figure emerged and briskly walked through the exit gate of the cinema house. He was now completely transformed and no longer dragging his left leg. He was wearing a dark jacket instead of the brown jacket he had been wearing when he first entered. He was wearing a bead and was now without his hat. It would have been completely impossible for any observer to identify this individual as the same figure who had walked slowly through the cinema gate twenty minutes earlier.

He walked smartly along the pedestrian path to cross the road to the other side. Once on the other side, he stopped and turned around nonchalantly. He scanned the street with his eyes for anything unusual. Convinced that no one was showing any interest in him, he turned around once more and started walking towards the gas station ahead of him. He got to the gas station and went straight to the parking lot beside the entrance. As he entered the parking lot, he encountered a man and his wife trying desperately to locate their car. The man was cursing loudly as he tagged behind his wife. He could see the frustration on his face as his wife zigzagged through the multitude of cars.

The figure had no such problem. He knew exactly where he had parked his car. It was part of his job to know. He walked directly to a position sandwiched between two palm trees. His SUV was exactly as he had left it. He brought out the car key and opened the door. He suddenly felt as if someone was watching him. He could almost feel the pair of eyes piercing through him. He paused, reckoning that whoever was watching him was not too far away from his position. Using his body as a shield, he reached forward and adjusted the side view mirror on the driver's side. He waited for a moment, then picked up the foot mat from the car and turned around to dust it.

That was when he saw her — a young lady in her late twenties standing four cars away and looking intensely at him. She was tall and slender, with an oblong face that was beautiful but ordinary in a way. As their eyes met, the woman quickly turned away. He kept his eyes fixed on her as he continued to dust the foot mat. He reckoned that the woman was a hustler, looking to nail an evening with a man. Nothing more, and nothing less.

He placed the foot mat back and entered his car. As he made to start the car, he purposely glanced at the sideview mirror. The woman was still there, staring at him. It was only when she realized that she was being watched that she opened the door to a Honda Civic and entered. This was when his sixth sense kicked in. If the lady was the owner of the car she had just entered, then she couldn't possibly be just another hustler. Who was she, and why was she staring so intently at him? He didn't know what to make of it. He knew his mind sometimes played tricks on him when people stared unusually at him. It helped him stay alert. It helped him prepare for any emergency.

He started the car, engaged the gear, and began driving slowly out of the parking lot. As he did, he turned his head to an angle of forty-five degrees to see if there was an oncoming vehicle approaching his driveway. Seizing the opportunity, he zeroed in on the Honda Civic. Just as he suspected, the car was slowly edging out of its parking position. Now, he was alert.

As he drove his SUV along Apapa Expressway, he caught sight of the Honda Civic. He was now dead sure that the car was tailing him, even though the lady was doing her best to conceal that fact. She had deliberately positioned her car as the third car behind the SUV and was driving at their pace. He glanced at the rearview again and again. The lady in the Honda Civic seemed to be reading his every move and using the cars in front of her as shields. He knew for a fact that the young lady was driving the Honda Civic, but was she alone?

He got to an intersection and noticed that the car behind him was signaling to turn right. He also signaled to turn right but, at the last moment, drove straight through the intersection. The car behind him made the right turn, as indicated, leaving one car between him and the Honda Civic. He started driving slower than the pace of traffic, trying to get the car behind him to overtake. The lady in the Honda Civic seemed to have guessed his motive; she reduced speed considerably, allowing a car to overtake her. The Honda Civic was once again back to position number three behind the SUV.

Thinking of his appointment with Tommy Anderson and the USB stick he had to hand over to him, the figure in the SUV decided it was time to get rid of the lady and her Honda Civic. He stared at the traffic light at the intersection some hundred meters ahead. He calculated that the light should be turning red by the time he got to the intersection. He maintained a constant speed, reaching the traffic light at the exact moment it turned red. He stopped and plotted his next move.

When the traffic light turned green, the SUV didn't move, prompting the cars behind to blast their horns. As the car directly behind the SUV began to maneuver its way from behind, the SUV suddenly made a terrifying left turn, causing oncoming cars to blast their horns repeatedly. The two cars that were behind the SUV hurriedly drove straight ahead. The light turned red as the Honda Civic reached it.

As the SUV, now driving in the opposite direction, sped past the Honda Civic, the figure in the driver's seat turned his head to look at the car. He caught sight of the lady driving the car, and their eyes locked momentarily.

"The next time I see you, it will be a different story, bitch." the figure said to himself. A sadistic smile stole across his lips as he drove away to keep his appointment with Tommy Anderson.

Chapter Seven

It's Friday morning, and Deputy Director Shola Davies was sitting behind his desk, his hands folded across his chest. He was staring at Smith the way one would stare at an irritating bug just before smashing it. He couldn't comprehend what he was hearing. He had read the report Edobor had hurriedly drafted and sent to him late Thursday night. He was anything but impressed.

"You arrived late for the meeting with Anthony," Davies said, his eyes burning deep into Smith's. "Explain to me how and why this happened."

Smith went on to describe in detail the incident with the bike rider, up until when he arrived at the Western House complex. Edobor sat still and listened, his eyes on the deputy director, not once looking sideways towards Smith.

When Smith had finished, he turned slightly towards Edobor, trying to make eye contact. Edobor turned sharply to meet his gaze and then turned his face once again to the deputy director.

Smith felt alone.

"And what do you make of all this?" Davies asked Edobor when Smith was done talking.

"I was wondering at first if the accident with the bike rider was a coincidence," Victor replied, his voice low but steady.

"Go on," Davies urged.

"The bike man is still in police custody. We interviewed him. He confessed that a man in a black Jeep asked him to race against a car he would point out to him. The bike man became interested when the man offered him some money in U.S. dollars." He paused, took a deep breath, and continued. "He was instructed to create a scene that would cause a delay for the car. He pocketed some easy money and did as he was instructed."

"Just like that?" Davies asked in total disbelief.

"Just like that, sir. I think the whole setup is directly related to what happened to Anthony. The plan was to delay Banji, to give the killer enough time to get to Anthony's office." Edobor explained.

"And you're convinced that the bike man was not a party to the plot?" Davies asked.

"I am convinced that he was just a pawn in the whole scheme, sir. The money was the motivating factor for him." Edobor said, carefully picking his words.

"And I want to assume that this bike man didn't get a description of the man in the Jeep?" Davies said sarcastically.

"He didn't, sir. His undivided attention was focused on the money rather than taking a proper look at the man." Edobor said meekly.

Davies now turned towards Smith, who had been listening attentively while the deputy director quizzed Edobor.

"The report says you scanned the office but couldn't find the material you were supposed to retrieve from Anthony?"

"That is correct, sir."

"You think the killer somehow got hold of the material?" Davies asked rhetorically.

"I strongly believe so, sir." Smith replied.

Davies continued to stare at Smith the way a father would stare at an erring child. Then he shifted his attention back to Edobor and regarded him. He was about to say something when Smith beat him to it.

"It's obvious, sir, that the unfortunate incident with the bike man was staged to give the killer enough time to get to Anthony. The question is, how the killer got to know about my meeting with Anthony."

Smith watched as Edobor turned to see Davies' reaction. Davies' stone-like face remained fixed on Smith, his eyes piercing through him.

"The meeting with Anthony and the fact that I was to collect the dossier from him were known only to the three of us," Smith said tensely. "And now he is dead, and the dossier is gone. What am I supposed to think in terms of trust?"

Edobor gazed at Smith in total disbelief. His statement was a direct accusation. He reminded himself, however, of the need to remain calm for the duration of the meeting. He had planned to raise the issue of trust with the deputy director, and now Smith was running his mouth.

"It's not just the three of us," Davies corrected. "The director general is also aware of it. I briefed him personally. That makes the four of us by my count."

Smith nodded his head. He had made a smart move. He had succeeded in diverting attention away from himself. Everyone except him was now a suspect. This was good for him. He started to breathe evenly again.

"Someone obviously leaked the information to some interested party. We need to find the leak quickly." Edobor said with a great deal of emphasis.

"Shut up! Let me think." Davies said in a cold, flat voice.

He reached for the report and examined it, then pulled open a drawer and deposited the report into it. He pushed back his chair and got to his feet. He took seven steps away from his desk and then turned around to trace his footsteps back—seven steps. Then he glared at both men sitting uncomfortably in front of him.

"Listen to me, both of you! It's too early in the investigation for us to imagine that we have a mole within us. This is unacceptable to me." Davies paused; his brain was busy trying to craft his thoughts into words. "We have to find this person, mole if you will, in order to prevent any future sabotage." Davies deliberately stressed the word "sabotage" for emphasis.

Seeing Davies' expression, Edobor nodded his head quickly, acknowledging the fact that he understood the urgency of the matter. Smith looked on, his swift mind alert. He had no reason to doubt the integrity of Edobor, nor was he ready to consider the possibility that Davies could somehow be the mole. The director general was a different ball-game altogether. His thought was cut short by Davies' cold voice.

"Bring in the bike man. We need to find out if he remembers something else aside from what he already told the police. Persuade him if you must."

"I will see to that at once, sir." Edobor said.

"The police will be making a big issue out of this, but I will handle that end. I don't need to remind you to keep the press out of this for as long as possible."

Davies sat down noisily in his chair, rested his back, then inclined his face towards Smith.

"This is your case now, Banji," he said crisply. "Victor will oversee the investigation; however, it's your job to find the killer of Anthony and recover the dossier. I don't give a damn how you accomplish the task. Do I make myself clear?"

"Perfectly clear, sir." Smith replied.

"We should take into consideration from this moment onwards," Davies continued, "that we are up against formidable opponents, ready to do whatever it takes to hinder the investigation. They must not succeed."

Davies got to his feet once more. He pointed the two men in front of him towards the door, signaling the end of the meeting. The two men stood up simultaneously, nodded to Davies, then turned and started walking towards the door. They stopped abruptly as Davies' cold voice reached them.

"I will be meeting with Director Abubakar this evening. He is going to be furious, as expected, about the catastrophic beginning of the investigation. I will try and reassure him of your ability to handle the case. In the meantime, find Anthony's killer and the missing dossier."

The two men left the office on that note. Neither of them said anything to the other as they walked together to the parking lot.

*****

If there was anything Raymond Westland was exceptionally good at, it was in covering his tracks. He was conscious of the fact that he was virtually "untouchable" in Nigeria, as in many other African countries within his area of operations. Despite this, he took great pride in knowing that he was well able to cover his tracks. Over the years, nothing whatsoever has ever been traced to him directly. His pride was not misplaced, as he had personally directed covert operations to cause mass unrest and topple governments in many

African countries for nearly two decades. He had gotten away with his many atrocities, unscarred. He was invincible.

Westland was the perfect puppet master with many strings to pull. The strings were people scattered across major cities in Africa, used for the achievement of what Westland regarded as the "greater good." His definition of the so-called "greater good" was often limited to the interests of his handler and what his handler considered the "interests" of the United States of America.

Westland was nobody's fool. He was clever and had ways of venting what his handler considered "the interests" of the United States before making a move. On at least two occasions, he had deliberately allowed the missions to fail because he felt his handler's assessment and conclusion about the missions were not in the best interest of the United States. On both occasions, the foot soldiers had taken the blame. The leaders of each team had been punished. They had died, shot in the head at close range. As a result, the President of Burkina Faso and his counterpart in Mali, two men whom Westland's handler in the United States felt were not doing enough to fight the insurgencies ravaging the two countries, had lived.

They had lived because Westland wanted them to live.

On this Thursday evening, Westland had remained in his office until nine-thirty when Tommy Anderson walked in, looking as serious as ever. Tall, heavyset, and with a certain level of seriousness around his face, Anderson was Westland's right-hand man, with an unrivaled ability to hunt down fugitives fleeing from the United States' justice system. The two men had come a long way, working many covert operations together. It was a common saying among operatives that wherever Westland was, Tommy was nearby. Their method of operation was usually the same. Westland called the operation and provided the logistics while Anderson put together the men needed to carry it out. Logistics support, as far as Westland was concerned, was not limited to providing abundant resources for the operation. It also involved cleaning up any mess resulting from such operations using the powers of the United States. It was a tough job, but one Westland had mastered over the years.

The reopening of the Halliburton case and the orders given to Westland by his handler had necessitated the need to draft Anderson back into the operation. Anderson had previously worked as the fieldman in this same case and was responsible for digging up dirty secrets about the then-President of Nigeria. It was these secrets, presented to his handler by Westland, that were subsequently used as leverage to get the President to discontinue the Halliburton bribery investigation. The President had refused to pursue the case any further and had paid the price when the people voted him out of office.

Westland had commissioned Anderson to be on standby during a brief security meeting at the U.S. embassy a few days earlier.

"We may need to move fast and at a moment's notice." Westland had told Anderson.

When Westland finally got a call from his informant on Thursday afternoon about a meeting scheduled to take place within an hour, in which a dossier with vital information would change hands, Westland had no choice but to leap over Anderson. He got hold of one of his most trusted "foot soldiers" and instructed him to go fetch the dossier.

This done, he put a call across to Anderson, instructing him to provide the necessary logistics needed to facilitate the job. The instruction was simple enough.

"Make sure Banji Smith gets to his appointment late."

"How late?" Anderson had asked.

"An hour should do."

The rest had been left to Anderson, who wasted no time and spared no expenses in making sure that Smith arrived late for his rendezvous with Osaro.

Now sitting in front of Westland, Anderson reached for his briefcase and took from it a brown envelope. He handed the envelope over to Westland. He watched as Westland carefully examined the envelope before opening it to retrieve a USB stick.

Westland's first instinct was to insert the stick into the computer, but he decided against it. There was plenty of time to check what was saved on the USB when Anderson was gone.

"How did the operation go, Tommy?" Westland asked distantly.

Westland needed to know. He needed to assure himself first that there were no loose ends. Only then would he be in a proper position to reassure his handler.

"It was tight, but we managed to pull it off. This is obvious from the fact that you're holding the USB stick in your hands right now," Anderson replied, grinning slightly.

Westland kept a straight face, staring intensely at Anderson. His question had not been answered. Anderson, realizing this, quickly continued.

"I got a guy; this guy got another guy who got another guy. The last guy in the chain made an offer to a bike man. It was an offer too good to resist. The bike man acted as the obstacle, preventing the subject from arriving for his appointment on time. The delay bought the lone wolf enough time to get to the destination and retrieve the USB."

"What was the bike man's role?"

"He simply ran into the subject's car as he headed for the meeting and caused some damage to the car. A chaotic situation ensured until the police arrived to restore order."

"The police?" Westland was alarmed.

"Yes. They came to restore order. The bike man was taken away by the police."

"I will assume that this bike man cannot be traced to any of the guys in your chain."

"Definitely not. There are no loose ends, I assure you." Anderson said confidently.

"And the lone wolf?" Westland asked, starting to relax.

"We met at the club. He delivered the USB stick to me in that very same envelope. I had a talk with him. It was a clean job."

Westland knew what "a clean job" meant. The original owner of the USB stick was now a guest at the undertaker's chambers. Westland thought of the lone wolf and was glad that he had picked him for the job. He was extremely efficient and good at leaving no trace behind. Westland was reassured.

Westland nodded slowly. Anderson had done a great job despite having less than one hour to put the whole operation together. He deserved some praise.

"Good job, Tommy, very good job," Westland said, smiling genuinely. He got to his feet. Anderson stood up as well, and the two men shook hands like old friends.

"You see now why I'm finding it hard to sign your transfer papers to the States?" Westland said, starting to laugh.

Before Anderson could register his objection, Westland continued.

"I might let you go when this Halliburton thing is over. Emphasis on the word *might*." Both men laughed loudly.

Westland walked Tommy Anderson to the door, and they shook hands again.

"Stand by for any fallouts, okay?"

"I most definitely will, Ray."

Westland locked the door behind Anderson. He went back to his desk and picked up the USB stick. He wanted to be doubly sure that the content was relevant to the Halliburton case, as the owner had claimed. He inserted the stick into the computer and then grabbed his coffee mug. He poured himself a generous amount of coffee, after which he moved the cursor to the file and clicked.

Westland stared curiously at its contents. The content was presented in an orderly manner, with footnotes. Westland spent the next two hours going through the file in total disbelief. The content was more incriminating than anything he had ever seen on paper. The sheer magnitude of the evidence against the individuals listed was mind-blowing. This document could easily pass for the Nigerian version of Pandora's box. He observed that the name of his handler appeared very frequently in many of the transactions as the main facilitator.

Westland made up his mind to notify his handler immediately. It was up to him to decide the next line of action. This was one call Westland was looking forward to making. He had handled his end perfectly well, and his handler should be pleased. He checked the wall clock: twenty-five minutes after midnight local time. The call would have to wait until around eight o'clock in the morning.

Westland suddenly felt tired as he reached for the coffee mug. He knew he needed some sleep. The activities of the past couple of hours have had a tiring effect on him. He closed the file and then retrieved the stick from the computer. As he dropped the stick into the envelope, it occurred to him that he would not be going home. He was too tired to drive. He got to his feet and staggered to the extra room within his office that served as a sleeping room. He dropped onto the bed in full gear, too tired to remove his clothes. Sleep came almost instantaneously.

Chapter Eight

The atmosphere in the conference room was tense. The rivalry between the Department of State Services (DSS) and the Nigerian Police was about to rear its ugly head once again. On one side of the large oval table sat Deputy Director Shola Davies, flanked on both sides by Victor Edobor to his right and Banji Smith to his left. On the other side of the table sat a smallish, pigeon-chested man in his late fifties. His smallish eyes were bright and very alive. His hair was beginning to thin, but his face bore the hardness of a seasoned police officer. He was Police Commissioner Michael Armani. Sitting in the same row with the police chief were Superintendent Lekan Ajeni and Detective Tina Bucknor, both looking very serious.

Director General of the DSS, Hamzat Abubakar, had initiated the meeting to try and work out a compromise between the police, who wanted the DSS to hand off the case since it was a homicide investigation, and the men of the DSS, who were insisting that the police had no jurisdiction over matters concerning the DSS. Since neither side was willing to shift ground, the DG had stepped in to arrange for a sit-down.

The tension relaxed the moment DG Abubakar entered the conference room. The DG walked straight to take his seat, nodding to his deputy and Commissioner Armani as the others hurriedly got to their feet. It was only when he reached his seat that the DG lifted his head to acknowledge the presence of the others. Then he sat down and watched as the others did the same.

The DG moved his head slowly, his eyes scrutinizing. His gaze finally rested and remained fixed quizzically, on the only female present.

Bucknor hurriedly got to her feet.

"I am Detective Tina Bucknor, an Inspector from the CID unit, police headquarters, sir."

Abubakar nodded. "Please, have your seat."

Detective Tina Bucknor was twenty-nine years old. She was tall, square-shouldered, and wearing her hair low. She was not what one would describe as pretty in the traditional sense, but there was a certain compelling handsomeness about her face that could get her onto the cover page of most beauty magazines. She loved her job as a police officer and was a sucker for details. As she sat down, she gently pulled out a tiny notebook from her side pocket.

At the same moment, DG Abubakar reached for his writing pad and flipped it open. He fixed his eyes momentarily on a page, then looked leftward towards some imaginary object. Thereafter, he turned to gaze at Davies.

"I want to assume that the police team is in the know as to why Banji went for the meeting with Anthony?"

Team DSS nodded in unison.

Abubakar turned to the police team, seeking confirmation on that point. He got his confirmation with a nod from the police chief.

"I also want to assume that everyone here is familiar with the events that unfolded on the day Anthony was killed." The DG paused long enough to stare at each person present in the room. Each nodded without saying a word.

"I have read the memo I received on the matter." Abubakar turned to his writing pad. "There are some grey areas that need clarification," he turned his attention then to Smith. "You had an appointment, and a specific time was agreed upon. What stopped you from immediately looking for an alternative means of transportation after the incident with the bike man?"

Smith shifted in his seat. He had had time to wonder along that line of reasoning. It was a reasonable thing to do in a normal situation. The situation on that day, however, was far from normal, as he recalled.

"Sir, the situation became chaotic very quickly." Smith replied, confident that he could talk his way out of any blame.

"Chaotic, very quickly? Please explain."

"Shortly after the bike man ran into my car, dozens of bike men surrounded the place in their usual manner. They blocked the main road and threatened to attack me." Smith explained calmly.

"It never occurred to you that you should call the police as soon as the situation began to degenerate?" Police Commissioner Armani asked rather sarcastically.

"The situation degenerated so fast—too fast, if I may. It was completely unexpected, sir."

"You have not answered my question," Armani said, frowning. "Even if I agree with you that the situation degenerated very quickly, that in itself becomes the main reason to involve the police."

"Like I said, it happened so fast, sir," Smith insisted.

The police chief shook his head slowly, registering his disagreement.

"When my men eventually arrived at the scene, what stopped you from asking one of the officers to drive you over to Western House for the meeting? This could have saved you a great deal of time."

"My car was in perfect working condition, sir, and besides, the police men—"

"I am talking about a police car with sirens. I am talking about time and time management." Armani said in his hard cop voice.

Davies shifted in his seat. He knew exactly what the police commissioner was doing. The police commissioner was trying to make the meeting as hellish as possible for Smith and by extension, for the DSS.

DG Abubakar looked on, his face hard and expressionless. This was the essence of the meeting—to apportion blame where necessary and then agree to work together to find a killer.

Edobor, who had been listening attentively, suddenly turned towards Deputy Director Davies.

"If I may, sir?"

"Go ahead." Davies said calmly.

"I am suggesting that we focus more on the murder of Anthony," Edobor said. He looked from Davies to Police Commissioner Armani. "If Anthony had not been killed, the dossier would have been in our possession by now…"

"But Anthony is dead, and the dossier is missing," Armani snapped. He glanced at DG Abubakar, who stared back blankly. He turned towards Edobor, his eyes cold and penetrating.

"You think it is inconsequential to dwell on the incident with the bike man?" He shook his head. "No! It's not. Most times, those little details that seem inconsequential may carry the clues in cracking a case."

"We have interviewed the bike man, and we can reach him anytime we want, Commissioner," Davies said to the police chief. "I understand your concern, but we are leaving no stone unturned."

"I will ask my men to bring in the bike man after this meeting for another talk. Who knows?" Armani said flatly. He had been warming up for a showdown with Davies. He had baited him as much as he could with his lines of questioning, but the deputy director seemed unwilling to take the bait.

DG Abubakar, who had been listening patiently all the while, suddenly cleared his throat.

"I want the killer of Anthony found, and fast too. No expense spared." He looked down at his writing pad before continuing, "The killing of Anthony should tell everyone here present that we are up against some formidable entities. If Anthony's dossier was damning enough to get him killed, then it must have been damning enough to scare some powerful individuals."

"Powerful individuals, both within and outside Nigeria, if I may add, sir." Edobor said. He spoke from the position of someone who had investigated the case before.

The DG nodded in agreement.

"Absolutely right, Victor. I really don't care who these individuals are. Just get me the evidence and leave the rest to me."

"We are ready to cooperate with the DSS to unmask the killers of Anthony and, by extension, get to the bottom of this matter." The police chief said.

"Cooperation is very essential. I want a team made up of both the police and the DSS." Abubakar said with an edge of finality in his voice.

"Victor and Banji here are members from our end." Davies said. He couldn't help but notice Commissioner Armani staring across the table at Smith. The look was anything but friendly.

"From the police end are Superintendent Lekan Ajeni and Detective Bucknor. They have my absolute trust." Commissioner Armani said. He shifted his eyes reluctantly away from Smith.

Davies ignored the last part of Commissioner Armani's statement. He knew full well that the commissioner was looking for a showdown. He was not ready for any showdowns just now. The time for that would certainly come.

"A four-member team for now is acceptable," Abubakar said. "The team may be expanded if the need arises. Is that clear?"

Both Commissioner Armani and Deputy Director Davies nodded in unison.

Detective Bucknor leaned over and whispered something to Commissioner Armani, who kept nodding his head as he listened. The DG gestured towards the police commissioner, forcing Detective Bucknor to quickly arrange herself back in her seat.

"I know, as a matter of fact, that Western House has no CCTV cameras," Armani said, following the signal from the DG. "However, the Defense House, which is adjacent to Western House, has CCTV coverage as far as Western House."

Armani pointed to Detective Bucknor. "My inspector here thinks it will be good to start by requesting the CCTV recording from the Defense House for the day Anthony was killed. This could potentially point us to the killer."

Abubakar looked from the commissioner to Detective Bucknor. He liked her. She was a fast thinker and anxious to begin the hunt. His face softened. He looked across at Davies and raised an eyebrow.

"I will request the CCTV footage for that day from the Defense House as soon as this meeting is over." Davies said.

"Perfect." The DG glanced at his wristwatch. "Davies and Commissioner Armani will liaise with me and inform me immediately of any new developments."

With that said, DG Hamzat Abubakar got to his feet, an indication that the meeting was over. He pulled back his chair and started his slow walk towards the exit door. The next moment, the door opened, and the DSS' number one man walked through it. The door closed noiselessly behind him as those left behind began to strategize on their next line of action.

*****

Westland came awake with a start. He slowly lifted his head to look around. This was certainly not his home. He was starting to wonder when he remembered. He had spent the night in the office's spare room because he was too tired to drive home. He lifted his head a bit higher to check the wall clock. It was seven o'clock in the morning. He could hear noises steadily coming from the direction of the entrance gate. They were the voices of the early morning visitors to the embassy, who were mainly visa applicants. He ignored the noises, choosing instead to freshen up. He got up from the bed and headed straight to the tiny bathroom.

Now feeling refreshed and sipping a cup of coffee, Westland, who was sitting behind his desk, decided it was time to make the call to his handler. He picked up his secured phone and dialed. The phone rang twice before Westland heard the voice from across the continent.

"Updates?"

"We acquired a USB stick. Originator down." Westland said, trying hard to keep his voice steady.

"Contents?" the voice asked.

"Halliburton. Very damning and incriminating." Westland replied.

There was a long pause as the one on the other end of the line reflected on the words "damning and incriminating."

"Single stick?" the voice finally asked.

"Yes, sir."

"Clean-up at the originator's place?"

"The place was cleaned, sir."

"Explain."

"The originator's computer no longer exists. Computer corrupted and totally wiped clean."

"And the press?"

"They are keeping it away from the press for now, sir."

"I want the stick ASAP. Use the official channel."

"Understood."

"Potential problem?"

"None that I can think of right now, sir. We are watching and constantly a step ahead of them."

"Supposing there's another copy of the stick? A cause for concern?"

Westland had thought of this possibility but was quick to dismiss it. He was almost certain that no other copy existed. Of course, there could be copies scattered in small pieces, but not in one single document, as was the case with the USB stick now in his possession. Moreover, the computer that was used to manufacture the document had been destroyed.

"I don't think there was another copy, sir."

"Do not underestimate anyone, especially not a man like the originator."

"Understood." Westland said, now wishing the conversation would end abruptly.

"I do not want a mess over this matter, especially if such a mess could be avoided!"

"I understand, sir."

"Let's hope you do."

The line went dead.

Westland noticed that his hands were sweating, as usual. He tucked the phone away and rubbed his hands together. He glanced at the wall clock; it was fifteen minutes before eight o'clock. He grabbed his cup of coffee but noticed that it was now cold. He felt a bit agitated. The call to his handler never failed to unnerve him. He stood up and walked over to the coffee jug to refill his cup. A sip of the warm coffee did him some good, and he started to get a grip on himself. It was the last statement from his handler that seemed to unnerve him the most. He was starting to wonder if his handler was beginning to lose faith in him. This was an unimaginable scenario. He had so far never failed to deliver on an assignment, and he was not about to fail on this one. He tried to rationalize the reason his handler was getting agitated. He pinned it down to the dossier with its damning content. This was understandable.

His mind shifted to the USB stick. He had to dispatch it as soon as possible and reach his handler within the next twenty-four hours. He pulled open a drawer and took out an envelope with the inscription "Priority" printed on the top right-hand corner. Just below the inscription was a logo of an eagle eye with the inscription "Eagle Eyes" written across it.

Westland took a pen and wrote down the details of the recipient on the envelope.

His eyes caught the inscription "Eagle Eyes." The inscription was an indication that the contents of the envelope were not to be seen by anyone other than the addressee. He looked intensely at the logo depicting the eye of an eagle and grinned. He knew the eagle was a super-intelligent bird, and the image of the eagle eye staring rather inquisitively at him conveyed that exact same message. It was as if the eye was alive.

The phone buzzed. Westland walked slowly over to where he had tucked away the phone to retrieve it.

It was a message from his handler.

He opened the phone to read the message. It was just seven words.

Seven words which gave Westland all the power he needed to carry out a ruthless campaign against anyone who stood between him and the achievement of his objective.

The message read: Take no prisoners. And no holds barred.

Chapter Nine

Detective Tina Bucknor stared intensely at the computer screen in front of her. A woman in a police uniform stared back at her. The woman staring back at her was her mentor and a source of great inspiration. The woman was her mother, Adesua Bucknor, a retired police officer who, despite being in active service for thirty years, managed to raise six children with her husband. Bucknor, who was the last and only girl among the six children, grew up as a tomboy, preferring to play with toys handed down to her by her older siblings.

Adesua Bucknor was a devoted Catholic who saw nothing wrong in forcing her children to go to church on Sundays despite the occasional protests from her husband, Segun Bucknor, who was a more liberal Catholic.

"You don't have to force the kids to go to church," Segun Bucknor would often say to his wife. "Just tell them why they need to go; that's all you need."

"My job is to get them to church," Adesua would respond. "It's the preacher's job to convince them as to why they need to keep coming."

Not wanting to start an argument on a Sunday morning, Segun Bucknor would turn to the children, a smile on his face, and say, "You heard your mother; let's go visit Jesus." This was a way of stamping out any potential revolt by the kids against their mother for continually forcing them to attend church services, even as they grew older.

When Detective Bucknor decided to enroll in the police academy, she went to her parents to inform them of her decision. Her father shrugged, then shook his head sadly.

"Why police?" he had asked. "I always thought you were going to be a lawyer, a good one at that."

"Papi, being a police officer is not in any way different from being a lawyer. They are both custodians of the law." she had replied, stroking her father's head.

"It's the job of the police to get criminals off the street. I will choose the police any day." Her mother had said.

Bucknor noticed her father starting to shake his head in disagreement with what her mother had said. She was sure that a long argument was about to ensue.

"Papi, I promise that I am going to be a lawyer someday, but for now, I want to enlist in the police."

Her father smiled, nodded his head, then shrugged in resignation. The matter was settled. She went ahead to join the police. The rest is history.

As she sat staring at the picture displayed on the screen, she couldn't help but wonder about her new assignment. She needed some kind of inspiration from staring at the picture on the screen. It had worked for her in the past when faced with difficult assignments.

Bucknor glanced away from the computer screen and reached for her phone just as it began to ring. She looked to see who was calling. Seeing it was Police Commissioner Armani on the line, she quickly hit the answer button.

"Detective Bucknor, sir."

"The CCTV footage will be available for viewing this afternoon." Armani informed her.

"The team is ready to review the footage, sir."

"I must warn you; it's about 200 hours of footage."

"I estimated that, sir."

"Good. I want you guys on top of this. A killer is on the loose, and we need to find him before he kills again." Armani said, an edge of urgency in his voice.

"We will find him, sir." Bucknor assured him.

"Good. Keep me posted." Armani said before disconnecting the call.

Bucknor waited a few minutes, the phone still in her hand. Then she put a call through to Superintendent of Police Lekan Ayeni.

"I've been expecting your call," Ayeni said as soon as he answered.

"I was waiting to hear from the commissioner before calling you, sir. We should be leaving for Western House in about twenty minutes if it works for you." Bucknor said.

"I am ready when you are." Ayeni said.

"The commissioner said the CCTV will be available this afternoon."

"That's good news."

"Get ready for about 200 hours of CCTV footage." Bucknor said sarcastically.

"I will prepare myself." Ayeni muttered.

Bucknor smiled and hung up. She knew from experience the enormous task involved in scanning through CCTV footage. It was a task dreaded by many police officers but one she enjoyed. She was a sucker for details. She was ready for the CCTV footage, but first, she needed to visit Western House. The visit should help her get an idea of what to look out for in the footage.

*****

The three-member investigative team arrived at the Western House complex simultaneously in two separate cars. After a brief meeting outside the building to strategize, Detective Bucknor led Ayeni and Smith into the complex to meet with the chief security officer, John Adejobi.

"I am John Adejobi, the chief security officer at the complex." Adejobi said as he approached Bucknor, hand extended. Adejobi was a tall, well-built man in his mid-forties. He was clean-shaven and blessed with a near-perfect set of teeth that were guaranteed to win him a place at the Mr. Maclear Men audition.

"I am Detective Bucknor, and this is Superintendent Lekan Ayeni." Bucknor said, taking Adejobi's outstretched hand.

The chief security officer shook hands with Ayeni, then looked towards Smith, who was busy studying the map of the complex attached to the wall along the corridor.

"I am Banji Smith from the DSS," Smith said, moving closer to Adejobi to shake hands. "I am told that you do not have CCTV cameras in the complex."

Adejobi smiled sheepishly. He had been the chief security officer of the complex for the past five years and from his first day on the job, had fought tirelessly to have CCTV cameras installed within the vicinity of the complex, all to no avail. Management just wasn't sold on the idea.

"While we do not have CCTV cameras in this building, we do have a security arrangement in place," Adejobi said calmly. He was thinking to himself that perhaps this unfortunate incident could serve as a push factor to finally convince management to install CCTV cameras around the complex. "Visitors are screened," Adejobi continued, "and are required to fill out a visitor's form before entering the building."

"We would like to see the visitors register for the day of the murder." Bucknor said politely.

"Absolutely. The register also has an exit column to record when the visitor leaves the building."

"How many entrances do you have to the building?" Ayeni asked.

"There are two entrances," Adejobi replied. "We have security personnel stationed at both entrances."

"I see." Bucknor said. She shifted her attention to the map of the building attached to the wall.

"We want to talk to the security personnel on duty on that day." Smith said.

Smith noticed that Adejobi was constantly rubbing his hands together. He willed himself to ignore the irritating habit.

"I have arranged for the six of them to meet with you today. They are waiting at the security office on the left wing of the complex." Adejobi said. He folded his hands across his chest. He had noticed that Smith was doing all he could not to stare at his hands.

"How many offices do you have on the fifth floor, Anthony's floor?" Bucknor asked.

"Seven offices altogether." Adejobi replied.

"We would also like to talk to some of the staff working in these offices," Bucknor said. She glanced at her wristwatch. "Especially the ones that were present between four and five-thirty on that Thursday afternoon."

"That shouldn't be a problem. I will notify the respective offices immediately."

"That would be all for now, John. Be kind enough to lead us to the security personnel." Bucknor said, almost pleadingly.

Chief security officer John Adejobi nodded his head. He turned and walked to the door to open it, then stepped aside to let Detective Bucknor walk through, followed closely by Ayeni.

Smith was the last to walk out of the office after staring at the map one final time. He had been studying the design of the fifth floor while the meeting with Adejobi was going on. His aim was to determine which of the offices would most likely hear any sound originating from Anthony's office. He had figured it out before walking out the door.

*****

The six security personnel were waiting at the security office situated on the left wing of the Western House building. The office was not only spacious but had four large windows on each side of the walls. These windows allowed natural light to find its way into the room unhindered. A large conference table was positioned at one end of the office, with chairs arranged on both sides. The chairs on one end of the table were arranged in such a way as to allow the occupiers a clear view of the lagoon front. The chairs on the other end of the table were arranged to give a panoramic view of the car park and the surrounding areas.

When John Adejobi led the team into the security office, the six security personnel stood up in unison. They stood still, hands by their sides, looking straight above the chief's head in a manner that only ex-service men would relate to.

"Good day, chief." They echoed.

Adejobi lifted his hand swiftly to his head in salute.

"Detective Tina Bucknor and Superintendent Lekan Ayeni." Adejobi said to his men. The six men nodded their heads at the pair without saying a word.

Turning towards Smith, who was standing slightly behind him and to his right-hand side, Adejobi pointed. "Banji Smith from the DSS."

Smith smiled and said, "I like the view from up here."

The six men looked on, expressionless. It was a compliment they heard often. The area view from up here was breathtaking, with a calming effect on people on a normal day. Today, however, was not a normal day, and the view was anything but calm. The guys standing in front of them were here to investigate a murder case. Nothing more, nothing less.

"Gentlemen, these guys are investigating the murder of Anthony Osaro. They will be asking questions, and I expect you to provide them with answers to the best of your knowledge." Adejobi said in a voice a military commander would envy.

As soon as Adejobi left the room, the investigative team took their seats. They were seated on the chairs backing the lagoon front. Their sitting positions allowed them to look directly into the parking lot far below and its surrounding areas.

The investigative team had decided to question the security personnel one at a time. The security personnel were to be in the waiting room, from where they would be summoned one at a time for the interview. A glass door between the security office and the waiting room gave the team an unhindered view of the waiting room. Once questioned, the security personnel would return directly to his duty post. This was to prevent him from revealing to his colleagues the nature of the questions.

The interview lasted until midday when the last of the security personnel was released. The interview, though thorough, failed to provide anything significant that could lead to a breakthrough in the investigation. It was a setback for the team. The team spent an extra two hours going through the information extracted from the security personnel to see if they had missed anything. Nothing of importance was missed.

"My only concern is that visitors to the building can easily sneak out if they decide to do so without being noticed." Smith observed.

"That's correct." Ayeni affirmed.

"It's impossible to gain access into the building without filling out a visitor's form." Bucknor said, flipping through her notepad.

"That's right, detective. Let's try and pin down everyone that visited the complex during the period in question." Smith suggested.

"Let's hope that the CCTV cameras will assist in this regard." Ayeni said.

Detective Bucknor suddenly lifted her head. She sighed and then rested her chin on her left palm, deep in thought. Her two companions looked at her, wondering what she was thinking. She stared right ahead, her face revealing nothing.

"I think the killer could have entered through the main entrance and exited through the left-wing entrance." Bucknor said almost in a whisper.

"Or vice versa." Ayeni said.

"I am pondering something." Bucknor said grinning.

"We begin by tracking down visitors who failed to sign out from the building on that day?" Smith ventured.

"Absolutely. This will help narrow down our search." Bucknor said.

"It's a good way to start. Let's get on with it." Ayeni said.

"First, we have to talk to some folks on the fifth floor." Bucknor said, and once again grinned.

Ayeni got to his feet, followed immediately by Bucknor as Smith hurriedly made some last-minute notes. As soon as Smith was done, he stood up and nodded to indicate that he was finished. The three of them walked out of the office to navigate their way back to the fifth floor.

*****

The team, together with a middle-aged woman, disembarked from the elevator when it stopped on the fifth floor. The middle-aged woman walked swiftly ahead of them to push the entrance door open and walked through. As Bucknor, who was ahead of the others, reached the door, she was surprised to find the woman standing by, holding the door open for her. Bucknor smiled at the woman as she reached to grab the door from her. The woman smiled back before turning and walking away. Bucknor observed the woman walking along the corridor until she entered the first office on the left-hand side.

"I think we should begin with the offices closer to Anthony's." Bucknor said as soon as the other two walked through the door.

"Agreed. It's a long corridor, and the offices closer are the ones most likely to hear any sound coming from Anthony's office." Ayeni said.

Smith nodded, walking towards office number 506. As he moved closer, he began to feel as though he was reenacting the whole experience all over again. He tried to push the feelings from his mind. His face hardened as he approached number 506, which had now been barricaded with police tape. A policeman in uniform stood outside the barricade to protect the crime scene. The policeman regarded Smith suspiciously but said nothing. As Detective Bucknor and Superintendent Ayeni approached, the policeman lifted his right hand to his head in a swift salute. The pair returned the salute nonchalantly. The policeman, now appearing more serious than usual, resumed his patrol around the barricaded area.

Smith couldn't push aside his feelings of nostalgia any longer as he stood in front of office number 506. The memory of that day came flooding back. He remembered vividly the shock he felt when he walked into Anthony's office to find him dead. It was one of the few occasions that something had truly shocked him in his adult life. It wasn't until Smith heard a knock on the door to office number 507 that he snapped his mind away from office number 506. He turned in time to see the door swing open. Holding the door was a young woman in her mid-twenties, grinning from ear to ear. The woman stepped aside to let Bucknor in.

Once inside, the woman closed the door behind them. She turned slowly to face Bucknor.

"Good day," she said in a very melodious and confident voice. "My name is Kate Adeyemi, and I am the customer service officer. How may I help you?"

The trio regarded her. She was dark and of average height. The two dimples dotting both sides of her cheeks made her beautiful without being overly sexual. She radiated a certain kind of aristocratic confidence by the way she held her head high, arms folded across her chest.

"I am Detective Bucknor," Bucknor said, pointing her hand. "Superintendent Lekan Ayeni and Banji Smith from the DSS."

"We are investigating the murder of Mr. Anthony Osaro, who was the occupant of the office directly opposite you." Ayeni said.

"I see." Kate said, her voice still melodious. "How can we be of help?"

"We need to talk to some of your staff, especially those who were present between four o'clock and five-thirty on that evening." Bucknor said calmly.

"I suggest we go to the conference room," Kate said in an impersonal tone. "I was in the office during the period in question with two of my colleagues."

Kate led the team to a well-furnished conference room with enough space to accommodate about a dozen people. She stepped back, folded her hands across her chest, and allowed Bucknor and her companions to enter the room. Kate, looking studious and very businesslike, sat across from them. She stared intensely at Bucknor as if trying to read her mind.

"Was there anything unusual you observed or heard during the time in question?" Bucknor asked her.

"Absolutely nothing. I was busy working on some files. It was almost closing time, and I needed to finish with them." Kate replied.

"On a normal day, would you hear if some noisy activities were to take place in Anthony's office?" Smith asked.

"Not unless the noise was really loud." Kate answered calmly.

"Surely, one of you must have heard something," Bucknor countered. "There was a gunshot. It's hard for me to believe that none of you heard anything."

"I can't speak for the other two," Kate said shrilly. "You will get to speak to them. As for me, I didn't know about it until the next day."

Watching Kate stare unflinchingly at Bucknor, Smith got the feeling that her answer was final. He turned to meet Ayeni's gaze, and the latter raised an eyebrow, indicating that he understood what Smith was thinking.

The next forty-five minutes was spent interviewing a thick-set man in his mid-thirties with a thin, hard face and large eyeballs, which seemed too large for their sockets, and a tall, insipid-looking young woman in her late twenties. Kate had introduced the two as the colleagues who had been with her on the day in question. The interview ended without producing any leads, as neither of them had seen or heard anything unusual that day.

Around four o'clock, the team walked out of office number 510 into the corridor. Bucknor stood with her back against the wall, checking what she had written down on the last page of her pad. She drew a circle around the second to the last line. When she lifted her eyes away from the pad, she caught sight of the middle-aged woman who had ridden the elevator with them earlier. The two women looked at each other.

"We meet again, ma'am." the woman called out, her face brightening with a smile.

"Yes, we did. I am Detective Bucknor, and these are my colleagues. We are here investigating the murder of Anthony Osaro, office 506."

"That's the office opposite mine."

"Then you work in the same office as Kate Adeyemi?" Bucknor asked.

"I do. My name is Titilayo Johnson."

"Do you know the late Anthony?" Bucknor asked.

The woman hesitated, her smile fading. She started weighing the pros and cons of volunteering information to the police.

Bucknor read her mind.

"I assure you that whatever we discuss here will be strictly confidential." Bucknor said quickly.

"I know him," Titilayo said after taking a deep breath. "We often meet in the elevator whenever he's here."

"On the day he was killed, were you at the office between four and five-thirty?" Bucknor asked.

"Yes, I was. I got to the fifth floor at about four-thirty-five. I had earlier seen him as he entered the building around four o'clock that afternoon."

Bucknor's heartbeat began to race. She was almost certain that her persistence was about to pay off. Titilayo could end up being their most promising lead so far.

"Are you certain about the time? I mean, the time you saw Anthony?" Smith asked.

"I'm one hundred percent certain about the time," Titilayo replied, eyeing Smith in a not-too-friendly manner.

Smith felt a certain level of animosity from Titilayo towards him. He wasn't overly surprised. He had raised his voice when he asked his question. He tried to make amends.

"I believe you, okay? No offense intended."

"None is taken," Titilayo said, staring Smith down one last time.

Bucknor shot Smith a quick look of disapproval. She wanted her most credible witness so far to be handled with care and respect.

"Did you notice anything unusual about him when you saw him entering the complex that day?" Bucknor asked, smiling encouragingly.

"Nothing unusual. We exchanged pleasantries like we often do when we run into each other. I was on my way to the DHL office to dispatch some documents."

"At around four thirty-five, when you got back here, did you observe anything unusual?"

"Nothing out of the ordinary."

"The elevator that brought you up, were you the only occupant to disembark on this floor?" Ayeni, who had been listening quietly, asked.

"No. There was this physically challenged man too," Titilayo replied. "I held the entrance door open for him to walk through."

"Physically challenged man? Was he someone you have seen before?" Ayeni asked sharply.

"Never seen him before." Titilayo replied, alarmed.

"Do you know which of the offices the man visited?" Smith asked, keeping his voice leveled.

"I have no idea. He walked towards the direction of Anthony's office. I watched him go, but I can't tell which of the offices he entered."

"The corridor was empty except for you and the man?" Bucknor asked.

"That's correct. It was almost closing time. Visitors should be leaving the building, not coming in." Titilayo answered.

Smith processed this information. His eyes roamed from where they were standing to Anthony's office. It was a long corridor, alright, but not long enough that a gunshot wouldn't be heard unless the killer used a silencer. Just out of curiosity, he asked,

"The man you held the door open for— I want to assume you got a good look at him?"

"He was dragging his right leg and holding a brown bag. The type of bag Jehovah's Witnesses carry along with them," Titilayo said. "He was wearing a hat, a cowboy type."

"A cowboy hat?" Smith asked, making a face.

"Yes. I did try to get a good look at his face but couldn't. The upper part of his face was concealed by the hat."

"Why would a physically challenged man try to conceal his face?" Bucknor wondered aloud.

"It beats me, but like they say, different strokes for different folks," Titilayo replied.

Bucknor knew instinctively that they had just found a lead. They needed to find the man quickly. She took out her card from her side pocket and handed it to Titilayo.

"Feel free to call me anytime if you remember something else, okay?"

"I hope you catch the killer if only to give his family closure." Titilayo said. She took the card from Bucknor.

"We will catch him. Thank you so much for your time." Bucknor said. She shook hands with Titilayo.

Bucknor then led the way out of the office, with Ayeni and Smith walking shoulder to shoulder behind her.

The next half hour was spent retracing their steps. Bucknor led the men back to every office they had previously visited to ask if anyone remembered seeing the physically challenged man on the day in question. No one seemed to remember seeing him.

"No one else saw the man except Titilayo. It was as if he was never here, a ghost." Bucknor said in frustration.

"We need to find him, ghost or no ghost." Smith said.

"Hopefully, the CCTV footage should capture him entering and leaving the building." Bucknor said, her eyes glittering with hope.

"Let's call it a day. We'll meet tomorrow morning to view the CCTV footage. Top priority is to identify our ghost using the footage." Ayeni said.

Ayeni pointed to the staircase and smiled. Then he started jogging down, taking the stairs two at a time, towards the ground floor.

The other two tagged along.

The hunt for the ghost was about to begin.

Chapter Ten

Banji Smith was completely exhausted. He was not a man to sit staring at TV screens, hoping to find something that would help crack a case. The trio had been going through the CCTV footage for hours, trying hard not to miss anything of significance. From the outset, Smith had suggested that the footage be restricted to a three-hour timeline, covering the period between four and seven o'clock. It was a suggestion that Bucknor had vehemently rejected, with the support of Ayeni.

"I think we should go through the whole coverage. We can't afford to miss anything." Bucknor had argued.

"The timeframe suggested is where I think we might find something of interest." Smith had countered.

"It's a painstaking exercise, and I wouldn't want us to miss anything," Bucknor had fired back. "Better to go through the whole coverage."

"If we can get what we want in three hours, why do we have to waste time going through the whole thing?" Smith asked Bucknor.

Bucknor stared at him, her eyes narrowing. Noticing that the pair was about to take their rivalry to the next level, Ayeni stepped in.

"Banji is right. The information we seek may very well hide within the stipulated timeframe." He took a step forward and pointed his forefinger at the screen. "I think, however, we should watch the whole footage, if only for the fun of it. Who can tell what else we could find before getting to the crucial three-hour timeframe?"

Ayeni caught a glimpse of Smith, who nodded his head in agreement. He was glad that he had somehow convinced Smith about why they should do it Bucknor's way. His main objective was to make sure the team was always on the same page.

With that matter resolved, the team sat for what felt like an eternity, watching the CCTV footage. Bucknor had a notepad in front of her and was taking notes. Every now and then, she would request that the video be paused so she could make certain observations. Even though Smith didn't agree with her method, he managed to keep his cool.

At around two o'clock, Ayeni called for a forty-five-minute break. This was a great relief for Smith. He just couldn't wait to get away from Bucknor. Her CCTV viewing method was too time-consuming as far as Smith was concerned. He would rather have the guys at the DSS—hard, efficient, and fast.

"We should be back here by two forty-five sharp." Ayeni said as he pulled back his chair.

"Okay, fine by me." Bucknor assured, stretching her arms above her head and yawning.

Smith said nothing. He got up and walked hurriedly out of the office. Some fresh air should help him regain his sanity, he thought to himself. Ayeni hurried after him, catching up just as he was about to step out of the building and into the parking lot.

"We should try and accommodate some of her excesses if you know what I mean." Ayeni said, jabbing Smith with his elbow.

Smith turned his head slightly, smiling.

"I get it, Lekan," Smith said calmly. "I know her type. Everything must be perfectly done and, according to the book. It could be irritating at times, but I totally agree with you about accommodating her." His smile widened.

"Then, see you soon," Ayeni said. He turned and walked towards his car.

Smith understood that Ayeni was trying to foster a better working environment within the team. He appreciated that and decided right then to be more accommodating towards Bucknor, no matter the circumstances.

*****

In Detective Bucknor's world, there was no difference between night and day as far as police work was concerned. Her mother had somehow instilled in her the notion that a police officer was required to be on active duty twenty-four hours a day, as long as there were people out there ready to break the law at any given time. No one had warned neither Ayeni nor Smith about this. The trio had returned as scheduled to resume viewing the footage. Though the process was slow and time-consuming, the atmosphere in the room this time around was more cordial, allowing for occasional jokes and comments. By the time Ayeni called for a second break, it was well past midnight.

Detective Bucknor went away for a couple of minutes and returned with three cups of fresh coffee and some snacks. They spent the next twenty minutes eating in silence, each wondering if the CCTV idea was an exercise in futility.

"C'mon, guys, we're almost done," Bucknor said as she finished her coffee. She went back to resume her position in front of the screen.

"I do hope you're right," Ayeni said jokingly. He signaled with his head to Smith that they should join Bucknor.

It was around four o'clock in the morning when Bucknor, who was so focused on the screen, suddenly froze. Her heart began to race. She moved her face closer to the screen and, after a moment, pointed at a moving figure. It was a man wearing a brown cowboy hat. He was dragging his right leg as he slowly made his way towards the entrance of Western House.

Bucknor immediately hit the pause button. The image was captured at five minutes past four.

"This is undoubtedly our subject of interest." Smith said in a cold, flat voice.

"That's right. Notice the way he positioned the hat. It's obvious that he's deliberately using it to conceal his face." Ayeni said, leaning over and staring more intensely at the screen.

"See if you can zoom in to enlarge the image." Smith urged.

Bucknor enlarged the image, so it covered the whole screen. The man's face was too obscured to make anything out of it. After a few minutes, Bucknor pressed the play button once more.

When the video started playing again, the man had reached the entrance of Western House. He appeared not to have any difficulties climbing the stairs. Then he started dragging his right leg again as he covered the short distance between the staircase and the entrance door. The big revolving entrance door opened automatically as he reached it.

"Did you see that!" Bucknor exclaimed.

The two men nodded. They had seen the man in the video navigate the stairs without much difficulty, only to start dragging his leg as he approached the entrance to the building.

"We have to find this guy." Smith said quietly.

"Let's do a re-watch, from when the camera first caught this guy all the way until he entered the building." Ayeni instructed.

Bucknor immediately pressed the backward tab. Then they watched the footage from the time the man appeared on the video until he entered Western House, twice. The actual time from when the man was caught on camera until he entered the building was four minutes and forty-seven seconds.

"The footage is not good enough for identification. We know, however, that this individual is a person of interest." Ayeni said, looking from Smith to Bucknor.

"Why fake disability if he's not up to something mischievous?" Bucknor wondered out loud.

Ayeni looked briefly at Bucknor. He figured they would have to watch the video to the very end to get the answer to that question.

"Let's keep watching," Ayeni said calmly. "Let's find out when this individual exited the premises."

Bucknor hit the play button, and the video resumed playing. It was the closing hour, and a stream of people could be seen rushing out of the premises. The video continued playing, and by fifteen minutes past six, two security officers appeared on the screen, did some security checks, and locked the gate. Without being prompted, Bucknor pressed her finger on the rewind button to take the footage back to when the camera first captured the suspect. The video played once more until it was paused at the point where the security officers were seen locking the gate.

"There is no sign of the man leaving the premises." Ayeni pointed out.

"He never left the building through this exit." Smith said.

"Perhaps the CCTV coverage of the left-wing will capture him leaving." Bucknor said.

Bucknor switched to the camera covering the left wing. They watched until the security personnel appeared to lock the left-wing gate. There was no record of the man leaving the premises. They were now convinced that their prime suspect had never left the building that evening through any of the gates.

"It's clear that the suspect never left the premises using either of the two gates," Bucknor said, waving her hands in the air.

"He left the premises for sure, one way or another. It's up to us to find out how." Smith said indifferently.

"True, Banji. He left one way or another." Ayeni reiterated.

Smith got up from his seat and started pacing around the room. Bucknor ignored him, choosing instead to focus her attention on the screen. Ayeni followed him briefly with his eyes before deciding to ignore him. He joined Bucknor in staring, absent-mindedly at the screen.

"I think we should call it a day," Ayeni said, finally breaking the silence that had engulfed the room. "We need to get some rest. The good thing is, we now have a suspect to track down."

Bucknor's attention was still glued to the screen. Ayeni hesitated, then reached forward and grabbed the remote control. The movement of his hand caught Bucknor's attention, making her turn her head towards him.

Ayeni switched off the TV. It was only then that Bucknor took a deep breath and realized it was time to call it a day.

"You go home and get some rest," Ayeni said to her. "I don't want you back in the office before ten o'clock."

"I will get some rest," Bucknor said, forcing a smile. "I'll be in the office by eight o'clock."

"I want you to get enough rest. See you in the office by ten o'clock, not before," Ayeni insisted.

Ayeni turned towards Smith, who was standing motionless with his hands in his pockets.

"I'll be meeting Commissioner Armani by eight o'clock later this morning for a briefing. I'll see the both of you by ten o'clock."

Smith nodded. He noticed, from the corner of his eye, Bucknor slowly getting to her feet. She gathered her writing materials and did a quick check.

"See you guys later." she said as she walked noiselessly out of the room.

Smith watched as Ayeni extracted the CCTV disk, walked over to a safe, and deposited it there. Once the safe was secured, Ayeni picked up his jacket and a bunch of keys. He walked past Smith to stand by the window, looking directly into the street. Smith joined him.

"We both know that the suspect left the premises that night, one way or another." Ayeni pointed out, his eyes fixed on the street.

"Absolutely," Smith said. "The how, is what we need to figure out."

"Our job becomes much easier once we figure that out."

"If he disguised himself to get into the building, what's to stop him from disguising himself to get out?" Smith wondered.

"Good point, Banji," Ayeni said sharply. He nodded his head towards the door. "Let's call it a day. We'll try and figure that out in our next meeting."

The two men shook hands. Smith was the one who led the way out of the office. He waited outside the door for Ayeni to lock up before walking rapidly away into the dark night.

*****

Davies had spent most of the day jumping from one meeting to another. He finally got back to his office as the clock was turning six to find Jessica waiting for him. This was not unusual as Jessica sometimes had to wait behind in the office while Davies was out attending meetings. It was her job to write a summary of what transpired in such meetings after being briefed by Davies. Such a summary is then presented to Davies to read through and approve before being filed away for future purposes.

As with any such day, Jessica had sat in front of Davies, engrossed in the notes she was typing. It was towards the last part of her jottings that she suddenly felt Davies' eyes roaming all over her body. She smiled a knowing smile. Davies reached forward and ran his hand through her hair. She looked up, her smile widening. It was as if she had been expecting this to happen. She stood up and immediately pulled down her skirt.

Davies gasped.

Jessica was now naked from the waist down. Davies observed that she had recently shaved. The sight of Jessica, half naked and smiling from ear to ear, had a paralyzing effect on Davies. Jessica moved her right hand to cover her virginal, teasingly. Then she touched Davies' lips with her middle finger before inserting the finger deep inside her virginal. Then, slowly and deliberately, she removed the finger from her virginal and pointed it towards Davies's mouth. Davies opened his mouth and swallowed the finger, sucking it the way a baby would a feeding bottle. He sucked eagerly for a moment before pulling Jessica towards him. She gently pushed him backward, then took some steps away from him. She moved her waist seductively as she slowly took off her clothes. Now completely naked, she took two steps towards Davies. Then started slowly rubbing her breast before sliding her right hand down her virginal. The moment her hand reached the virginal; she inserted two fingers into her virginal and started to do a rapid in-and-out moment with her fingers.

Davies, who was by now completely naked, took two steps towards Jessica to wrap his hands around her. He wasted no time bending her over. He penetrated her from the rear as deep as he could, making her let out a loud scream. The more she screamed and moved her waist from side to side, the more he pounded her. Eventually, Jessica fell forward and to the ground. She crawled on all fours to a chair to sit down. She lifted her right leg and rested it on the right arm of the chair; she did the same with the left leg on the left arm of the chair. Her virginal was now wide open. Davies gazed, zombie-like, at the virginal and marveled as to how beautiful it looked. As if in a trance, Davies went on all four to taste the virginal with his mouth, and Jessica lost control.

"Eat my wet pussy!" she screamed as she rocked her waist back and front.

Davies needed very little prompting. He buried his head between Jessica's legs and did exactly as he was commanded. He sucked the virginal so passionately as if it was something he was born to do. It was only when Jessica had reached a loud orgasm that Davies moved his head from between Jessica's legs. Thereafter, he lifted Jessica's legs up and penetrated her. He felt her wetness all over his penis even as he went deeper. Even though Jessica cried out every time Davies went deeper, Davies was not letting go. He continued to pound her even when Jessica started pleading for him to stop. It wasn't until Davies ejaculated that he stopped, falling limply over Jessica.

Davies slowly stepped away from Jessica to sit on the chair beside her. He was satisfied and happy. He wished he could get this kind of happiness and satisfaction from having sex with his wife. This, he knew, was wishful thinking. His wife-Mariam was a good wife and a good mother to their children. That was about it. Their sex life was a boring one, but Mariam was content with it.

"Humans shouldn't engage in sex as if they were animals." She would often say when they were newly wedded. It was a belief she still holds dear to this day.

Davies turned to steal a look at Jessica. She was now fully conscious and smiling at him.

"That was amazing." Davies said as a matter of fact.

Jessica rolled her eyes and smiled.

"I am wondering when you are going to leave that husband of yours and come marry me."

"Let's keep it this way for now, okay." Jessica said, her smile widening.

The phone started to ring.

Davies walked naked to pick up the phone. He listened.

"Victor on the line, sir."

"Victor, you are calling rather late. I was about to leave the office."

"Am sorry sir. Just wanted to give a quick update on the CCTV coverage."

"Listening."

Edobor gave Davies the update.

"The prime suspect disguised himself to gain access into the premises?"

"Yes, sir."

"He was not recorded leaving the building?"

"No sir, he was not."

"If he disguised himself in order to gain access to the premises, what's there to stop him from altering his disguise before exiting the premises."

"Exactly our line of thinking, sir."

"Find this guy. He has some questions to answer."

"We will find him, sir."

"What about the woman who gave the hint about the suspect?"

"We are planning to bring her in for more questions, sir."

"Do that."

"Okay, sir."

Good."

Jessica was fully dressed by the time Davies dropped the phone. She was going through the notes she had made. Davies picked up his clothes and slowly started to dress. Jessica walked over and gave him a kiss. She helped him adjust his tie, then turned and walked out of the office without saying another word. She needed to make an urgent call before closing for the day.

It dawned on Davies that it was time to go home to his lovely wife to give her the usual story of "too much work at the office."

His wife was a good wife, but their sex life was practically dead. She doesn't even seem to realize that fact. Well, he has Jessica and was enjoying regular sex with her. So long the arrangement with Jessica takes care of his sex life; he doesn't see any reason why he shouldn't continue to be the loving husband to his wife.

He was still thinking of his wife as he left the office and wandered to the parking lot, where his driver was waiting in the car to drive him home.

Chapter Eleven

Jessica opened the door to her second-floor apartment and walked into a massive living room. She closed the door behind her and unconsciously looked around. Her eyes drifted from the fireplace to the built-in book shelve, where she had left books scattered around the previous evening. The books were now neatly arranged in the book shelve. Her eyes travelled across the floor, taking in the different rugs, French, English, Persian, and Orientals arranged in such a way to form a unique pattern with a breathtaking effect. She shifted her gaze to the large windows, which were strategically positioned to allow sunlight into the living room. A sitting area besides the window gives her a vintage position to observe the heavens and its stars. She could sit in this section and watch the moon and the stars staring directly at her. It was a sight like no other. She had poured in a great deal of time and with no expense spared to make her apartment look the way she wanted it- elegant.

She removed her shoes, then walked to the kitchen to get a bottle of cold water from the refrigerator. After drinking a full glass of water, she went straight to the bathroom to remove her makeup. She needed to freshen up before calling out to Harry, whom she knew was busy in one of his studio rooms.

When Jessica stepped out of the bathroom, she was startled to find her husband staring at her from across the room. He was leaning against one of the pillars in the sitting room, hands folded across his chest. He smiled as their eyes locked. She smiled back meekly.

"Hope my beautiful wife had a wonderful day at work?"

"You startled me, Harry." Jessica said.

"I didn't mean to. How was your day?" Harry walked over and kissed her affectionately.

"My day was as hectic as always." Jessica managed to say as Harry released her.

"I understand that. Now you are home, and the workday is over."

"And how was your day, Harry?" Jessica asked.

"Let's not even go there." Harry warned her.

"Hectic and crazy, I presume."

"That's why I said that we should skip that part." Harry said, shaking his head as if feeling sorry for himself.

"Let me change my clothes. I will be right back." Jessica said. She patted Harry on both cheeks as she walked away.

Harry Olaniyi followed Jessica with his eyes until she entered the dressing room. As the dressing room door closed behind her, he turned and walked swiftly to the kitchen. He opened the refrigerator and brought out a packet of pineapple juice. He poured juice into two glasses, then added some ice cubes.

Jessica walked into the kitchen to find her husband standing with two glasses of pineapple juice. He handed her a glass. They drank in silence.

As soon as Jessica finished her drink, she dropped the glass. She then looked over at Harry who was just drinking down his last swallow. Harry finished his drink and looked quizzically at Jessica.

"Am thinking of food." Jessica said

"Anything should do, honey." Harry opened the dishwashing machine to deposit the two glasses into it.

"There's chicken stew in the fridge; I just need to cook some rice."

"Rice and chicken stew sound perfect." Harry said. He opened a cupboard and brought out a packet of rice.

By the time dinner was over, Jessica was completely relaxed. She had gotten over the feeling of guilt, which always occurred whenever she had a sexual encounter with Davies. Her head was now cleared enough to focus on her husband. She listened as he told her the story about the moon and the old woman trapped inside the moon. It was a tale she had heard many times before. It was a tale Harry's grandmother had told him often as a child. Jessica knew quite well that there was no old woman trapped on the moon, but she let Harry tell the story anyway while she listened patiently. It brings back memories of his childhood, so she lets him relive his childhood by telling the tales by moonlight, as it was called back then. They would then argue back and forth as soon as the storytelling was over. The story would be told again the following month, if they happen to catch the full moon together.

Jessica yearned as Harry finished telling the story. She was tired and needed some sleep. She dragged herself closer to Harry, to rest her head on his chest. She was trying hard to keep awake. Harry noticed it. He lowered Jessica's head on the pillow beside him and slowly got to his feet. Jessica adjusted her head to settle it properly on the pillow, she opened her eyes but couldn't keep her eyes open for more than a few seconds. Harry bent over and carried Jessica to the bedroom. He gently laid her on the bed, then covered her with the bed sheet. Harry then dimmed the light before walking out of the bedroom. He walked back to take his position once more by the window, to continue to stare at the imposing moon, and reliving the many memories it brings.

*****

The last fifteen hours have been both busy and hectic for Westland. The news that the Boko Haram terrorist group had kidnapped five Red Cross workers, two U.S citizens and three French nationals, had sent a shock wave through the intelligence community. The abduction along the Nigerian border with Chad had completely caught the intelligence agencies by surprise. Westland and his counter-terrorism team at the U.S. embassy had acted swiftly, by establishing a task force to liaise with Nigerian security organizations, to establish a parameter and to block the terrorists from getting their captives into the Sambisa Forest, where rescue mission would be near impossible. Westland had then activated his network of informants all over Nigeria, to go fish in troubled waters and get him usable information, by any means necessary.

It wasn't long before information started flooding in, with Westland being the main recipient. A few hours later, of all the info he received, one of them was able to give the location of the terrorists and their captives. His quick intervention and the initiative to immediately co-opt the Nigerian security agencies, without waiting for the approval of his superiors had paid off, by slowing down the terrorists' attempt to move the hostages into the Sambisa Forest. The terrorists and their human cargo were now holed up somewhere, but that somewhere was nowhere near the Sambisa Forest. It was this one vital information of exact location that Westland needed as a trigger, to go after the terrorists.

Westland had come under tremendous pressure from his superiors within hours of the abduction. The first call came from the CIA director, Alex Cowley, who demanded that the counter-terrorism team go after the terrorists immediately to secure the captives. This was followed almost immediately by a call from the FBI director, Greg Roadman, practically making the same demand on Westland. The US Secretary of State Matt Owens was the last to call, preferring to speak instead with Ambassador Rich Miller.

When Westland eventually got words that the terrorists and their victims were holed up in a residential quarter somewhere in Maiduguri, the Borno State capital, he quickly dispersed Tommy Anderson to Maiduguri to meet with the informant for an on-the-ground assessment. It wasn't until he got words from Anderson corroborating the informant's info that Westland notified both the CIA director and his FBI counterpart of the development. Ambassador Miller, who was not directly involved in the planning and execution of the mission, was the last to be informed. His role was limited to that of damage control after the mission.

Director Cowley had insisted that a rescue operation be carried out immediately, when Westland notified him of the exact location of the hostages. Secretary of State Owens was, however, not convinced that it was a good idea, since a failed mission might result in a political backlash to the US President. It has taken Westland a great deal of time to convince Secretary Owens, that the mission needed to be carried out immediately, to prevent the terrorists from moving the hostages into the Sambisa Forest.

"As the man on ground, I agree absolutely with Director Cowley that we act now. We have the element of surprise on our side." Westland had argued in a Zoom meeting, which included CIA director Cowley, FBI director Roadman, Secretary Owens and Ambassador Miller.

"It's easy for you to say. Have you thought of the political backlash if this mission fails?" Secretary Owens had asked crossly.

"It's best to act now than to wait, sir." Westland had insisted.

"How trustworthy is your source? How can you say with certainty that the hostages are in that location?" Owens asked, not willing to let go.

"My source is impeccable. The hostages are in the location." Westland replied calmly.

"Do you agree that we should go ahead and drive this mission? Alex, Rich, Greg?" Owens asked. He was hoping that at least one of the men would object to it, giving him a chance to cancel the mission.

To Owens' surprise, the three men nodded without hesitation. The Secretary of State closed his eyes for a brief second. Damn it, he thought. His political career was now hanging in the balance and depending on the outcome of the mission. He took a deep breath.

"Let's do it, gentlemen." He said finally. "I have to go brief Mr. President immediately."

The die was cast.

*****

Westland arrived in Maiduguri by ten o'clock on that warm Tuesday night, in a small spy plane camouflaged as a passenger plane. The plane, equipped with the state-of-the-art gadgets necessary for counter-terrorism operations, transported a team of highly trained and heavily armed members of the US counter-terrorism squad into Maiduguri. These men had been hastily assembled from their respective stations within the West African sub-region and transported to Nigeria, without being told the specific nature of their mission. It wasn't until the plane touched

135

down in Maiduguri, that the nature of the mission was revealed to the men on board.

The team was subsequently divided into three groups for easy coordination. The first group, which consisted of eight men, was assigned the role of locating and neutralizing any potential threat, to accessing the house where the hostages were kept. The second team, made up of five men, was assigned the role of neutralizing any real or imagined threats once inside the building. The third team, made up of three men, was assigned the role of physically removing the hostages from the house and transporting them to safety. Westland and the squad commander, Joseph Williams, were to remain on the plane to coordinate the operation from there. Westland had tried but not succeeded in convincing Tommy Anderson not to follow the squad into action. Tommy had insisted on going and had been assigned alongside the group responsibly for removing the hostages from the house.

In the early hours of Wednesday, two o'clock to be precise, men from the squad stormed an ordinary-looking residential building, standing a few meters away from a mosque, in a popular residential area in Maiduguri. The occupants of the house were never told to expect visitors. The five men stationed to guard the building were not in a combat mood when the men struck. Perhaps due to fatigue or the notion that their hideout was never going to be discovered, the men felt secure. So secured to the extent that the two men, guarding the entrance to the house, had their eyes glued to their mobile phones, as a man dressed in a native attire and carrying a small kettle approached them. One of the guards eventually looked up, but by then, the man with the kettle was within striking distance. The guard sensed that something was amiss as he tried to focus. The man lifted the kettle a little bit and pointed it in the direction of the guard. The guard felt something hit him. He fell backwards, hitting his head on the wall behind him.

It was only then that the second guard shifted his gaze from his phone and looked to where his partner had fallen. He was almost immediately able to register what had happened. He reached for his gun, which was placed standing by his side and to his left. Just as his fingers touched the gun, he felt something hit him on his neck. The hand that was almost grabbing the gun, made a quick U-turn, choosing instead to grab at his neck. He felt warm liquid rushing down his hand even as his body suddenly began to vibrate in a dance of death. The other three terrorists guarding the house had equally seen men carrying small kettles and had died shortly afterwards.

By the time the signal to enter the house was given, the combat-ready team assigned the role approached the entrance door in a V-formation. The leader of the team reached for the handle of the door, and surprisingly, the door opened. He paused and lifted his fist, signaling the men to stop. He listened but heard nothing from the inside. Moments later, he gave the signal to advance. The men entered the house quietly, quickly scanning the place. Their night vision glasses, equipped with a special feature to detect heat form, allowed the men to easily detect and headcount the people inside the house. Twelve in total.

The leader of the team passed a tiny wire through a little space underneath the door of one of the rooms. He looked into the small TV-like box he was carrying. He could see clearly seven individuals, five hostages huddled together in a corner of the room, and two men wearing bulletproof vests with AK47s dangling on their shoulders. They were awake and playing cards. The leader of the team lifted his hands above his head to draw the attention of his men. The men moved closer to him and looked into the TV box, quickly registering the situation. The team leader then pointed his index finger to his head, indicating that the terrorists were to be shot in the head. He folded his hands into a fist and pointed the index finger to his head a second time, to emphasize the importance of the headshot. He did a circle with his right hand, and his men dispersed in different directions, leaving him behind. Less than five minutes later, the men reconvened in front of the room, leaving five terrorists dead in different parts of the house.

Westland and Commander Williams watched as the events unfolded on a giant screen, in one section of the plane. The fact that the two terrorists in the room with the hostages were awake, was a source of worry for Westland. One of them could be wearing a bomb and wouldn't hesitate to detonate it, should they be cornered. He looked over his shoulder at Williams and almost envied his calmness.

Commander Williams was staring intensely at the screen, his hands folded across his chest. He was as calm as an expert chess player. Though he had no doubt that his men would rescue the hostages, but like all expert chess players, he was holding his breath until the very end. He had played out the different scenarios that could happen in his mind, and the only outcome each scenario resulted in was success. This was reassuring for him and was the rock upon which his calmness was based.

Williams suddenly pointed his finger at the screen. Westland pushed forward to look. One of the terrorists was moving towards the door. This was a dicey situation. He turned to look at Williams and thought he saw what looked like a smile flanked through his face. Williams lifted his thumb without shifting his gaze from the screen. Westland relaxed and refocused his attention on the screen in time to see the terrorist open the door, then stepped into the hallway. He had the AK47 dangling nonchalantly across his right shoulder as if he had no care in the world. He took a couple of steps along the hallway, then stopped abruptly. He listened. It was as if some sixth sense was warning him of some impending danger. He started to turn around, automatically reaching for the AK47. He succeeded in turning his body to an angle of forty-five degrees, before he was shot in the head. He died standing. As he started to slide to the floor, two powerful hands grabbed him and gently laid him down. The men moved swiftly back to their position in front of the door. The leader of the team motioned with his hands, and the man next to him, went down on his knees. He gently maneuvered the tiny wire through the door once again. Both men stared at the TV screen, to judge the distance between the door and the terrorist's position.

When the door opened, the terrorists didn't react initially. He was facing away from the door and must have reasoned that his colleague was returning to the room. Suddenly, he looked sideways to see two men standing motionless, a short distance from him and pointing something, he couldn't yet recognize, at him. By the time the reality of what was happening dawned on him, it was too late. Five bullets rammed into his body almost simultaneously. He fell to his left side, dead. The two men rushed towards the terrorist to confirm that he was dead, just as two other members of the squad, rushed past them to the hostages. The fifth man maintained his position outside the room, ready to neutralize any threat.

"We are members of the US counter-terrorism squad. We are here to rescue you. You are in safe hands now." The leader announced rapidly to the hostages.

The hostages, who were understandably in shock, didn't respond to the announcement. The two words that registered right away were "The US" and "rescue". The men worked quickly to unshackle the hostages. Once the hostages were freed from their shackles, one member of the squad stepped forward and rubbed a substance on the faces of each of the hostages. Their faces immediately turned black. The same substance was rubbed on their hands, up to their elbows. The other man retrieved from his backpack five native caps, used by the average person in Maiduguri. He placed one on each of the hostages' heads. He adjusted the caps to fit in such a way as to conceal the hair of the person wearing it. The dark color of their faces, the dark color of their hands, and the caps, did the trick of transforming these Caucasian men into Africans.

It was time to exit the building.

*****

The rescue team successfully reached their rendezvous with their human cargo without further incident. Anderson, who was sitting in one of the four bulletproof Jeeps, waiting to ferry the men back to the jet, sprang into action when the message came through the radio.

"Cargo intact. We are with you in five minutes."

The vehicles transporting the squad members, and the rescued men arrived in a convoy, exactly five minutes after the radio message. Anderson quickly loaded the men into two of the Jeeps. A lead Jeep then drove away, followed closely by the two Jeeps carrying the men. The fourth Jeep followed behind, deliberately allowing for some distance between it and the three Jeeps ahead. The leader of the squad and his men remained behind until the Jeeps had disappeared. He then gave the signal for the lead car and the other cars in the convoy to follow the Jeeps, towards the airport.

When every man and every vehicle had been accounted for and subsequently loaded into the Jet, Westland walked over to Commander Williams, who had just finished giving instructions to a tall, broad-shouldered Army Captain. The two men shook hands with Commander Williams, allowing what looked like a smile to steal across his face.

"My job here is done, Raymond." Williams said calmly.

"Mine too. Great working with you, Joe." Westland's voice was packed with admiration. Westland and the members of his team arrived in Lagos by nine o'clock on Thursday morning.

The rescued men were already on a flight to Charles de Gaulle Airport in France from where the three Americans would catch a connecting flight to the United States. The other members of the squad, including Commander Joseph Williams, had flown back to their various locations from the Abuja International Airport, having completed their assignment in Nigeria.

Westland sat in the back seat of the embassy car that picked him up from the Airport. He was staring out the window as the driver maneuvered his way through the heavy traffic, onwards bound for the US embassy complex on Victoria Island. Westland shifted his gaze back to the car and the TV screen that was right in front of him. It was News time. The News anchor had just started reading the News, when it was suddenly interrupted. There was a breaking

News. Westland watched as the President of the United States gave an update on the rescue mission. He listened as the President presented the story to the American people and the rest of the world.

Westland frowned. He thought of Commander Williams and the men who took part in the rescue mission. He remembered Tommy Anderson. He remembered the trauma the hostages went through. He remembered the tension he felt throughout the duration of the rescue operation. In all of it, it was only fair that he and all the men fighting to keep America and the rest of the world safe, receive the accolade they so rightly deserved. They were heroes in every sense of the word.

Westland was trying hard to figure out the extent to which the President on the screen, fits into his definition of "hero" when the driver announced:

"We are here, Sir."

"Thanks, Kent." Westland said as he reached for his briefcase.

Ambassador Rich Miller and a small group of top officials were waiting to receive him. As soon as Westland stepped out of the car, they all started clapping their hands and shouting:

"U.S.A! U.S.A.!! U.S.A.!!!"

Westland walked towards the group, a fixed smile on his face. For a man like Westland, this was the best he could do under this slightly embarrassing situation.

Chapter Twelve

As soon as the initial reception for Westland was over, Ambassador Miller ushered him to his office for a debriefing. The Ambassador needed to get a grip on the situation in case he had to do damage control. The meeting was long and detailed, with ambassador Miller personally taking notes. It wasn't until late in the afternoon that Westland was finally able to escape from the custody of the ambassador.

Westland checked his wristwatch as he stepped out of the ambassador's office and noted that he had thirty minutes before his meeting with the intelligence corps in conference room B, located down the hall from the ambassador's office. This should give him enough time for a light lunch and a big cup of coffee, he thought to himself, as he hurried towards the restaurant on the second floor of the building.

The meeting with the intelligent corps was not as long as Westland had anticipated. He was quick and to the point, and because those in attendance were familiar with the issues, he didn't have to spend too much time on useless details. As Westland stepped out of the conference room, he almost ran into Ambassador Miller. He looked quizzically at the ambassador, who beckoned him to follow, before leading the way back to his office.

Once in the office, Ambassador Miller picked up the phone on his desk and casually handed it over to Westland.

"Raymond!" It was the strong and unmistakable voice of CIA director Alex Cowley.

"Sir."

"Good job, Raymond! Very good job!"

"That is to the whole team sir, including Ambassador Miller who helped with certain aspects of the logistics." Westland was not one to corner credit to himself.

"Absolutely correct, Raymond. Good job to the whole team."
"Thank you, sir." Westland said, pleased.

"The President sends his appreciation to the whole team, too." Cowley said.

Westland hesitated, not sure of what to say. He looked towards the ambassador, who was pre-occupied with the document in his hands, seemingly not interested in the conversation taking place.

"Thank you, sir." Westland repeated.

"I would expect a detailed report from you by tomorrow morning at the latest. I got a sketchy report from Ambassador Miller but, I need a first-hand report."

"You should get it before midday tomorrow, sir."

Westland knew full well that the report would be ready first thing in the morning. He didn't, however, want to be under any kind of pressure, hence the need to play on time.

"I shall be expecting the latest report by eleven thirty tomorrow morning." Director Cowley said with a note of finality.

"Copied, sir."

"That will be all for now." Cowley said and cut the line.

Just then, Ambassador Miller stood up and walked to where Westland was standing, to retrieve the phone from him. He smiled at Westland in a new, admirable way. It was not lost on him that Westland had mentioned his name to the CIA director as one of the people worthy of commendation.

*****

Westland collapsed into a chair when he finally got back to his office. It dawned on him that he hadn't slept for the past thirty-six hours and was beginning to show signs of fatigue. He tried and succeeded in blanking out almost all the events of the past couple of hours. It was now "work accomplished" and needed to be saved deep down in his "work accomplished bank" situated somewhere in his brain. It was something he had developed very early in his career and had perfected over the years. There was no need dueling on a mission already accomplished; it was a huge distraction.

Once his mind was cleared, Westland didn't feel so tired anymore. He felt somehow reborn and re-energized. This was nothing strange to him. It was his body's way of fighting stress. This has helped largely in preventing any form of post-traumatic stress disorder (PTSD) over the years.

Westland turned his head slightly when he heard the secure phone ringing. He got slowly to his feet and walked to the drawer where the phone was kept. By the time he got to the phone, it had stopped ringing. As he reached for the phone, a message came in. He opened the phone and read the message.

"Been trying to reach you. Updates on our case?" He read the previous message.

"Good job with the rescue, Raymond. Updates?"

Westland turned and walked back to his desk. He sat on the edge of the desk as he looked through the phone call list. He studied the list for a few seconds before dialing a number. As the phone began to ring, he immediately cut the call. It was his tactics. The person at the other end would take this as a signal that Westland was free and ready with some new updates.

It didn't take long before the phone rang. "Updates."

"CCTV footage watched. The recording was not very clear to reveal anything significant." Westland paused.

"That wouldn't be all, would it?"

"A lady working in one of the offices on the same floor, encountered a physically challenged man, around the time the target was neutralized." Westland paused again.

"The physically challenged man is your man?"

"Yes, sir." Westland replied.

There was a deafening silence. It was as if the man on the other end had ended the call. Westland waited patiently.

"And this lady?"

Westland had anticipated this question.

"The crew are interested in her. Hoping to bring her in for questioning."

"Same floor with the target?"

"That's correct, sir."

"You have this woman's name?"

"Yes, sir."

"Think she's going to be a problem?"

"No, sir. She couldn't possibly id the physically challenged man."

"Would that be all?"

"For now, sir."

"Good job with the rescue mission."

"Thank you, sir." Westland said calmly, careful to keep his voice as flat as possible.

"You will do well to clean up this mess just as you did with the rescue mission."

Westland said nothing. There was nothing to be said. He listened as the man on the other end of the phone disconnected the call. He dropped the phone and looked away. He was dead certain that the physically challenged man seen by the lady was his man. He was caught on CCTV camera entering the building, though the recording was bad. The possibility of identification using the CCTV may be slim, but the lady was something else altogether. Could she possibly identify the individual she saw on that day? Westland didn't think so. He was certain that his hitman would have taken certain precautions, to make it nearly impossible for anyone to identify him.

Westland got up and started pacing round the room. He started to reflect on the conversation he just had with his handler. He suddenly found himself standing in front of the cabinet housing a bottle of whiskey. He pulled the cabinet open and brought out the bottle of whiskey. He stared at it longingly. He opened the lid and, without hesitation, gulped down a mouthful. He swallowed hard and could feel the burning sensation of the whiskey in his throat and chest, as the liquid cruised through his system.

This lady, could she possibly be a cause for concern, as his handler had hinted? Most likely, the answer was negative. Westland knew from experience that there was always a one percent probability that the lady could pose a problem. Always, there was.

Westland reached for his phone and dialed a number. Almost immediately, a voice answered.

"Boss man."

"Were you a physically challenged man at the Western House?"

"Affirmative."

"Would you say the lady you encountered on the subject's floor is in a position to zero down on you?"

Westland knew it was extremely unlikely that the woman

could, but he needed to ask the question. The fact that the woman was still alive was a testimony that she was not a problem. The remote chance that she could identify the man on the phone would most definitely have gotten her killed.

"Negative, sir. But I remember the woman."

"The police had a talk with her. She remembered seeing you heading towards the subject's office. Her recollection is vague. The police are planning to question her again at the station."

Silence.

Westland was the one to break the silence.

"Do you think you have anything to worry about, concerning her?"

"I don't think so. Always safer though to take preventive measures."

"At this stage, I wouldn't say preventive measures. I would think countermeasures fit more appropriately." Westland corrected.

"Totally agreed, boss."

"Then go ahead and take countermeasures. You have my approval. Her name is Titilayo Johnson, office number 507."

"Noted, boss."

Westland disconnected the call. He walked slowly towards the drawer. As he dropped the phone in the drawer, he heard a sound coming from outside his office. He moved swiftly towards the door. He pressed his ears against the door to listen. The methodic and deliberate pacing along the corridor convinced him, that the security personnel were doing their routine patrol.

Westland decided it was time to call it a day. He needed to eat some homemade food, and he needed some sleep. He picked up his jacket and his set of keys, then walked over to switch off the lights, before leaving the office.

Westland glanced at his wristwatch as he stepped into the warm night, the time was eight forty- five.

*****

The white convertible Mercedes Benz navigated its way into a reserved section of the underground parking lot. The occupant of the car adjusted the rear-view mirror so she could look her face over in the mirror. She automatically reached for her hair to do some adjustments. She checked her face from different directions and was satisfied that her make-up was perfect. She smiled. Then, she opened that car door and stepped out calmly, it was Titilayo Johnson.

She took some steps backwards to look the car over. The traffic this morning was unusually heavy, with cars driving almost bumper to bumper. Satisfied that no damage was done to her car, she walked towards the staircase that would lead her directly to the entrance hall of Western House.

Titilayo was always vigilant whenever she walked towards the staircase, careful not to be caught by any car that might make a sudden swerve. She was walking alone and hated it whenever she was alone, in this underground parking lot. She always gets a creeping feeling that someone might be watching her, from any of the many stationary cars. She had been watching too many American true crime movies lately, and this, she believed, was largely to blame for the uneasy feelings she got, whenever she was in certain places. She reached the entrance to the building and seeing the familiar faces of the security personnel, the feeling of creepiness left her.

Titilayo entered the cafeteria just before the entrance, to buy some candy and a cup of coffee to take with her to the office. The salesgirl, seeing her walked in, waved happily towards her.

"Good morning, sister Titti," The salesgirl called out to her.

"Good morning to you, sweetheart!" Titilayo called back. She started to pick some candies into a small paper bag.

By the time Titilayo reached the payment counter, a large cup of coffee was waiting for her. She made payment before taking a sip from the coffee. It was after this that she turned around to scan the cafeteria for some familiar faces. She smiled at some and waved at others. She failed, however, to notice a lone individual sitting in the far-left-hand corner, drinking a cup of coffee with a newspaper in front of him. The man, though appearing to be reading the newspaper, was in reality just sitting and observing everything around him.

Titilayo stepped out of the cafeteria and walked through the security post heading for the elevator, as the man slowly dropped the newspaper. He took his cup of coffee and pretended to drink from it. He checked his wristwatch as he got to his feet. He observed a queue beginning to form at the entrance to Western House, as people rushed out of the cafeteria to secure a place on the queue. The man mingled with the crowd and was out of the cafeteria in a jiffy. Once out, he nonchalantly followed a group of people hurrying towards the security post. His gaze was fixed on Titilayo, who had already crossed the security post and was moving unhurriedly towards the elevator.

The man was almost at the security post when a hot argument suddenly broke out between an elderly woman and security personnel. The old woman was accusing the security personnel of deliberately causing human traffic at the entrance. Many people in the queue sided with the old woman. This didn't go down well with the security officials. As the argument ranged, a few people used the opportunity to jump the queue and walk past the security personnel without clearance. Among this set of people was the man from the cafeteria, his eyes fixed on Titilayo as she boarded the elevator.

The man took the stairs to the second floor before stopping to observe. He was alone on the stairways, he took a deep breath and then started running upwards towards the fifth floor. He was confident he would make the fifth floor before the elevator.

*****

The man reached the fifth floor just as the elevator opened its

153

door on the fourth floor. Once on the fifth floor, the man paused to catch his breath. He then quickly scanned the long corridor for any human traffic, it was empty. He could hear voices coming from some of the offices in front of him. His attention shifted to the toilet areas, then back to the elevator door. He walked quickly to the male toilet area to judge the distance to the elevator. He realized then that the female toilet area, which was situated on the opposite side from where he was standing, was much closer to the elevator. He also realized the risk of drawing unwanted attention to himself, if seen entering or leaving the female toilet area. He stayed where he was and waited.

Judging that the elevator would be stopping at any moment, the man pushed the toilet door open and stepped inside. It was large inside, ten doors on each row indicated a total of twenty toilets. He observed four wash-hand basins on each row. He quickly pushed open every single door, to make sure the toilets were empty. Satisfied that he was alone, he looked up and stared at himself in the big mirror. He reminded himself that he was here to carry out a routine job and nothing more.

The man peeped through the slightly opened toilet door when the elevator came to a halt. He could see a man rushing out of the elevator and running down the corridor. He watched as two ladies stepped out. One of them was in her early twenties, beautiful but insipid looking, in every sense of the word. She touched her face a couple of times before walking hurriedly, into the female toilet area. The other lady, walking slowly and carrying a cup of coffee in one left hand, was Titilayo.

The man gazed at Titilayo the way a predator would a prey, then braced himself. He silently closed the toilet door as he stepped out, walking quickly but noiselessly towards her. The man was within a striking distance when Titilayo suddenly turned around, to see a man reaching out to grab her. In shock and total disbelief, she was on the verge of screaming, when she realized that she was staring at the muzzle of a .44 revolver. The man was pointing the gun directly to her head. She collapsed into the man's hand, the coffee cup falling to the ground.

The man quickly led Titilayo into the male toilet area. Once inside the toilet, the man dragged her to the toilet on the far end, right row. As the man reached forward to open the door to the toilet, Titilayo suddenly woke up from her slumber and started fighting back. The man hit her hard on her shoulder, with the butt of the gun, making her fall backwards. She screamed out in pain, as the man viciously hit her again, this time across the face. She tried to scream, but her scream was muffled by the shock her body was going through. Suddenly, she lashed out at the man, aiming for his stomach. The punch to the stomach landed, making the man gulp for breath, from the unexpected strength behind the blow. Titilayo then tried to reach the man's face, but he reacted swiftly by parring her hands away from his face. He hit Titilayo twice, in quick secessions, with the butt of the gun across her face, making her crash against the wall. Then she fell to her knees, the fall taking the breath out of her. Titilayo began to float between conscious and unconsciousness.

The man brought out a silencer from his breast pocket and carefully attached it to the gun. He steadied the revolver in his hand and shot Titilayo twice in the head. She died from the first shot. The second shot was only intended to guarantee that she stays dead.

The man dragged Titilayo's lifeless body and positioned it in a kneeling position with her head resting on the toilet seat. The blood from the gunshot wounds began to pour into the toilet. The man closed the door to the toilet, then walked calmly to the nearest wash basin to wash his hands. He checked himself all over for any sign of blood. Satisfied that he had no blood stains on him, he walked to the exit door. He listened. There was no movement. He brought out a handkerchief from his pocket and quickly wiped clean everything he had touched, not wanting to leave any fingerprints behind. Then he opened the door a little and peeped. The corridor was as silent as a graveyard. He stepped out and moved around the corner to access the nearest staircase. He took the stairs and began his downward movement, strolling casually towards oblivion.

Chapter Thirteen

The queue at the Western House entrance hall was long when Detective Bucknor arrived. She had to make a decision: jump the queue or join the queue. She decided on the latter. She was not in any form of a hurry. Her mission was to come to Titilayo's office, to personally invite her over to the station for a talk. During her last conversation with Titilayo over the telephone, it became clear that Titilayo was not looking forward to any further interaction with the police, especially not at the police station.

"This is why I dislike the police!" She had screamed. "They have a way of messing up your life the moment you try to assist them."

"We just want to ask you a couple more questions, that's all." Bucknor had pointed out.

"And for that, I have to come to your station?"

"I assure you, it's just routine and nothing more. We won't keep you more than necessary."

"I don't think I want to come to the station for anything, but I will think about it and get back to you."

"That's fair enough, okay."

Bucknor was all too familiar with the general distrust the Nigerian public had for the police. They sum up this distrust in a general slogan, which is often used to describe the police:

"Come today, come tomorrow."

"Come today, come tomorrow."

This was coined from the fact that the police, as a routine, often invite suspects and witnesses to the station for meetings with investigative officers, as many times as is deemed necessary, during the cause of an investigation. The public generally sees this as a waste of their time and hates the police for it.

It was when Titilayo had not gotten back to Bucknor after two days, that Bucknor decided to pay her an unscheduled visit, to formally invite her to the station.

Standing in the queue, Bucknor busied herself, observing everything happening around her. She observed that the security at the entrance was rather relaxed, as some individuals were able to jump the queue. She suspected that these individuals were business owners, judging from the way the security personnel reacted to them. One other thing that caught her attention was the fact that, a few others seized the opportunity to slip through security, pretending to be in the company of these business owners.

Bucknor shifted her attention back to the queue. She was now second in line. A man was standing in front of her, talking to the security man. Bucknor regarded the man. He was a tall, suit-wearing, powerfully built man, in his mid-thirties. He was holding a briefcase in his left hand while his right hand was tucked away in his right pocket. He looked distinguished. One of the security men greeted him respectfully, bowing his head each time he asked the man a question. After a few questions, the man was handed the visitor's form to fill out. As the man was filling the form, Bucknor looked away from him to glance at an over-dressed middle-aged woman, who was talking loudly on her mobile phone as she hurried towards the exit.

By the time Bucknor's attention shifted back to the man, the security man was holding the man's form in his left hand and respectfully pointing out to him which way to go. As the man started walking away from the security post, the security man gave him one last bow, grinning from ear to ear. Bucknor eyes hovered around the man for a while as he walked away. Then her eyes, for no apparent reason, travelled from the man to lock onto a man wearing thick glasses and a dark shirt, who was walking calmly towards her. The man looked towards Bucknor momentarily, then looked straight ahead towards the exit.

"It's you, Detective Bucknor!"

Bucknor half-turned, to see chief security officer John Adejobi pushing past two security men, trying to get to her. The two security men quickly stepped aside, to let their chief through.

"What brings you here, detective?"

"Routine investigation."

"Why are you on queue if you are here on investigation?"

"Just to kill time, I guess." Bucknor replied.

The "thick glasses" wearing man reached Bucknor and adjusted his glasses as he walked, soundlessly passed her. His attention was forward-looking. Though he didn't look back, the reflection on the glass door ahead enabled him to see all that was happening behind him. He was able to get a good description of the lady the man had addressed as "Detective Bucknor." He had encountered her before; he was sure of it. He tried but couldn't remember where he had seen her before. He let her slip out of his mind to concentrate on getting to his car and away from Western House.

It wasn't until he was sitting in his car that he remembered. The lady was unmistakably the same lady he had encountered that evening at the parking lot, after the hit at Western House. He had suspected that the lady was tailing him that night, and now, he was dead certain he had been right. It dawned on him at that instance, that the detective was on her way to see Titilayo and possibly take her to the station, for further questioning.

"Good luck to you, detective, but dead men don't talk," he muttered to himself as he maneuvered his car out of the parking lot.

*****

Detective Bucknor had spent some minutes with the chief security officer before hurrying off to catch the elevator. She headed straight for Titilayo's office as soon as she stepped out of the elevator, walking deliberating behind a young lady who was carrying a little baby in her arms. The baby was crying uncontrollably, stopping every few seconds to gather enough strength, for the next crying session. Bucknor reckoned that the baby was either extremely hungry or in need of a fresh diaper.

The lady, seeing a vacant seat stationed between two pillars, rushed to take possession of it. Bucknor smiled as she saw the lady looked from left to right, before unzipping her dress to fish out a breast, which she guided into the baby's mouth. The baby stopped crying immediately and started sucking frantically. The lady, who had been completely engulfed with her baby, suddenly looked up to find Bucknor smiling at her. Her eyes immediately went to her breast, and realizing that her breast was largely exposed, she quickly folded her arms across her chest, trying to shield her breast. At the same time, she began pulling at her dress in a bid to cover her breast while still breastfeeding. Seeing that her efforts to conceal her breast were not working, she turned sideways, away from any preying eyes. Bucknor walked on, the smile still on her face.

Bucknor entered office number 507 and nearly ran into a man, who was hurrying out of the office. He quickly stepped aside to let Bucknor in.

Bucknor looked around until her eyes rested on a familiar face. Kate Adeyemi walked briskly to Bucknor, an inquisitive look on her face.

"Hello Kate," Bucknor said, stretching forth her hand.

"Detective Bucknor." Kate shook her hand. "What brings you hear today?"

"I am here to have a word with Titilayo. I assure you that I won't take much of her time.”

“I hope not.”

“Is she in the office?”

“No, she is not. Meaning she’s running late.” Kate checked her wristwatch. Bucknor beat her to it.

“Time is eight thirty-two.”

“She is usually here by seven forty-five. She’s never this late.” Kate sounded surprised.

“Maybe the traffic is keeping her.” Bucknor wondered.

“Maybe and maybe not. Let me check with her team members. Perhaps, she has an out-of-office meeting, booked for this morning.”

Kate walked off.

Bucknor watched her go. She could hear her talking in a low voice, to a couple of her colleagues. Satisfied she had the information she needed, Kate walked back to join Bucknor.

“Nope. No out-of-office meeting today.”

“Okay. Do you know if anyone had tried to reach her on phone?”

“Yes, but she’s not picking up her calls. She will call back as soon as she sees the calls.”

“Can I hang around for a while?”

“Sure, over there.”

Kate pointed to a small reception area where two middle-aged men and a girl were seated. Bucknor nodded her thanks and walked off to the reception area. She picked a sitting position that gave her an unhindered view of the entrance door. Then she turned slightly and regarded the girl. The girl was tall, slender and hippy in a way that would make her stand out among her pairs. She was wearing a tight blue jean trouser and a top that was rather too small, to conceal her oversized breast. She busied herself adjusting her long and freshly made hair repeatedly, as she stared at the big wall mirror in front of her.

Bucknor turned her face away from her, as an elegantly dressed lady stepped out of a V-shaped office and moved briskly towards the reception area. She had on a smile that would shame an air hostess. She stopped a few inches from where the two men were seated, her smile widening. The two men stood up and walked up to her. She shook hands with them, said a few words, then turned around and led the men to her V-shaped office.

*****

Detective Bucknor had spent her time going through a copy of an Ovation magazine she had picked up from a shelf at the reception. She had looked through every single page of the colorful magazine, without reading any of the stories attached to each page. One thing that was remarkably worrisome for her was the fact that most of the celebrities featured in the magazine were out to deliberately flaunt their wealth, nothing more. This was a turn-off for Bucknor.

When Bucknor dropped the magazine, she took a deep breath,

then got to her feet. She was now alone in the reception room. The girl had been led away into one of the offices some fifteen minutes ago. Bucknor looked up at the wall clock and realized that she had been waiting for the past forty minutes. There was still no news about Titilayo or her whereabouts.

Bucknor walked out of the reception room as her waiting time was over. She had to get back to the station where a workload was waiting for her. She was halfway across the office when an unsmiling Kate emerged.

"Any news?" Bucknor queried

"No. Her phone kept ringing, but she's not picking up. I am worried. It's unlike her."

Bucknor folded her arms across her chest and stared intensely at Kate.

"Have you tried to reach any of those closed to her: friends, family members?"

"I called the husband personally. He said she left for work before seven this morning."

"Yet, she's not here?"

Bucknor could see that Kate was becoming agitated.

"Maybe she's involved in an accident. Do you think?" Kate asked.

Bucknor could sense that Kate was beginning to enter a panic mood. She reached forward to grab both her hands and squeezed gently.

"Kate, I've to get back to the station, right now. If you don't reach her in the next two hours, give me a call. I will mobilize a team to go and search for her. Do you understand?"

Kate tried to say something, but no words came. She nodded her head rigorously.

Bucknor released Kate's hands. She patted her on the shoulder and walked away towards the exit door. Kate walked slowly behind her, convinced that something terrible had happened to Titilayo.

*****

Etim Fredrick heard a phone buzzing the moment he walked into the restroom. He paid no attention but instead, walked into one of the toilets to urinate. The phone kept vibrating repeatedly. Fredrick, who was becoming irritated, couldn't understand why the owner of the phone was refusing to answer the call. Then it occurred to him that the phone might have been forgotten in the restroom.

The phone stopped ringing as Fredrick stepped out of the toilet. He stopped to glance in annoyance towards the direction the sound had been coming from. Then he moved to the wash-hand basin, opened the tap and started washing his hands. The phone started buzzing once more. Ignoring the irritating noise, Fredrick finished washing his hands. He checked himself in the mirror, after which he began walking towards the door. He stopped abruptly. If someone has forgotten the phone, the least he could do was to get the phone across to the security post, from where the owner could pick it up anytime. This was the reasonable thing to do.

Fredrick turned around and walked to where he suspected the sound was emanating from. Standing in front of the toilet, he knocked but didn't get any response. Convinced that no one was using the toilet, Fredrick slowly pushed the door open. Nothing could have prepared him for what he saw next. A woman was in a kneeling position, her head inside the toilet. The toilet was bloody. Blood was pouring out of the woman's head into the toilet and on the floor. The woman's blood was slowly meandering its way towards the door. The sight was bizarre.

Fredrick stood motionlessly for a moment, mouth wide open, staring at the scene in front of him. His body was going into a shocked mood, and there was nothing he could do about it. Just then, he heard voices as two men walked into the restroom. The two men were talking on top of their voices, each trying to talk over the other. One of the men noticed Fredrick, looking as white as a ghost. He grabbed his companion by the elbow, then pointed a finger towards where Fredrick was standing, in shock and motionless.

The companion halted. He looked across at Fredrick and knew instantly that something was wrong with the individual standing some distance away from them.

"Everything okay, mate?" He yelled.

Fredrick suddenly came alive. He turned and stared blankly at the two men. He tried to say something but couldn't. He pointed to the restroom in front of him several times. Then he screamed and started running towards the men. He ran past them, screaming all the way.

A few moments later, the two men hurried out of the restroom in total disbelief. They, too, had seen what Fredrick saw, to make him behave in such a bizarre manner.

*****

Detective Bucknor stepped out of Titilayo's office to see Fredrick running towards her and screaming on top of his voice. Kate, who was right behind Bucknor, quickly turned around and dashed inside her office. Bucknor waited until Fredrick was within reach, then charged him and slammed him against the wall.

"I am a police officer. What is happening with you? Speak!" Bucknor barked. She slapped Fredrick hard on the face.

Fredrick tried to speak but couldn't. He pointed hysterically towards the toilet area.

Bucknor tried to calm Fredrick, but nothing could calm him down at that moment. He was shaking fervently as if he had seen a ghost. Bucknor forced him into a sitting position. Once in that position, Bucknor released him and glanced towards where he was pointing. She saw two men hurrying towards her direction and looking as if they had both seen a ghost. She stepped over to block their way.

"Police, stop!" She snapped.

The men stopped. They looked at each other and then stared, distantly at Bucknor.

"Officer, I think you should go and have a look at the restroom. Something terrible had happened there!" The taller of the two men screamed.

"What happened? Speak!" Bucknor was now all cop.

"There is a woman in there! There's blood all over the place!" "Take me there!" Snapped Bucknor.

"Never! I have seen enough. Right ahead of you is the restroom." The man said frantically.

"You are the police. Go check it out for yourself!" The shorter of the two men snapped at Bucknor.

"Do yourselves some good and stay right here. Don't move till I get back." Bucknor warned, as she dashed towards the restroom.

The two men watched in bewilderment as Bucknor began running towards the very same scene they had fled from. They looked at each other but said nothing. It was obvious that the whole situation was embarrassing to them. People were now gathered around in small circles, whispering to each other. A few were tending to Fredrick, who was still in shock.

"What right has she got to order us to stay here, until she gets back?" The shorter of the men wanted to know.

"She is the police and that gives her the right. Swallow your pride, mate. Let's just wait for her." The taller man answered.

"Police!" The shorter man hissed, waving his hands in frustration.

They waited.

*****

Detective Bucknor pulled out her gun before entering the restroom. She was not taking any chances. Once inside, she quickly looked around, but there was no one in sight. She pushed open the door to each of the toilets, one after the other, until she got to toilet number ten. It was here she found Titilayo, in a kneeling position. Her face was inside the toilet, and she was literarily drowning in her own blood.

Bucknor gulped. She examined the body closely without touching it. There was an entrance hole to the back of the head. This was execution. Blood from the hole was beginning to thicken. Whoever had killed Titilayo, had deliberately positioned her so that the blood from the wound would flow into the toilet. The killer needed time to get away before the blood flow could attract attention. Bucknor almost jumped when a phone suddenly buzzed. She took a step backward. As she reached to pick up the phone, the phone stopped vibrating. She picked up the phone and examined it. Titilayo's driver's license and a bank card were tucked away in the phone case.

Bucknor stepped out of the toilet, shaken but calm. She dialed Ayeni's number, to give him the news and to request an ambulance.

Then, a man walked into the restroom. He was surprised to find a lady in the restroom who was staring unblinkingly at him. He stared back, not sure of what to make of it.

"Ma'am!" The man finally said. "I think you are in the wrong place. The "ladies'-restroom" is on the other side, if you don't mind."

"I am a police officer. This is now a crime scene. I suggest you find some other place to go and do your thing." Bucknor said coldly.

It was then that the man noticed the gun in Bucknor's hand. He turned and walked away, as fast as he could.

Chapter Fourteen

Janet Osazuwa sat on a grey colored sofa in her sitting room. She stared blankly at the wedding picture hanging majestically on the wall, behind the Tv set. It was her wedding picture. In the picture, she was all smiles and looking extremely happy. Standing by her side, was her prince charming- Anthony, equally looking very happy. The picture had never failed to bring joy to Janet's heart, that was up until now. All that was left now was a memory and the sad reality that she was now alone, without her husband of thirty-five years.

Janet was extremely saddened by the murder of her husband. The sadness was amplified by the fact that she had, on numerous occasions, warned Anthony to desist from pursuing the "Halliburton criminals," as he often referred to them, without success. She knew her husband was an honest man, determined to make a bunch of corrupt individuals answer for their crimes but, she wished her husband had heeded her advice to let the matter go. Now, Anthony was dead, and she was alone.

Janet recalled how Anthony had reacted, when the then President gave the order that the criminal investigation be discontinued for *"lack of sufficient evidence"*. Anthony was beside himself with grief.

"The President is a traitor." He would tell anyone who cares to listen. "His election was financed with corruption money, and now, he's returning the favor."

Janet watched helplessly as Anthony slumped into depression and a near mental breakdown. It was a very difficult period for Janet, who stood by Anthony and helped nurse him back to good health. Anthony snapped out of depression to embrace a new hobby, research. He started to spend a lot of time researching financial crimes, and the agencies that were saddled with the responsibilities of punishing such crimes. It was during this period, that he started to prepare a dossier on Halliburton's financial crimes against Nigeria.

"My laugh would come soon enough, when these bunch of criminals are hoarded off to jail." Anthony would often tell Janet.

"Don't you forget that these individuals are powerful." Janet would warn. "They wouldn't go down without putting up a stiff resistance."

"I understand you perfectly well, but my dossier would scare every single one of them into hiding."

"They will fight you, and they will fight you in a very dirty manner. Keep that at the back of your mind, as you wage this war."

"You worry too much, my beautiful wife. I am a big boy and can take care of myself."

Janet would repeat this same episode with Anthony every time a new piece of evidence was uncovered and included in the dossier.

When the President was defeated in his reelection bid, Anthony was one of the happiest men in Nigeria. His one wish for the new president was that the Halliburton case be re-opened. His wish was granted barely six months into the new administration, when it was announced that the Halliburton bribery case was going to be reopened for investigation. Anthony's joy knew no bounds. He immediately started reaching out to certain individuals and agencies that he figured might be interested in his dossier.

Janet was not too surprised when Anthony came home on that Monday afternoon, to inform her that he held a brief meeting with an agent of the DSS. Anthony confided in his wife that he felt he could trust the agent.

"Just be careful and don't trust anybody." Janet had warned.

"I know. I promise to be careful." Anthony assured. Thereafter, he narrated to Janet about his initial meeting with Banji Smith.

"We are scheduled to meet again on Thursday afternoon at my office. I intend to hand over my dossier to him. I assure you that heads will roll."

"When you hand Banji the dossier, do you have a backup copy for yourself?" Janet enquired.

"Yes, I do. I will be sending a copy to my lawyer before my meeting with Banji."

"That is good to hear. Now let's go have lunch."

Janet did not like the development. Deep down in her heart, was the awareness that her husband was playing a dangerous game, but like every good wife, she was stuck with Anthony and all his baggage, no matter what.

On that fateful Thursday, Janet recalled that the day had started like every other day. Anthony had prepared breakfast for two, singing to himself while in the kitchen and joking about how he was a better cook than Janet. Janet sensed that Anthony was only doing his best to reassure her that everything was under control. But Janet had a nagging premonition that something terrible was about to happen.

Anthony had hurried out of the house at eight o'clock as Janet was dressing up for her doctor's appointment.

"Make sure to call as soon as you get to the office." Janet had said as Anthony hurried towards the door.

"On my honor, ma'am." Anthony had promised.

True to his words, Anthony had called as soon as he got to the office. Janet had listened as Anthony talked about traffic and how the traffic was surprisingly light for a Thursday morning. Janet listened, but she wasn't really interested in traffic. All she wanted was to hear Anthony's voice, nothing more.

When Janet's appointment with the doctor ended by ten o'clock, she immediately called Anthony for a welfare check. They had talked for ten minutes with no indication of any impending doom. Janet had again called by two o'clock in the afternoon, to do a "welfare" check. She had spoken with Anthony for a third and final time by three thirty, this time to ask what he would like for dinner.

"Anything will be just fine." Anthony had replied, laughing. He knew his wife was just checking on him.

"Then I will prepare some Jollof rice with chicken."

"That will be great." Anthony took a deep breath. "Darling, I am fine. You worry too much. Nothing is going to happen to me in my office."

"I am not worried. Just finish your meeting and come back home."

"I have some things to tidy up after the meeting before coming home."

"Just don't stay too long." Janet had insisted.

"I won't. I must get back to work. Talk to you later. Love you." Anthony said softly, aware of the need to reassure Janet.

"Love you too, darling." Janet had said, relieved. Anthony is fine and there was no basis for her to be unnecessarily paranoid, she thought to herself.

Janet's anxiety would reach a frightening dimension, when Anthony wasn't back home by seven o'clock. Janet had dialed Anthony's number, preparing to scold him for being late for dinner. The phone rang, but Anthony hadn't answered. Janet was furious. She waited for Anthony to call back.

Twenty minutes later and still with no call from Anthony, Janet became concerned. She called Anthony's phone again. It started to ring. Janet prepared herself, trying to think of the most terrible thing to say as soon as Anthony picked up the phone. She was once again disappointed. Anthony didn't pick u p her call. She could feel panic beginning to set in even as she was desperately trying to keep herself under control. She dropped the phone in anger and walked to the refrigerator, she needed a glass of cold water.

But, as she made to open the refrigerator, her phone started to ring. The sound was shrill and urgent, startling Janet. She ran all the way back to where she had left the phone.

She answered the phone to the sound of an unfamiliar voice. "Am I speaking with Mrs. Osaro?"

"That's me!" Janet replied automatically. "I am Janet Osaro, and this number belongs to my husband, Anthony. May I ask what you are doing with my husband's phone?"

"My name is Victor Edobor with the DSS. There has been an accident with your husband, Anthony."

"What accident are you talking about? Is my husband, okay?" Janet was shaking uncontrollably. She forced herself to sit on the sofa nearest to her.

"He is on his way to the hospital," Edobor had said. "And we are on our way to your residence."

"Hospital? What are you talking about? Which hospital?" Janet could hardly breathe. She was screaming on top of her voice.

"We will give you all the details when we arrive." Edobor had replied to Janet's many questions.

"Tell me this is all a bad dream!" Janet had screamed as she collapsed to the floor, sobbing.

*****

When Edobor walked into the large living room, his eyes immediately drifted to where a group of people were gathered round a woman. The woman was sobbing uncontrollably, and the people gathered were doing their best to console her. The woman, he concluded, must be the one they had come to see.

He moved towards the group, stopping only when he was standing directly in front of the woman, he assumed to be the wife of the deceased.

"I am Victor Edobor from the DSS. You must be Mrs. Osaro." Janet nodded her head. She stared absent-mindedly at Edobor.

Janet, it would seem, had been busy making some distress calls after receiving Edobor's call. She had managed to reach out to some friends and family members, many of whom were now crowding around her, to offer support. Their attention shifted from Janet to Edobor, the moment he introduced himself. Everyone wanted to hear what he had to say about Anthony's condition.

"Is it okay if we go somewhere private to talk, ma'am?" Edobor asked. He turned slightly to see Ayeni standing rigidly midway into the room. Smith was standing just inches away from the door.

A man in his early thirties suddenly stepped forward. He was dark, tall and athletic without being muscular. He looked dignified in his well-ironed dark suit. He walked to where Janet was sitting, and bent over to whisper something into her ears, before turning to face Edobor.

"My name is Greg Osaro." He held out his hand towards Edobor, for a handshake.

"Is there somewhere private we can talk?" Edobor asked, looking from Greg to Janet. He could see the strong resemblance between mother and son.

"Absolutely." Greg replied.

Greg gently grabbed her mother by the arm and pulled her up. As they walked away from the living room, Greg waved for Edobor to come along. In turn, Edobor signaled both Ayeni and Smith to tag along. Greg led Janet into a small room, followed closely by Edobor, who held the door open long enough for Ayeni and Smith to walk in, before closing the door behind him.

"These two are my colleagues," Edobor announced as soon as everyone was seated. He pointed to Ayeni, who was sitting on his right-hand side, "Police Superintendent Lekan Ayeni."

Edobor turned to his left-hand side. "Banji Smith, DSS."

Janet came alive. She started to get up from her seat, then decided against it. She pointed a finger towards Smith, then a fist.

She projected her anger towards Smith.

"You are the one my husband was scheduled to meet!" She roared with distraught and hysteria. Before Smith could say anything, Edobor responded.

"That's correct, ma'am. Anthony and Banji were scheduled to meet."

"Scheduled to meet?" Janet barked. "Didn't they meet?"

"They didn't." Edobor answered without hesitation. He watched, as Janet leaned forward, mouth trembling.

"What are you talking about?" She screamed.

"Anthony was shot in his office before Banji arrived for the meeting," Edobor said without mincing words. "I am sorry, but Anthony is dead."

Edobor watched as Janet collapsed back into the chair. She stared blankly at Edobor, then turned slowly towards Greg.

"I warned your father to stop pursuing this Halliburton matter, but he wouldn't listen." She began to bang her fist against the table until Greg reached over to grab her hands.

Edobor watched, allowing Janet to process her loss the way she deemed fit. It was a difficult situation, for both the bearer of the bad news and the receiver of the news.

"He was obsessed with this case. He told me about the planned meeting with Banji. I had a premonition that something bad was going to happen, and now, he is dead."

"I am deeply sorry for your loss." Edobor said, "We will do everything possible to bring those responsible for his death to justice."

"Will such justice include bringing Anthony back to life?" Janet asked rhetorically.

Greg, who had been listening, too shocked to utter a word, suddenly found his voice. "Are you saying that my father was killed in his office?"

"He was shot and killed in his office." Edobor replied, his face deadpan.

"And for what? What was the motive?" Greg was becoming hysterical

"Your father was planning to hand over a dossier to Banji. We strongly believe that the killer was after the dossier. The killer ransacked his office after killing him."

Greg was dumbfounded. He looked at his mother pitifully and could almost feel her pain. He shook his head in total disbelief before turning his attention towards Smith.

"If my dad was supposed to meet with you, how on earth did the killer get to him before you did?" Greg screamed. "And most importantly, how did the killer get to know about the dossier?"

"We are trying to figure it all out, Greg," Smith replied calmly. It was the best answer he could think of at that moment.

"One of your guys sold my father out," Greg said, looking from one man to the other. "This is a possibility, isn't it?" He rested his gaze once more on Smith, eyebrows raised.

Ayeni, who had remained quiet all the while, suddenly cleared his throat, deliberately drawing attention to himself. Convinced that all eyes were now focused on him, he adjusted his seat and addressed Janet directly.

"May I ask, ma'am, if your husband discussed the scheduled meeting with anyone apart from you?"

Greg was instantly offended at the line of question. In anger, he started to get up from his seat then checked himself and collapsed back into his seat. He regarded Ayeni the way a hawk would a chick.

"And you think my mum is in a position to answer such an irrelevant question, right now?"

"It's a very relevant question, Greg," Ayeni said without shifting his gaze from Janet. "It will help our investigation a great deal, ma'am."

"He didn't, I assure you. He would have told me if he did. It's unlike him." Janet answered tearfully.

"And you didn't, by any chance, mention it to anyone?" Ayeni continued.

Greg looked at his mother and then across at Ayeni. He was beginning to dislike Ayeni. The "rat" was within their ranks, they should be looking within themselves, not outside.

"No. I never mentioned it to anyone; why should I?" Janet rose slowly to her feet. She regarded the three men in front of her. "If you are serious about finding out how the meeting between my husband and Banji was leaked, I suggest you look inwards. There's a mole within your team."

Greg stood up and Janet immediately reached to hold Greg's hand for support.

"We will be looking at all the possibilities, ma'am," Edobor said, rising to his feet. He knew the situation was upsetting for Janet, and he didn't want to overstay his welcome. "Perhaps, it's better if Greg comes along with us to identify the body."

"I will come along with Greg. I need to have a word with my husband."

Janet started to walk away, heading for the door. Smith hurriedly got up from his seat and walked to her.

"I am deeply sorry for your loss, ma'am." Smith said, his head bowed.

Janet stopped to face him.

"You know, he trusted and believed in you. He risked his life because he was trying to bring those criminals to justice." She paused as tears dropped freely from her eyes. "Find his killer and make them pay. That's the least you can do for a man who believed so much in you."

Smith stood transfixed. He wanted to speak but the words were taking too long to form in his brain. Janet stood in front of him, waiting. Finally, the right words came.

"I swear to you, ma'am, I will find the killer of Anthony if it's the last thing I do on earth. It's a promise."

"That's all I ask for." Janet said, before continuing her walk towards the door.

"Do you have any idea if your husband kept a copy of the dossier somewhere?" Smith asked as Janet was about to step out of the room.

"I don't know. But I promise to check and get back to you." Janet replied without turning back. Then she stepped out of the room.

Greg held the door open for his mother to walk through. He held it open long enough for Smith to reach him, then he left the door to Smith. He hurried after his mother, back to the living room, where sympathizers were waiting and hoping for any iota of good news.

Edobor and Ayeni exchanged glances as they listened to the conversation between Smith and Janet. They watched as Janet walked out of the room in a slow and dignified manner. It becomes apparent to both men, that Janet considers Smith, as well as her now deceased husband, victims of a setup.

Chapter Fifteen

Detective Bucknor carved a parameter around the crime scene as soon as she ended the call to Superintendent Ayeni. She stood guard around the parameter and waited for back-up to arrive. Then, the gravity of the murder of Titilayo began to dawn on her. It occurred to her that her visit to Titilayo was unofficial. She had merely strolled in to have a chat with her and to convince her to come to the station for further questioning. What a coincident that the killer decided to strike at about the same time, she was in the building. She would have to explain this part to the police commissioner and her teammates. But then, how did the killer got wind of the fact that Titilayo had volunteered information to the police? This information was only circulated within her team and their superior officers. Yet, it has somehow leaked to a third party outside the cycle. How? Bucknor wondered.

Ayeni arrived exactly ten minutes after he received the call. He was accompanied by a team of policemen, including the forensic experts. The men quickly spread out to begin the tedious job of looking for and gathering clues from the crime scene. Two ambulance nurses moved over to examine the body for any trace of life. They took a look at the body, looked at each other, and then quietly stepped aside. It was clear to the nurses that the only job they would be required to do, in this case, was to evacuate the corpse to the morgue. They stepped further away, to allow the forensic team to comb the crime scene. They could afford to wait patiently like the vulture, and like the vulture, return to clean up the carcass.

"The three men who alerted me to the crime scene are just around the corner." Bucknor informed Ayeni, as soon as they were alone in a quite section outside the parameter.

"Let's go over everything. From the moment that you got here, to when you were alerted by the men." Ayeni said flatly.

Bucknor noted the coldness in Ayeni's voice. This was to be expected. The police commissioner was sure to be on Ayeni's neck over this turn of events. She took a deep breath, then went ahead to tell Ayeni everything, from when she first walked into Westen House until she found the body.

Ayeni listened attentively as Bucknor told the story, frowning every now and then. When Bucknor was done, Ayeni regarded her, then nodded his head slowly.

"Let's go have a word with the men while the boys comb the scene." Ayeni said.

The talk with the men yielded no lead. None of the men had seen anything. They had merely gone there to relieve themselves, only to find a woman in a pool of blood.

"I walked in there to hear a phone ringing, non-stop." Etim Fredrick had said. "My first thought was that the owner must have forgotten the phone in there. I decided to take the phone to drop it at the security post. That was when I found the woman."

When questioned, the two men went ahead to describe how they had found the lifeless body of Titilayo. Ayeni was quick to realize that each man was trying hard, not to say anything that could potentially be incriminating. Their account of the event was completely useless as far as Ayeni was concerned.

"Get their details and let them go." Ayeni instructed Bucknor. He was about to walk off when the shorter of the two men stepped forward.

"Sir, do you think her ghost is going to hunt us?" He asked.

Ayeni regarded him. He was a short, pigeon-chested man with a voice that belonged to a much bigger man. He had a small mouth compared to his heavy voice, and his eyebrows were constantly blinking.

Ayeni was about to tell him to get lost, but the taller man beats him to it.

"What kind of a stupid question is that? Did you kill her?" His lean but handsome face couldn't hide the contempt he felt towards his companion for asking such a question. Realizing that Bucknor was eyeing him, he softens his voice. "Her ghost should go after her killer, if there's such thing as a ghost going after someone."

"Like I said, get their details and let them go for now." Ayeni said and stepped away.

"Are we in any sort of trouble?" The shorter man asked.

"No. Unless you are hiding something." Bucknor replied, calmly.

"We have nothing to hide. It's just that I personally don't feel comfortable dealing with the police." The taller man said, his face revealing nothing.

Bucknor ignored him. She went ahead to collect their details, starting with Etim Fredrick. Ayeni's phone started to ring as Bucknor was closing her notepad.

"Banji is here. I gave him a call earlier on my way here, to update him." Ayeni was walking away as he spoke.

Bucknor tagged along silently behind Ayeni. Her mind was racing. A killer was on the loose, and they had to stop him before he struck again. She lifted her head to look straight-ahead, right-on time to see Smith, who was standing with his back towards her, stepping hurriedly aside. The coroner appeared and looked instinctively towards Ayeni, before stepping aside as the ambulance guys came hurrying through, with Titilayo's lifeless body on a stretcher and on its way to the morgue.

*****

The impromptu meeting was held at the request of Commissioner Armani. The news of the murder of Titilayo came to him as a rude shock. He couldn't fathom how the only potential witness to a murder investigation could be so dastardly murdered, virtually under the nose of the police. He recalled that Titilayo was to have been brought in for further questioning before she was killed. This enraged him even further.

"I want everyone involved in this investigation in my office by three o'clock this afternoon!" Armani had screamed at Ayeni over the phone, after Ayeni called to inform him of the death of Titilayo. The police boss had then called deputy director Davies, to request that he be present at the meeting. The urgency in the commissioner's voice had prompted Davies to accept the invitation.

The meeting commenced the moment the police commissioner walked into his office accompanied by Deputy Director Davies. A police sergeant had earlier led: Superintendent Ayeni, Edobor, Smith and Detective Bucknor into the commissioner's office and had kept guard, until the commissioner walked in. The police sergeant swiftly saluted the police commissioner before walking out of the office and closing the door behind him. Ayeni and the others, who had hurriedly got to their feet, remained standing until the police commissioner waved his hand, to motion them to be seated.

"Titilayo, a potential witness in this investigation, was killed earlier today." The police boss was not attempting to hide his anger and frustration at the turn of events. "There's something very wrong here, and I want someone to tell me what it is."

"My question is, how did anyone outside of the four of you get to know that Titilayo was a potential witness in the investigation?" Davies barked.

"We do not have all the answers right now, sir," Edobor said, his eyes on the police commissioner. "We think we might have a mole within us."

"A mole? What the hell are you talking about?" Armani asked, irritated.

"It will be hard to explain this as a coincidence," Bucknor explained. "First was Anthony, and now, Titilayo. In each case, the killer had foreknowledge of our next move. We need to look at the possibility that someone among our rank is passing information to a third party."

"Do you all agree with the detective on this absurd assertion?" Davies queried, staring at Smith, then shifting his eyes to Ayeni before finally resting the eyes on Edobor.

The three men nodded in the affirmative.

Armani regarded Bucknor keenly and deduced that she was still upset over the murder of Titilayo. He gazed at Ayeni, and their eyes locked. Then, very slowly, Ayeni nodded his head twice and wiped his mouth with the back of his hand. It was a signal that the police boss quickly deciphered. There was an accusation to be made, but Ayeni was not in a position to make such an accusation.

"If the team says there's a mole within the rank," Armani said, turning sideways to face Davies. "I suggest you look inwards. The mole is most certainly from your end."

Davies was taken aback by this open accusation. He eyed Armani all over, leaned back to adjust his seat, and then pointed a finger at Armani. But before he could say anything, the police boss raised his hand as a way of asking for permission.

"My men were not on ground when Anthony was murdered. This is the premise that led to my conclusion that the mole is from among your ranks."

Davies was shocked, but he quickly got himself together. There was no need to start an argument with the police commissioner in front of subordinates. The premise upon which the police boss had based his argument was valid and couldn't be faulted.

Davies cleared his throat and adjusted his seat once more. He glared at the four sitting across the table from him.

"I find it hard to believe your accusation," Davies said to Armani, without looking at him. "But I want to assure you that we will do everything possible to smoke out the mole. That's if the leak is coming from our side."

Commissioner Armani was satisfied and at the same time, relieved. He had directly accused the DSS of trying to sabotage an investigation and had gotten away with it. Though he had cleverly coined his words, he had expected a counter. He was glad that Davies was not in a mood for any such counter.

Ayeni decided to defuse the tension that had enveloped the room after Armani's accusation.

"Our boys were able to retrieve the bullets that killed Titilayo. Two shots to the head, fired from a .44 revolver."

"I don't get it," Davies said. "Why kill Titilayo? From what I was told, she didn't have any new information to share."

"That's true, sir." Bucknor concurred.

"Then, what was the essence of inviting her to your station, when you knew she had nothing new to share?" Davies queried.

"We were trying to talk her through the whole process, in a controlled environment. We have done this before. Some people usually provide additional information once they are in such an environment."

Davies leaned forward to rest his elbows on the table. His every attention was now on Bucknor.

"Correct me if I am wrong. You were the one that was present around the time she was knocked off, right?"

"I was in the complex, but not in her office." Bucknor corrected.

"May I ask what your mission to Western House was about?" Davies continued

"We had earlier invited her to the station, but she was a little unsure if it was a good idea, for her to come down to the station. I was there to persuade her to honor the invitation."

"I see," Davies said.

Bucknor shifted her gaze from Davies to Commissioner Armani, who stared back woodenly, his facial expression refusing to give away anything.

"And was your visit official?" Davies asked, he sounded as if he genuinely wanted to know.

"No sir, it was not," Bucknor replied. She couldn't find any fault with the question. It was a question she knew was bound to come up. "It's a common routine in my line of duty. We sometimes need to present our "police is your friend" side to witnesses, to convince them to do the needful."

Davies was impressed but not convinced. Bucknor, he noted, was not one to be easily intimidated. This speaks volumes as far as Davies was concerned. He stared absently at Bucknor for a moment, before shifting his attention away.

"We have to catch this killer as soon as possible." Armani said, poking the table with his index finger.

"This is the top priority for now. The killer will lead us to the dossier." Davies added.

"We will find the killer and the dossier, sir." Ayeni promised.

"Time is of the essence, too. Let's not forget that." Armani said, poking his finger against the table once more. "I will obtain a warrant by tomorrow to enable you to access the surveillance camera for the period…"

"There won't be any need for a warrant." Davies interrupted. "I view it now as a matter of national security. I will make a phone call after this meeting to request the surveillance camera. It will be available immediately afterwards."

Smith, not looking forward to the prospect of sitting for hours watching surveillance footage, shifted uneasily in his seat. From the corner of his eyes, he looked over at Bucknor who was busy taking notes. The thought of having to sit for hours with her, staring at video footage, when he should be out hunting for a killer, scared the hell out of Smith.

"I think I should go have another talk with Janet." Smith said, looking from Edobor to Ayeni.

Both men said nothing; they focused their attention on the two men in front of them. It was almost as if Smith never said a word.

"That's a good idea, Banji." Davies said, turning to glance at Armani.

Armani's eyes were expressionless as he said, "One little thing, though." All heads turned towards his direction. "See to it that Janet doesn't end up dead as well.

*****

As soon as the meeting ended, Commission Armani walked over to Davies. They shook hands and talked in a low voice for a moment, before both men walked out of the venue. Edobor waited until the two men had left, and then he cleared his throat loudly to attract the attention of the members. Once he was sure he had their attention, he began.

"The next time we have a meeting in which both the deputy director and the police commissioner are present, I expect us to report a breakthrough in the investigation. Is that understood?"

"That is exactly what I was thinking." Ayeni said. He eyed Bucknor thoughtfully, as if he needed to impress it mentally on her. Bucknor looked back absently, telepathic message received.

Ayeni shifted his eyes to Smith. They exchanged glances. They both knew why Smith was choosing the option to pay Janet a visit. He couldn't fault him, not everyone was cut out to sit patiently in front of a TV screen watching surveillance cameras.

Ayeni swung his chair to face Edobor.

"When the "big boys" start nagging about the slow pace of progress in an investigation, it means they are beginning to get tired of us, the "small boys" in charge of such investigation. Believe me, I have seen this happen over and over again in my many years as a police officer. We have but a short time to get to the bottom of this. A short time, that's all we have."

Edobor was impressed by Ayeni's frankness. He had figured from the beginning that the team had but a short time to burst the case. However, hearing it from Ayeni at this moment gives it a completely new meaning.

"A short time is plenty of time, my friend," Edobor said, forcing a smile. "We are going to get to the bottom of this, sooner than expected. Let's see what's in the surveillance camera first; then, we go through everything we have, starting from the very beginning. Perhaps we've overlooked something."

"That's what we are going to do." Ayeni concurred.

"Let's meet by twelve o'clock tomorrow afternoon in my office to do a review," Edobor said as he grabbed his briefcase. "And don't forget about the leak, be careful who you share information with."

Smith got up, shook hands with Bucknor then, leaned over to shake hands with Ayeni. He got to his feet to hurry after Edobor, who was slowly walking towards the exit door. They both walked to the parking lot without saying a word.

When Edobor got to his car, he opened the car door and dropped his briefcase in the passenger seat. He closed the door, then turned to face Smith.

"Banji, we've made little or no progress as far as this investigation is concerned. Two killings that are connected and no clues as to a suspect."

"The leak is a major drawback in this investigation, sir." Smith said dryly.

"That's an understatement, Banji," Edobor said sharply. "We've to come up with a plan to either catch or derail the mole. We must have something concrete to present to the "big boys" the next time we meet them. Is that clear?"

"Absolutely, sir."

"Good. I should be on my way now." Edobor said as he jerked the car door open. He entered the car and started the engine without glancing at Smith. He drove slowly out of the parking lot, his mind on a killer who was out there and free to kill again.

Smith waited until the car was out of sight before walking to his car. He entered his car and sat in the driver's seat. His grip tightened on the steering wheel as he reflected on the events of the day. It has been one failure after another since his first meeting with Anthony. This was not good for his health and for his career. He needed a break, a positive break at that.

Suddenly, it dawned on him. Anthony Osaro was no fool. He was an intelligent and calculating individual. Why would he put all his eggs in one basket? Why would he generate a single file on a scandal as big as the one he was willing to expose? It doesn't add up.

There has to be a duplicate copy somewhere. That makes more sense.

Smith reached for his phone and without thinking, dialed Janet's number.

"This is Banji Smith, ma'am," Smith said, surprised that Janet answered the phone personally. "I was wondering if I could come over for a short meeting with you."

"Of course, we can meet." Janet said, calmly.

"I can be at your place tomorrow morning, if you give me a time." Smith said, pressing the phone tightly to his ear.

"Would nine o'clock, be okay by you?" Janet asked.

"Thank you, ma'am," Smith said and meant it. "It's okay by me."

By the time the call ended, Smith's mood had shifted on a positive note. He had a feeling that something was about to give. Janet was not one to let her husband die in vain. The killing of her husband had forced her to become a crusader, determined to carry on the legacy of her late husband. He needed a person with the kind of anger and determination of Janet on his side, if he hopes to crack the case.

He started his car and tuned the car radio to Lagos FM Station. The Station was playing Kenny Rogers' "The Gambler." He started to sing along happily as he drove, feeling as though he was a gambler himself.

Chapter Sixteen

Smith arrived at Janet's residence at eight forty-five. He checked his wristwatch as he drove slowly to a parking spot. He parked the car, turned off the engine and waited. When it was three minutes before nine, Smith got out of the car and walked to the huge black gate.

Smith was about to bang on the gate, when it opened as if by automation. Smith walked in, to find Greg standing behind the gate and holding it for him to come through.

"Good morning, Greg." Smith said, extending his hand.

"Good morning, Banji." Greg shook hands with Smith before closing the gate.

Smith couldn't help but notice that Greg was immaculately dressed, wearing a dark suit and a sparkly white shirt, with a navy-blue tie to match. He was mourning the loss of his father by wearing the dark suit as most people would, but he was mourning in style.

"You look good, Greg." Smith said, nodding in admiration.

"Thanks man. Even though I am mourning, I try to look good, just to keep my spirit high."

"That I understand, Greg." Smith said.

"My mother is waiting." Greg said. He forced a smile.

"And how is she doing today?" Smith asked.

"Not too good, as is to be expected. They were inseparable and married for decades."

"It's a tough one." Smith said, as Greg pulled the entrance door open.

Greg ushered Smith into the living room and pointed him to a chair. He then excused himself. He came back a few minutes later with Janet, who was dressed in black attire from her neck down. Her hair was hidden under a black head scarf, and her eyes were hidden by the dark glasses she had on.

Smith got up and remained standing until Janet came to sit on the chair directly in front of him. Smith nodded his head in salutation, before sitting down again.

Greg floated away silently. He returned moments later with a tray containing two cups of coffee and a cup of tea. He handed the cup of tea to Janet.

"Coffee, black or with milk?" Greg asked Smith.

"Little milk, no sugar, please." Smith replied, bowing his head slightly.

"Any leads?" Janet asked calmly.

"We are still going through everything we have." Smith replied.

"Last time, you asked if my husband had an extra copy of his dossier somewhere."

"Yes, I did, ma'am. You did promise to look." Smith said, dutifully.

"I suggest you talk to his lawyer," Janet said.

Smith leaned forward in his seat. This was one thing he hadn't thought of. A man who was willing to embark on a mission to fight corruption would most certainly need some kind of *"should anything ever happen to me"* back up plan as a way to make sure he stays alive.

"My husband told me on that fateful day," Janet continued. "That he was going send a copy to his lawyer, as a precautionary measure."

"That would be the ideal thing to do, ma'am." Smith said, trying hard to conceal his excitement.

"His name is John Oris." Janet stretched forth her hand. "Here's his card. Go talk to him. He should give you everything you need if he has it."

Smith reached forward and collected the card.

He examined the card. Then he said, "Thank you, ma'am."

"You don't have to thank me. Get the killer of my husband and the people he was after. We can thank each other after that."

Smith nodded his head. He picked up the half-emptied cup of coffee and drank down in one swallow.

"We will meet again for some coffee. That's after you have made some arrests." Janet said. She got up and started her slow walk towards the door, from where Greg had led her into the living room.

"I will keep you posted, ma'am." Smith said, hurrying to his feet.

"The best time to talk to the lawyer is from four o'clock in the evening. Before then, he is always busy with court cases and meetings." Janet said and left the room.

Smith glanced across at Greg, who was standing by the doorway from where his mother had just left. As their eyes locked, Smith bowed slightly, then let himself out of the house. Once outside, he stood and raised his face skywards, to feel the sun beat against his face, eyes closed. He stood motionless for a moment before deciding that he had had enough of the sun.

He suddenly felt hungry, as he strolled briskly towards where he had parked his car.

*****

It's no easy job sitting in front of a TV screen, watching surveillance videos for hours on end. A lot of patience and dedication is required if one is not to miss anything. Bucknor knew this for a fact. She had been sitting patiently for the past five hours scanning through surveillance footage, ignoring calls for coffee breaks on multiple occasions from Ayeni.

Bucknor was becoming increasingly frustrated; firstly, the surveillance camera's coverage of Western House was limited only to the entrance area. Secondly, the quality of the footage was poor because of the distance from the Defense House, where the cameras were located, and the Western House. These setbacks did not, however, deter Bucknor, who continued to stare at the screen, hoping to catch something of interest.

Ayeni returned from his third coffee break to find Bucknor staring at a fixed image on the screen. A group of four people apparently walking away from the direction of the surveillance camera. As Ayeni took his seat beside Bucknor, she pointed at the image on the screen, poking her tiny finger at a man wearing a dark shirt. The man was sandwiched between three men and was looking away from the direction the other three were facing.

"I recognized this group from when I was at the security post on my way to Titilayo's office." Bucknor said, her finger still poking the man facing away from the camera.

"Was there anything of significance that made you zero your interest on this group?" Ayeni quizzed.

"Nothing, except for this one guy." Bucknor answered. She stopped poking, but her finger remained on the man.

"And what about the guy?" Ayeni asked. He had a feeling that Bucknor was on to something.

"He's kind of familiar. I believe I saw him walking out of Western House while I was at the security post. I felt I had seen him somewhere but couldn't place it."

"Are you sure this is the same person you are referring to?"

"Absolutely. The shirt and the glasses, it's him. I locked on to him momentarily before the chief security officer created a distraction for me. The group of three had earlier walked by me."

"You don't think that the man was with the group?"

"Definitely not. I think he mingled with the group, in his bid to get away." Bucknor said confidently.

Ayeni stared at Bucknor for a long time, then at the screen. He was trying to make up his mind whether to believe Bucknor or not. Perhaps, she was tired and needed to get some rest. His thought was cut short as Bucknor began to murmur to herself.

"I have seen him somewhere. Where? Where? Where?"

Ayeni who was not about to embark on a wild goose chase, simply because Bucknor thinks she has seen a man somewhere and coincidentally on the day Titilayo was killed, decided to stir the conversation away from the man without offending Bucknor's pride.

"I think you should take a thirty-minute break, and rest the brain a little," Ayeni said. "We will go through everything together when you return. Maybe we have missed something we shouldn't have."

"I don't think I need a break, sir." Bucknor protested. "Am trying to remember where I have seen this individual before."

"I insist on you taking a break. It's not something for discussion. Besides, you have been here for hours, the brain is fatigued." Ayeni said, he stood up from his seat.

Ayeni motioned Bucknor to stand up. She complied reluctantly. She was tired mentally and felt she needed the break.

"I will see you back here in two hours' time."

"You said thirty minutes time, sir." Bucknor corrected.

"My bad. I meant to say two hours. Have lunch and get some rest. Then come back, so we can go through what we have got together." Ayeni said, his face expressionless.

Bucknor saluted swiftly and walked out of the office. As soon as the door closed behind her, Ayeni moved forward to sit on the seat Bucknor just vacated. He stared intensely at the image on the screen, trying to make some sense out of it. Then, he tapped on the play button and watched, as the small group of four continued to walk far away from the surveillance coverage area, until they were out of sight.

Ayeni pushed the play back button. The video started to rewind rapidly, until Ayeni pressed the stop button at the point where the small group was seen walking out of Western House. Ayeni took a deep breath and then hit the play button. The first thing he noticed was the three men walking out of the building together as a group. Then, a fourth man hurried to join them, tagging along but slightly behind the group of three. It appeared as if the man was deliberately looking away from the surveillance camera.

Ayeni did a replay, watching the footage a couple of times. He was trying to debunk his notion that the fourth man was not with the original group of three. The more he watched, however, the more he became convinced, that the man was free riding alongside the group. Then he concluded that the fourth man in the video, was definitely a person of interest. Bucknor was right.

"Bad surveillance footage or not," Ayeni whispered to himself, "we have to find this guy and bring him in for questioning."

As was the case when Bucknor left the room, Ayeni highlighted the image of the group of four on the screen. He unconsciously began to tap on the table with his middle finger, deep in thought. He caught himself and stopped the tapping. It dawned on him that he, too, needed to take a break. He shook his head slightly as if trying to clear his head. Then, he got up, picked up his mobile phone and walked out of the office to get some fresh air.

*****

Smith drove into Munchies eatery, feeling as if he had not eaten for days. He parked his car alongside a black Jeep and hurried into the eatery. He hung his jacket on an empty seat near a window overlooking the busy street, before going to join the line of people waiting to place an order.

He observed the queue and estimated that it would take about ten minutes before it got to his turn. Then he looked around and noticed a smartly dressed lady, busy typing away on her computer, as she waited for her order to be delivered. He regarded her and was impressed. He allowed an awkward smile to cross his face, at the exact moment the lady decided to look up from her computer. Both man and lady stared at each other with Smith's awkward smile quickly fading away. The lady's perplexed gaze was unsettling.

Smith quickly turned his attention back to the queue. There were now two people ahead of him. He checked his wristwatch and calculated that he had spent approximately seven minutes in the queue. He had estimated almost accurately. He got to the ordering point exactly nine minutes from when he joined the queue.

Smith allowed his eyes to roam freely as he started to eat. His eyes roamed and eventually settled on the smartly dressed lady once more. She was munching down a piece of meat pie, her eyes glued to the computer screen. Smith, who was not one to mix business with pleasure, couldn't help but wonder how it was possible for her to enjoy the food, when her attention was divided between the food and whatever it was, she was doing on the computer. He turned away to shift his attention to happenings on the busy street outside.

When lunch was over, Smith walked out of the eatery into the hot sunshine. He walked to his car and opened the car doors to allow the heat to escape. As he waited for the car to cool a little, he brought out the card Janet had given him and glanced at the lawyer's phone number. Janet had suggested to him the best time to meet the lawyer, but she never mentioned anything about the right time to put a call across to the lawyer. He decided to try his luck.

He brought out his phone and dialed the lawyer's number. The phone started to ring and, almost immediately, a woman's voice came across to him.

"This is Bose from Oris Chambers. How may I help you?"

"My name is Banji Smith, and I am with the DSS. I would like to speak with Barrister John Oris, concerning one of his clients."

"I am his secretary."

"I am wondering if you could book a time for me today, to meet him. It's urgent."

"Did you say that you are with the DSS?"

"That's right."

"Well, you are a lucky one. He is in the office right now. Hold the line and, let me check with him."

"Okay. Thanks."

Smith liked the term "lucky one". Hopefully, his luck would hold with the barrister. He knows how it was with lawyers and their over-oiled egos, always thinking that their time was so precious and needing someone to pay for every single minute of that time.

The voice came through once more.

"Like I said, you are a lucky one. The barrister is free now and can meet with you within the next one hour, if you can make it here."

"I can make it to your place in twenty-five minutes." Smith said, barely able to conceal his excitement.

"I assume you have the address to the office?"

"Yes, I do."

"Good. Then see you in, say, half an hour's time."

"I will be there. Thanks a lot."

Smith looked at the address on the card one more time before tucking it away in his pocket. He estimated that it would take him eighteen minutes to drive to the Barrister's office, from his present location. He was about to enter his car, when he saw from the corner of his eyes, someone walking towards him. It was the lady from the eatery. She was walking majestically, with the computer held tightly against her chest. As she neared Smith's car, she suddenly turned towards the black Jeep parked alongside Smith's car.

Smith turned to regard her. She was around twenty-five or six, tall, dark and slender. Her bright eyes, pointed nose, and full lips gave her a face of standard prettiness. Her full but average-sized breasts seemed a perfect fit for her slender body. She paused, turned her head sideways and regarded Smith, who was staring at her, in a way that would make most men wonder, but probably get no further than wondering.

Smith summoned up courage and walked the short distance between them, to stand in front of her.

"My name is Banji Smith, and I must confess that you are extremely beautiful." Smith told her, smiling. He held out his hand.

"My name is Angela and, thank you for the compliment." Angela observed Smith's outstretched hand for a moment before shaking hands.

"I noticed you inside, and coincidentally, your car is parked besides mine." Smith said sheepishly, unsure of himself.

"The space your car is parked was free when I arrived here." Angela said firmly.

"My apologies." Smith said, bowing a little.

"There is no need for apologies," Angela said flatly. "I must be on my way now as time is not my friend."

"I am pressed for time too. When next are you planning to come out here for lunch? I am hoping to see you again." Smith felt it was his lucky day.

"I will be here same time tomorrow." Angela said and got into the Jeep.

"Then see you tomorrow."

Angela didn't answer. She rolled her eyes and drove away.

Smith was excited at the prospect of meeting Angela again. It suddenly dawned on him that his commitment to work was gradually eroding the social aspects of his life. Too bad, he thought to himself. He needed to find a balance in his life. A balance that would possibly encompass a woman such as Angela.

It wasn't until Smith started the car engine that he bothered to glance at his wristwatch. He realized he had less than twenty minutes to make it to the meeting with Barrister John Oris. That was a lot of time, given that he was going to be driving against traffic.

He engaged gear and drove away with Angela on his mind.

Chapter Seventeen

Smith sat in front of Barrister John Oris fifty-two minutes after the appointment was booked. Oris, who was sitting behind a large mahogany desk, did not bother to stand up as Smith walked into his office. He motioned Smith to one of the three chairs neatly arranged in front of him.

"Good day, sir," Smith said as he advanced to Oris' desk, to sit on the middle chair.

"Good day to you, too. I understand that you are from the DSS." Oris said.

"My name is Banji Smith, and I am with the special operations unit of the DSS."

"You already know who I am." Oris said, as he unconsciously adjusted his blue tie.

Smith regarded him. A smallish, bald-headed man, in his fifties, with a set of eyeballs that were too large for the sockets that housed them. His thick, well-kept mustache ran all the way to meet his equally well-kept beads. His broad and shining forehead gives him the look of an aristocrat.

"Yes, I do. I also know that you were Anthony Osaro's attorney."

Barrister Oris looked Smith over, the way only lawyers could, trying to make up his mind whether to continue with the meeting or not. He unconsciously reached for his tie again, adjusting it slightly to his right.

"And what can I do for you? If I may ask?"

Smith was used to lawyers and their tactics. He looked directly at the lawyer sitting in front of him, who was trying to intimidate him with his superior altitude. It was an altitude he had seen several times when lawyers storm into his office uninvited, on behalf of one of their clients.

"I am part of the team investigating the murder of Anthony. His wife, Janet, asked that I talk to you…"

"Talk to me about what?" Oris interrupted.

"About the dossier. Anthony was supposed to send a copy to you on the day he was killed." Smith said calmly.

Oris was not impressed by Smith. He stared absently at him for a long time, before reaching for a red pen from a wooden pen holder, positioned on the left-hand side of his desk. He, thereafter, opened a drawer and brought out a writing pad. He began to draft something on the pad.

Smith waited patiently as Oris continued to write. He knew from experience that lawyers enjoy making notes, in order not to miss anything. It was their way of keeping records. Smith turned away to observe the interior of the office. His eyes immediately went to a big sculpture of Marcus Garvey, standing in the far-right corner of the office. Behind the sculpture was a large portrait of a canoe, with the inscription "freedom boat" printed across it.

Smith was still trying to figure out the connection between the sculpture and the canon, when he realized that Oris had stopped writing, and was now staring intensely at him. He stared back at Oris.

"What authority do you think you have, to burst into my office and ask me something that is strictly confidential between me and my client?" Oris asked, pointing the pen at Smith as he spoke.

"We are investigating a murder case. He was killed because of the dossier…"

"Why am I even having this discussion with you? Anthony never sent me any dossier on the day of the murder."

Smith was taken aback by this revelation. He was confident that the barrister wouldn't say such a thing if it weren't true. It was easier for lawyers to admit to having a document, and then hide under some law, in order not to produce such a document than a blatant denial.

"He told his wife that he was going to send a copy to you, as a protection in case anything should happen to him." Smith said, desperately.

"My client called me around eleven o'clock in the morning, to inform me that he would be sending a file across to me later in the day. He never did." Oris said, shaking his head sadly. "My assumption when I didn't hear from him was that he wasn't yet through with the file. I got to know the next day that he had been murdered."

"We had planned to meet on the day he was killed. He had a dossier on the Halliburton scam, which he was planning to hand over to me. I arrived at his office to find him dead." Smith said, deliberately omitting the fact that he arrived late for the meeting.

"I see," Oris said. He started writing frantically on the pad once again.

Smith watched in silence. He watched as he turned a page and continued to write. Just as Smith was reaching his breaking point, Oris suddenly stopped writing. He looked up and yet again, adjusted his tie. Smith concluded that the tie adjustment thing was a habit.

"Now, tell me what you and the DSS are doing to catch his killer."

"The investigation is ongoing," Smith said without hesitation. "I assure you that we are making progress."

"Making progress? I like your use of the term, *progress*."

Oris examined the pen he was holding, as if he was seeing it for the first time. It was obvious that he was not buying the *"making progress"* story. He let out a deep breath, then lifted his head to look across the table at Smith.

"I want to assume that the killer or killers went away with the dossier after the murder," he said, coldly.

"Your assumption is correct." Smith concurred.

"That's why you are out searching for a copy." Oris said, his eyes fixed on Smith. "Now, suppose there is no extra copy?"

"With or without it, we are determined to find his killer, and we will." Smith replied.

"That's comforting to hear." Oris said, then looked away.

Smith knew he was beginning to overstay his welcome. He could tell by the body language of Oris. He concluded that the attorney didn't have anything more to offer and decided to call it a day.

"Thank you for your time, sir," Smith said as he got to his feet.

"Wasn't it possible to extract the information from Anthony's computer?" Oris asked as he stood up and walked around the desk, to stand face-to-face with Smith.

"We are working on it." Smith replied. He noticed that Oris was not as small as he had imagined, now that he was standing in front of him.

"I see," Oris said, flatly. He walked to the door, jerked it open and pointed the way out to Smith.

Smith walked out of the office without saying another word. The meeting had not yielded the kind of outcome he had anticipated. But why didn't Osaro send a copy to his lawyer as promised? The only logical explanation that came to his mind was that Osaro was still working on it, when his killer surprised him. This certainly explains it.

*****

Bucknor was back in the office thirty minutes after the forced break. At first glance, she noticed that Ayeni wasn't in the office. She imagined that he had stepped out for a cup of coffee. Her eyes shifted to the TV screen, and the image of the group of four confronted her. She stepped over to stand in front of the screen, staring at the image for a couple of minutes, deep in thought. Then, she leaned over to focus all her attention on the man she believed to be a free rider.

She tried to recall, as much as she could, the face of the man she had seen walking out of Western House as she stood in the queue. Then, she transposed the image from her memory to the image staring away from her on the screen. She had a strong feeling that she was looking at the same person. She started to fantasize about the idea that she had come across the man somewhere else, before the sighting at Western House. But she couldn't place him. She shook her head slowly, then forced her eyes away from the screen.

Bucknor ranks herself top-class when it comes to remembering faces. She was dead certain that her mind wasn't playing any sort of tricks on her. She had seen the man whose image was now forming in her mind before. But where? She stared once more at the screen, as if expecting the image to speak to her.

"I have seen you before, but where?" She whispered, pointing at the man on the screen.

Bucknor took a deep breath, then pulled back her seat before collapsing on it. She stretched her legs under the table, closed her eyes and tried to blank her mind. She was in that position for roughly ten minutes before opening her eyes. Then, she jumped up from her seat, letting out a loud scream. She started to clap her hands and laugh loudly to herself. Her memory hadn't failed her, after all. She stopped clapping, bent over and covered her face with her hands.

When she removed her hands from her face, Ayeni was standing right in front of her, perplexed.

"I got him!" Bucknor screamed. She began to clap her hands again.

"You got who?" Ayeni asked, sharply.

"This son-of-a-bitch!" Bucknor replied, pointing to the man on the screen

"How? What do you mean?" Ayeni asked, almost simultaneously.

"On the day Anthony was killed, I ran across this man in a parking lot. It was dark, but I was able to get a good enough look at him."

"You are speaking in riddles," Ayeni said calmly. He motioned Bucknor to sit down. "Calm down and talk to me."

"This man was at the Western House the day Titilayo was killed," Bucknor explained. "I ran across this same man the day Anthony was killed in a parking lot…"

"Are you absolutely certain about that?" Ayeni interrupted.

"I am dead certain it's the same individual."

The noise of the door opening forced Ayeni and Bucknor to turn towards the door. Smith was standing by the door, holding it wide open. They had no idea how long he had been standing there. He walked into the room, closing the door behind him.

"Even if it were the same individual on both occasions. It still doesn't make him the killer." Smith said, as he strolled towards the pair.

"Exactly my thoughts, too," Ayeni said

"I understand that perfectly well," Bucknor said, undeterred. "But if we can ID this individual, then we bring him in for questioning, so as to rule him out or otherwise."

"You have a point there. However, finding him is going to be like trying to find a needle in a haystack. Don't you think?" Ayeni asked rhetorically.

"Even if they were one and the same person," Smith said, glancing from Ayeni to Bucknor. "The fact that you spotted him in a parking lot, far away from Western House and again, at Western House the day Titilayo was killed, doesn't place him at the scene of two murders."

"Your conclusion is logical, Banji," Bucknor said, coldly.

"I suggest we review the surveillance footage from the day Anthony was killed. The objective would be to see if the physically challenged man, caught on camera, bears any resemblance to this guy?" Ayeni said. He was not willing to rule out Bucknor's assumption just yet.

"We can get our forensic experts to do an analysis of the individuals, to see if they are one and the same person." Bucknor said, unwavering in her conviction.

"That's a very brilliant idea," Smith said, impressed.

"Let's do it." Ayeni ordered. He hurried away to retrieve the copy of the previous surveillance tape from the locker, where he had stored it.

When Ayeni returned with the tape, he placed it on a tray in front of Bucknor. He dusted his hand as if trying to get rid of some unseen dust particles. Then, he addressed Bucknor.

"Get the forensic department to send someone here immediately."

"Right away, sir!" Bucknor said, as she reached for the intercom on the desk.

Smith knew what Ayeni was thinking. It was faster to have a forensic expert come over and view the footage together with them, than having to send the tape over to the forensic lab, with their notoriously slow feedback time.

*****

Smith, followed closely by Bucknor, was the first to walk into Edobor's office. As Ayeni walked in, Bucknor glanced at him momentarily, then sat across the table from Edobor. Smith, who was standing by a window, watching the slow-moving traffic outside, turned around to acknowledge Ayeni with a nod. He walked back to take the seat to the left of Bucknor. Ayeni sat on the vacant seat to her right.

Edobor regarded the three of them emotionlessly. He had hurried out of a security meeting as soon as he got a call from Smith, informing him that the team wanted to meet with him urgently. Edobor was all too aware that Smith would never make such a call if it wasn't for something important.

"We may have stumbled upon a major breakthrough in the investigation." Ayeni began. He adjusted his chair, pulling it towards the table. "I think Bucknor is in a better position to present the breakthrough."

Edobor shifted his eyes to gaze at Bucknor.

"I think we are on to the killer, sir," Bucknor said, locking eyes with Edobor. "I was able to ID him. Our parts have crossed before, on the day Anthony was killed."

"Go on. I am listening." Edobor urged, not taking his eyes off Bucknor.

"On the day that Anthony was killed, I ran into a man in the parking lot at a gas station. There was something odd about him. I studied him for a while before he got into his SUV and drove away.

I followed him until I lost him. I saw the same man again at Western House on the day Titilayo was killed."

"How can you be so sure of this?" Edobor asked.

"I saw him walking out of Western House on the day Titilayo was killed. He was also caught on camera. We have verified it."

"Verified? What do you mean?" Edobor asked, shifting his gaze from Bucknor to Smith.

"We have had to watch the surveillance footage all over again, with two forensic experts present. They were able to analyze the video and concluded that the physically challenged man caught on the first video, was the same person on the second video, recorded on the day Titilayo was killed. He was the man Bucknor saw leaving Western House and who was later caught on camera, walking alongside three other individuals." Smith replied.

"Interesting. How on earth is this even possible?" Edobor asked, astonished.

"We doubted Detective Bucknor when she made the connection, until the forensic guys confirmed it." Ayeni said, a look of admiration on his face.

"Even at that," Edobor said. "Aren't we talking about three separate individuals here: The physically challenged individual, the man in the parking lot, and the individual on the day Titilayo was killed?"

"Actually, one individual but three different roles." Bucknor corrected. "The man who was faking physical disability was the man who was later seen in the parking lot. He was also seen again on the day Titilayo was murdered."

"I am still trying to figure it out for myself. How was it possible for you to connect a man you saw in a parking lot, to a man faking physical disability at Western House?" Edobor asked, quietly.

"Think along this line, sir," Bucknor advised. "The man in the parking lot and the man that I saw on the day Titilayo was killed, are one and the same person. The forensic experts have confirmed that the guy I saw on the day Titilayo was killed leaving Western House and captured on video is the same man captured on camera faking disability on the day Anthony was killed. This makes the three of them one and the same individual."

Edobor listened attentively as Bucknor explained. He was trying hard to put the jigsaw puzzle together. Finally, he stopped trying.

"Do we have a clear enough face?" He asked.

"Not at the moment, sir. We are planning on visiting the shopping mall that owns both the gas station and the parking lot. We plan to take a look at their surveillance camera." Smith replied.

"Bucknor, I want you to meet with one of our facial reconstruction artists and work with him, to give this man a face."

"Right away, sir," Bucknor said.

"And what about your meeting with Anthony's lawyer, Banji?" Edobor enquired.

"Anthony never got to sending the file to his lawyer before he was killed." Smith replied, a note of sadness in his voice.

"That's rather unfortunate," Edobor said. "However, that shouldn't slow down our momentum."

Edobor picked up his phone and dialed a number. His call was answered almost immediately.

"I am sending a Detective Bucknor over to you right away. I want a facial job done."

Edobor tucked the phone away in his side pocket after the call and got slowly to his feet.

"Banji will lead you to the facial reconstruction guys."

Bucknor nodded her head. She turned to Smith and said, "I am ready when you are."

"Then, let's go." Smith said.

Smith led Bucknor out of the office, leaving Edobor and Ayeni behind. Once, the two men were alone, Edobor said.

"I will be meeting with the deputy director this evening, to brief him."

"I will have to give the commissioner an update, too," Ayeni said, calmly.

"It's amazing how Bucknor was able to ID the suspect."

"I was amazed myself. She's got quite a talent." Ayeni said, proudly.

"We could use a person with such talent here at the DSS."

"And you think the police will allow you to have her? Not a chance."

"We will see about that. After this case, of course." Edobor said, a thin smile crossing his face.

"We will see." Ayeni said, as he rose to his feet.

Edobor walked over to him, shook his hand, and then led him to the door.

When Ayeni had gone, Edobor remained standing, his back against the door. He remained in that position for a moment; then, he took a deep breath before reaching for his phone.

He dialed Jessica's number to book a meeting with Deputy Director Davies.

Chapter Eighteen

It was raining heavily outside as Jessica was busy going through some files. She could hear the rain pounding mercilessly against the rooftop, making some irritating sound that Jessica was trying hard to ignore. The rain had started suddenly and without warning an hour earlier and was still pouring, with the same fury one hour later and showing no signs of slowing down.

Jessica paused for a moment, shaking her head regretfully. Rain! She recalled, as a child, how the sound of raindrops on the rooftop would make her fall asleep, always. As an adult, that effect was still there, but something else had been added: sexual urge. Whenever it was raining, Jessica usually got this strong sexual urge, especially if the rain persisted over a period of time. With the passage of time, she had learned to keep her feelings under control, but every now and then, the urge got so strong that it needed to be fed.

And right now, she was feeling the need to satisfy that urge.

She stood up and stepped away from the file she had been handling. She picked up another file from the shelf and checked its sub-title. It was a file that Davies had requested for earlier in the day. Now was the perfect time to take the file to Davies, she reasoned.

She picked up a mirror from her handbag to check her face, her hand automatically reaching to adjust her hair. Satisfied with the way the lady in the mirror looked, she gently dropped the mirror back into her handbag. She picked up the file and checked once more that it was the right file. She was heading for the door when the phone started to ring.

"Bad timing." She whispered to herself.

She took three steps backwards to pick up the phone.

"Jessica."

"This is Victor. We have an update on the investigation. I need to see the deputy director ASAP."

"Hold on. Let me check with him."

Jessica decided against using the intercom but instead, hurried towards the deputy director's office. She had dropped the file when she answered the call and had forgotten to pick it up, as she rushed to Davies' office. She had also forgotten her sexual urge, for the moment.

Davies was busy going through a file when there was a slight knock on the door. He paused, as the door was pushed open, and Jessica walked in.

"Victor would like to see you ASAP." Jessica walked over and gave Davies a light kiss across the lips.

"Did he say why?" Davies asked. He pulled Jessica to himself and rubbed his hands all over her body.

"There is an update on the investigation," Jessica replied, she took Davies right hand and forced it between her legs.

Davies was aroused. He opened Jessica's skirt and slid his hand further down until he located her clitoris. He started to stroke the clitoris slowly at first and gradually increased the pace. He succeeded in driving Jessica to a quick and violent orgasm.

The orgasm left Jessica breathless. She felt air clogged in her lungs, with a burning sensation that left her feeling weak. Davies gently rested her head on his shoulder. She was thankful for the gesture as her mind began to focus. She longed to have him make love to her immediately but was aware that the meeting with Edobor was of utmost importance. She would wait until after the meeting.

She shifted her head to look at Davies. He smiled. She realized that he was thinking exactly what she was thinking: sex.

"You will see him?"

"Tell him to make it here in thirty minutes, rain or no rain."

"Sure," Jessica said. She cat-walked out of the office, a smile flashing across her face.

*****

Edobor sat silently in front of Deputy Director Davies and waited. He had requested the meeting, but it was Davies' duty to start the proceedings. He didn't have long to wait.

"I understand that you've an update," Davies said calmly.

"That's correct, sir," Edobor said. He produced a small notepad from his breast pocket. "We can safely conclude that one individual was responsible for the two killings."

"What do you mean? Are you, by any chance, insinuating that the same person killed Anthony and then Titilayo?" Davies asked. He leaned forward towards Edobor.

"That's correct sir. It was the same person." Edobor replied. He looked away from the piercing eyes of the deputy director, staring instead at his notepad.

"Clarify that," Davies said, his voice barely above a whisper.

"Detective Bucknor was able to make a connection to pinpoint that fact. On the day Anthony was killed, Bucknor coincidentally crossed part with a man in a parking lot, far away from the crime scene. She saw the same man again at Western House, on the day Titilayo was killed."

"Is she willing to bet her badge on the fact that the two individuals seen in two different locations, are one and the same person?" Davies asked, frowning.

"Evidence from the surveillance camera revealed that the physically challenged man Titilayo described seeing, on the day Anthony was killed, was the same man that was seen again on the day Titilayo was murdered. This was confirmed by the lab boys." Edobor explained.

"Strange," Davies murmured. "And do we have a face?"

"Bucknor is at this very moment helping the facial boys get a face."

Davies looked away from Edobor, deep in thought. He couldn't help but acknowledge to himself that this was a giant leap in the investigation.

"Banji had a meeting with Janet, the late Anthony's wife," Edobor said, checking his notepad. "She directed him to Anthony's lawyer. Anthony had planned to send a copy of the dossier to his lawyer on the day he was killed."

Edobor felt Davies' eyes burning through him once more. He looked up, then quickly tucked the notepad away in his breast pocket.

"I want to assume that the lawyer never got the copy." Davies said.

"That's correct, sir." Edobor concurred. "He never got to sending the copy before he was killed."

"I want this killer!" Davies exclaimed, banging his fist on the table. "I want him alive, not dead."

Davies got up and walked across the office to one of the large windows with curtains drawn. He parted the curtains to look outside. The rain had subsided, but it was still very windy. He turned to gaze at Edobor, who sat motionlessly, his notepad back in his hand.

"He is useless to us dead." Davies continued, "Alive, we can squeeze out information from him before disposing of him."

Edobor nodded his head in agreement without uttering a word. He would also want the man to be brought in alive, if possible.

However, capturing a professional hitman alive was a near-impossible task, in his opinion. He kept his opinion to himself.

"I understand it's going to be difficult trying to capture this man alive," Davies said as if reading Edobor's mind. "Let's identify him first, then see how it plays out."

"That's fair enough, sir." Edobor said, pleased.

Edobor got to his feet. He didn't want to overstay his welcome. There was nothing more to be said, for now.

"Send Jessica to my office on your way out." Davies instructed.

"Have a nice evening, sir." Edobor said and walked out of the office.

*****

Jessica walked silently into the deputy director's office, locking the door behind her. She went straight to where Davies was seated, to stand in front of him. She began to slowly remove her dress until she was completely naked. Davies gulped for breath as usual, then pulled Jessica over to himself and kissed her passionately. He laid her on the desk, spreading her legs wide apart. He held his breath as his eyes locked onto Jessica's clean-shaven virginal. He felt for the clitoris, stroking it gently. He inserted his middle finger into the virginal, moving it slowly up and down. He felt the wetness as he added a second finger, going even deeper as Jessica moaned in ecstasy.

Davies suddenly stopped. He stepped back and quickly removed his clothes, starting with his tie. He positioned himself, then pulled Jessica gently by the waist towards him. His one thought now was to possess Jessica and to feel the vibration of her body against his. So, he penetrated her, deeply.

Jessica cried out, the pleasure intertwining with pain. She adjusted her hips to allow for easier penetration. Davies pounded her relentlessly and without mercy. He was not one to show mercy during sex, his aim being to possess and dominate.

"Oh gosh!" Jessica called out. "It's too deep, please!"

Davies was unperturbed by Jessica's pleas as he continued to dig deeper, with each stroke. His animalistic instinct knew no bounds until he started to vibrate violently as he reached orgasm. Jessica was holding him tightly when he ejaculated and collapsed on top of her. Jessica took a deep breath of relief and satisfaction as she listened to Davies' rapid heartbeat.

Jessica was fulfilled. Davies was happy. Now, it was time for Davies to tell her about the matter that necessitated the visit by Edobor. She waited.

*****

Westland was in a good mood as he headed to his office. He had just wrapped up a security meeting with top regional CIA operatives within the African command. His good mood was a direct reaction to the news that the CIA director had given the go-ahead, for regional operatives to start the mobilization of opposition elements, against President Muammar al-Gaddafi of Libya.

Westland was thrilled by this development. This was something he had advocated for many years without success. His superiors were not all sold on the idea. The consensus among the top hierarchy of the CIA was that a move shouldn't be made against al-Gaddafi in the absence of a reliable substitute. The substitute to be hand-picked by the US, must also enjoy the support of the Libyan people. The US had been searching for the right candidate for decades while al-Gaddafi waxed stronger.

The CIA had finally gotten the approval to act from the President of the United States. The President's directive, which was delivered by the Secretary of Defense, was clear: get rid of al-Gaddafi by whatever means necessary, even if it means risking an outright civil war in Libya. Westland, who had been waiting for this opportunity for decades, couldn't wait to set things in motion. He had men whom he could mobilize at short notice, scattered all over the region. These were men totally sold on the idea of getting rid of al-Gaddafi. The die was cast, and there was no going back.

He entered his office, and as soon as he had closed the door behind him, he dashed to one of the cabinets to retrieve a bottle of Johnnie Walker, which he had hidden away in a special container. He poured himself a mouthful and swallowed hard. He then walked to a small, padded chair by the window to sit down. He closed his eyes and tried to clear his mind.

He was in that peaceful position for approximately twenty minutes when his mobile phone suddenly started to buzz. Startled, he opened his eyes lazily and yawned. He got to his feet and was about to start making his way towards the drawer, when the phone stopped buzzing. Not dissuaded, he walked to the drawer and retrieved the phone. He started to check the caller ID as the phone started buzzing again. He hit the green sign.

"Updates," The voice on the other end said.

"Go ahead." Westland walked back to his seat, to sit down and to listen.

"Detective Tina Bucknor figured it out. The same individual carried out the two jobs at the same venue." The was a pause, perhaps intended to allow Westland to process the information.

"How's that possible?" Westland queried.

"The detective, by a stroke of luck, ran across the individual in a parking lot on the day of the first assignment. She was on a visit to Western House on the day the second assignment was executed. Brief encounters, but she was able to somehow make a connection."

"Any facial recognition?"

"Not from CCTV footage. Bucknor is, however, working with facial reconstruction experts to create a face."

Westland was silent. This was a whole new development and one he hadn't anticipated. A facial recognition would point the investigators to a hitman. Was this a slip on the part of his hitman?

It most definitely looked like one. The caller could hear Westland breathing evenly over the phone.

The caller waited. It wasn't the caller's place to break the silence.

"Send a copy of the facial work to me as soon as you have it." Westland said finally.

"Absolutely."

"Good job." Westland said, before cutting the line.

Westland put the phone away and realized immediately that his hitherto good mood had changed. He was now visibly upset. This thing about facial reconstruction was enough to upset him. His hitman was a professional. He had carried out many hit jobs for him in the past. He had never had any reason to doubt his ability. This issue of facial recognition was, however, making him feel uneasy. He was finding it hard to accept the fact that his hitman had slipped. But what else could it be, he wondered. In the case of Anthony, Titilayo described him. In Titilayo's job, a police detective not only recognized him but is able to connect him to both jobs. There was no other way to describe it but slipping, big time.

Westland picked up another phone and dialed a number. The phone rang once, and the person on the receiving end answered.

"Boss."

Westland managed to suppress his anger and frustration. He was trained to do that, no matter the level of provocation.

"You slipped yet again." He said flatly. "A lady detective recognized you and is able to connect you with the two jobs."

The person on the receiving end was silent.

Westland anger was reaching a boiling point after saying those words. He started to count mentally from one to ten, after which he took a deep breath. This helped calm his nerves.

"The detective saw you in some parking lot on the day of job one. She saw you again on the day of the second job. After watching the CCTV footages of both days, she was able to connect you to it." Westland paused, allowing the listener to grasp and digest the information.

"She is just now helping get a sketch of you. They are trying to get a facial identity." Westland said. "Are you worried?"

The question was harmless enough, but the man at the receiving end was no fool. He knew that the answer to this seemingly harmless question could spell the difference between life and death for him.

"I am not worried, not one bit."

"And why not?" Westland asked, flatly.

"We ran across each other in the parking lot on the day of job one, and coincidently, she happened to be at the entrance of the Western House on the day of job two. I recognized her immediately..."

"That doesn't answer my question!" Westland interrupted, impatiently.

"It was not me she saw on both occasions. Maybe the individual who carried out both jobs, but not me. So, I am not worried."

Westland knew instantly what this meant. He had disguised himself on both occasions and apparently wearing the same disguise, which was why the detective was able to make the connection.

"Her name is Detective Tina Bucknor. You must not underestimate her." Westland said casually. He was raising the red flag on a potential threat.

"I never underestimate anyone, Boss."

"I want to assume that you and I are both on the same page here."

"Yes, boss."

"Good. No more slips." Westland warned, then ended the call.

Westland returned the phone to its holding place. He was no longer as angry as he was before the phone call. He tried to envisage a scenario as it is currently playing out, in which a detective can accurately pinpoint the fact that two seemingly unrelated hits were carried out by the same hitman. It was difficult for him to imagine, especially when one is dealing with a professional hitman. But, as soon as he factored in the fact that the hitman might have slipped, it started to make sense to him.

He reached for the phone once more and dialed Tommy Anderson's number.

"Tommy Anderson." The voice was calm.

"Goddamn it. I know who you are, Tommy." Westland said, jokingly.

"I know you do, Raymond." Anderson laughed

"I think the lone wolf is getting old, Tommy."

Anderson knew exactly who Westland was talking about and what he meant. Every one of the field operatives has a code name depending on the modus operandi of the operative. The lone wolf was not only one of the best but also one of the few that had Westland's complete trust. If Westland, for whatever reason, thinks the lone wolf is getting old, it means he was beginning to make silly mistakes.

"Lone wolf getting old?" Anderson asked rhetorically.

"Getting old and beginning to make mistakes. The last two jobs were traced back to him by investigators though no facial ID."

"How is that possible?" Anderson asked

"I will give you the details when we meet," Westland replied.

Anderson knew all too well the implications of Westland's words. The lone wolf was going to be retired one way or the other if he kept showing signs of "old age", a term used to describe operatives when they start to make mistakes. A knock on his door, then a bullet through the head, was one very convenient way of retiring such operatives.

"Understood," Anderson said, emotionlessly.

"We've been given the clearance to move against al-Ghaddafi. I want you to be ready to leave for Libya at a moment's notice."

"My bags are packed and ready." Anderson hated the Libyan leader as much as Westland. He was glad when he got the news that the US was finally going to make a move against al-Gaddafi. It was long overdue, he thought to himself.

"It's going to be a big operation, Tommy. We have a once-in-a-lifetime opportunity to get rid of that son-of-a bitch; we cannot afford to fail. He will fight back, but he must never be allowed to win." Westland said, coldly.

"I am ready to fly down to Libya as soon as you give the go-ahead." Anderson reassured.

By the time Westland ended the call, he was fully back to his "original" good mood, induced once more, by the prospect of getting rid of the Libyan strongman Muammar al-Gaddafi.

Chapter Nineteen

Supervisory special agent Mark Dozie had just stepped into his office when the desk phone started to ring. Lifting an eyebrow, he slowly walked to his leather-padded chair and gently dropped his enormous body on it. The chair buckled under his weight, letting out a squashing sound as if in protest. He reached for the phone.

Dozie, a battleship in police uniform, was well above six feet in height. At forty-nine years old, he considers himself in great shape, which he attributes to the many hours spent in the gym. He delights in showing off his muscular biceps to the admiration of his colleagues, especially those within his age group. His stomach was the only part of his body that he believed was not as it should be. Dozie had been fanatical about keeping his stomach as flat as possible in the past, but not anymore. Years of uncountable bottles of beer had taken its toll on the stomach. His stomach was enormous, but his large size was helping to conceal it, that is, until one takes a closer look. But only very few officers dare to take a closer look.

As he pressed the phone to his ears, the unmistakable voice of Commissioner Armani barked.

"Mark!"

"On the line, sir."

"I want to see you in my office, immediately."

"Right away, sir," Dozie said. He got quickly to his feet, as the commissioner disconnected the call.

Dozie stood up, still holding the phone. The police commissioner doesn't often use the phrase "immediately," except when there are some matters, needing urgent attention. He wondered what it was. Realizing he was still holding the phone; he frowned before replacing the phone.

He checked his calendar to see his schedule for the week. He needed to be certain his schedule could accommodate the extra assignment, which he was certain the commissioner had in mind. He likes to anticipate and plan ahead. It makes his life easier. If the new assignment proves to be too demanding, to the extent of affecting his current assignments, he would suggest to the commissioner that he passes the job over to another officer. Ultimately, the final decision was that of the commissioner.

Satisfied that his schedule for the week could accommodate an extra assignment, Dozie walked out of his office, into the main office. As soon as he stepped into the main office, there was an immediate silence, punctured occasionally by a few whispers.

"Listen up!" He announced. "I am on my way to a meeting with the police commissioner. "All previously scheduled meetings are postponed until later today. Got that!"

The officers all nodded in unison. Some of them were already getting ready to storm into Dozie's office for consultations, before he stormed out to make the announcement. They realized as Dozie turned and walked away that they had only one thing to do: wait as he had instructed.

Dozie hurried out of the main office to ride the elevator that would take him to the fifth floor for his meeting with the police commissioner.

*****

Mark Dozie walked into Police Commissioner Armani's office to a warm reception, a handshake, and a genuine smile. It wasn't every day that one gets this kind of reception from the police boss. Dozie was wary. He had every reason to be. He had in the past received similar receptions after which, the police boss would dispatch him to fish in troubled waters. It was often that the police boss was not happy with the slow pace of an ongoing investigation or suspected that some of those carrying out the investigation had been compromised. Then, Dozie would get a mandate to step in.

Dozie made himself comfortable on a seat indicated to him by the commissioner and watched as Commissioner Armani started searching through a pile of files, until he found the one, he was searching for. He pulled out the file from the lot and examined it somewhat closely, before pushing it across towards Dozie.

Dozie took the file and waited. It was the job of the commissioner to do a brief of the content. He would do the reading later after the meeting. He didn't have long to wait as the commissioner cleared his throat, then began his sermon.

"I want you to suspend every other job at hand right now, to concentrate on this particular case," Armani said, pointing a thick finger at the file in Dozie's hand.

Dozie said nothing. He shifted his eyes briefly to look from Armani to the file, then back to Armani.

"The file contains the updates on the Halliburton case. A case of homicide at the Western House drew our attention to the fact that the DSS had reopened an investigation into the matter. Then, there was a second murder connected to the case. In both cases, the killer appeared to have had some privileged information on the victims." The police chief paused, then gestured towards the file.

Dozie unconsciously tightened his grip around the file.

"Everything you need to know is in that file. The case is a top priority for you as of this moment. I want you to find the mole who is leaking information to the killer. My guess is that the mole is within the DSS. Your job is to find him."

"The investigative team, sir, how many members are from our side?" Dozie asked

"There are four members in total. Two from each side. The two from our side report directly to me while the two from the DSS, report to Shola Davies, deputy director DSS."

Dozie opened the file and examined the names of the members of the investigative teams. He quickly memorized the names.

"I've worked with Detective Bucknor in the past. She's a good one." Dozie said, his eyes fixed on the file.

"The very reason she was drafted to the team," Armani said. "The team will eventually apprehend the killer; of this, I am certain. Your job is to smoke out the mole."

"Would that be all, sir?" Dozie asked, jerking his eyes away from the file to gaze at Armani.

"That's all I want you to do, plus go through the file to see if the team had overlooked anything of significance," Armani said, trying to keep it as simple as he could.

Dozie was taken aback by the seemingly uncomplicated task he was just saddled with. Smoking out a mole shouldn't be too difficult a task, if one knows what to look for, he thought to himself.

"Do I have your permission to interview the team members, especially the ones from our side?" Dozie asked.

"Absolutely." The police chief replied.

"I will see you again, sir, as soon as I unmask the mole."

Dozie stood up and saluted the police chief briskly. He turned and walked out of the office without looking back.

Dozie's hunt for the mole has begun.

*****

Detective Bucknor awkwardly held a copy of the final sketch of the suspect in her hand. She examined it closely, then nodded in satisfaction. The image of the suspect, which had existed only in her mind, was now in a concrete picture form. The artist had been meticulous and had worked her through every detail, before producing the final sketch.

"Is this your man?"

Bucknor shifted her eyes from the picture to see Smith standing by her side, a smile on his face. He was also holding a copy of the sketch in his left hand and poking it with his right index finger for emphasis.

"I think so. It's almost a perfect resemblance of him as far as I can recall." Bucknor replied, waving her own copy back at Smith.

"Great. I will get a copy across to Victor right away. We should be able to nab this guy any time now." Smith said, optimistically.

Bucknor said nothing. She shifted her gaze away from Smith. She wondered if she was truly able to recall every single detail, as she worked with the expert to create the sketch. She reassured herself that she hadn't missed anything. The face staring back at her was the face she had seen before, twice.

"I have a strange feeling that I am going to meet this guy very soon," Bucknor said abruptly, a frown on her face.

"When we meet him again, it's going to be game over for him," Smith said without hesitation.

"It's going to be game over for one of us, him or me," Bucknor said, she hesitated. "I do not expect a cold-blooded killer like this guy to go down without putting up a fight, do you? If he could kill two people within days, what is there to stop him from attempting to silence the only person he suspects could pick him out in a crowd?"

"That's the more reason we should get him before he makes his move." Smith said in a consolatory tone.

"He's going to come for me. I am dead sure of it. When he does, I will be ready."

Smith wasn't sure what else to say. He reached forward and patted Bucknor on the shoulder.

"We are a team, remember? If he's coming for you, then he's coming for the team. Don't you forget that."

Bucknor smiled and patted Smith's hand.

"I know, Banji. I know."

By the time Bucknor walked out of the DSS office, her survival instinct had kicked in. Convinced that an attack on her was imminent, she had decided to take every necessary precaution and to be ready to defend herself when the time comes. She was with this mindset as she walked towards her car. She scanned the surrounding area with her eyes without moving her head, in a bid to identify positions where an assailant might try to conceal himself. Satisfied that the immediate area offers no hiding place for a would-be assailant, she approached her car. Her eyes instinctively drifted to a brown-colored Volvo parked behind her car, and she froze. Her hand immediately reached for her gun. In an instant, the gun was out of the holster and in her hand, her finger hovering around the trigger, ready to shoot.

She tiptoed to the driver's side of the Volvo and stood silently beside the car. A man in his mid-forties was sitting in the driver's seat, his eyes glued to a pornographic magazine, oblivion of the fact that he was been watched. Bucknor lowered her head a little, to have a complete view of the inside of the car. Satisfied that the man was alone, she turned her gaze back to the man who, at that very instance, flipped over to the next page.

In disgust, Bucknor lowered her gun. She walked noiselessly to the back of the car to check its licensed plate number. She returned the gun to the holster, then slammed her fist as hard as she could against the boot of the car. She got the reaction she wanted.

Instantly, the man in the driver's seat opened the car door and jetted out, cursing under his breath as he ran towards Bucknor. He was slimly built, with a heavy moustache and a flat nose. He came across to Bucknor as a man who was unsure of himself.

"What's it with you, ma'am?" The man asked angrily. "What are you doing to my car?"

"Your car? Is this your car?" Bucknor asked, a latent viciousness on her face.

"What do you mean by that? Is that how you go about banging on people's cars?" the man asked angrily, his eyes glowing. He started to move slowly and menacing towards Bucknor, fists clenched.

"Stay back; I am a police officer!" Bucknor yelled.

The man stopped in his tracks as if he had hit a brick wall. All the anger and bravado in him evaporated in an instant. He unclenched his fists, letting his hands drop by his sides. He was no longer looking menacing but rather, subdued. He stared meaninglessly at Bucknor for a moment, shaking his head in disbelief.

"Police! How do I know for sure that you are a police officer?"

Bucknor did not border to answer. She brought out her gun and waved it at the man. The man, seeing the gun, took two quick steps backwards, hands raised.

"I don't want any trouble, ma'am." He muttered. You have no right whatsoever, to go about banging on people's cars, then threaten them with a gun."

"If I ever catch you again, openly displaying an adult magazine in a public place such as this, I will arrest you for constituting a public nuisance. Do I make myself clear?"

The man's jaw dropped. He couldn't fathom that he had literally been caught pants down, with a pornographic magazine. How was this possible? He was so damn sure he was alone before he started to indulge himself. He was addicted to pornography, and there was nothing he could do about it. It wasn't as if he hadn't tried to fight his addiction. He had, with little or no success. What else was he supposed to do? Kill himself? It wasn't as if he was hurting anyone with his addiction, so why should the police, or anyone else, care? Then he remembered the threat *"to arrest him for constituting a public nuisance"*. This was something else altogether. Police! He dislikes them and doesn't want to have anything to do with them. They have a way of making an issue out of every damn thing.

His hands were still in the air, as he started to slowly back away from Bucknor until he felt his back pressed against the car door, he had left open, as he rushed towards Bucknor. He entered the car and with a sweating hand, he managed to start the car. He stole a glance in the rear-view mirror to see Bucknor standing still and glaring at him. He quickly engaged gear, maneuvered the car out of its parking position, then drove rapidly away. He couldn't wait to get far away from Detective Bucknor.

Bucknor waited until the car was out of sight. She went to her car, opened the car door, and entered. She sat in the driver's seat, a sudden feeling of blankness overpowering her. She couldn't tell if it was because of her being fatigued or because of the disgust she felt towards the individual she just encountered. Why would a full-grown man go around with pornographic materials, she wondered? Perhaps, she should have arrested the man on the spot and have him investigated. Supposing he was a sex offender-just suppose.

Eyes closed, Bucknor groped for a pen from the car compartment. She wrote down the plate number of the car and a description of the man. She would instruct an officer to do a routine check on the man. Once she had reached this conclusion, she suddenly felt revigorated. She took a deep breath, then adjusted the rear-view mirror, before starting the car. As she began to slowly edge the car out of the parking lot, her mind drifted once more, trying to envisage the different possible outcomes in the event of a showdown with the "ghost." She wondered if the term "ghost" was still befitting for the suspect, since she had succeeded in unmasking him. For this singular act, she was convinced that the "ghost" wouldn't hesitate one bit, in putting a bullet through her head. She smiled.

A meaningless but sadistic smile. It was a smile straight from her heart.

Then she whispered to herself, "Not if I kill you first."

*****

Edobor patiently studied the sketch that Smith had handed over to him. He was impressed. The sketch in the portrait staring at him was detailed. He stared at the image, and the image that stared back at him looked rather harmless. He let the portrait slide from his hand, dropping noisily on the desk.

He took his mobile phone and positioned the portrait properly, before taking some pictures.

"It shouldn't be much of a problem finding this individual. The sketch is detailed enough." Edobor said, pushing the portrait towards Smith.

"It shouldn't be, sir." Smith concurred.

Edobor fumbled with his phone for a couple of minutes before putting it away.

"I have just sent copies of the sketch to Deputy Director Davies." Edobor said. "He gets a hard copy with the internal memo as soon as possible."

Smith said nothing, preferring instead to stare at the portrait in front of him.

Edobor regarded Smith for a moment, then cleared his throat, making Smith look up quickly.

"We keep this sketch thing close to our hearts for now. We don't want this guy getting tipped off. Do you understand?"

Smith nodded. "I understand, sir."

"I am worried about the possibility that there's a mole within us. It's not good for the agency." Edobor said softly, as if talking to himself.

"It's worrisome, sir."

"We need to find this person and fast, too," Edobor said, placing emphasis on each word. "We need a plan, a trap, to smoke out the rat."

"We will catch the rat soon enough, sir," Smith assured.

Edobor's phone vibrated. He picked up the phone to check the message. He read the message, then nodded.

"The deputy director has confirmed that he had received the copies."

"Okay, sir," Smith said. He got briskly to his feet. "I should be on my way now."

"Do that, Banji. The day is far spent. I have an early morning appointment, and I will not be getting back to the office until late in the afternoon. You can reach me from three o'clock, if the need arises."

"Ok, sir. Do try and get some rest." Smith said, before walking out of the office.

Alone, Edobor picked up the sketch and took a final look before putting it away. The image of the man in the portrait was now planted in his mind. He was almost certain that he could fish him out from a crowd. This gave him the assurance that it was only a matter of time before their suspect was apprehended.

For the moment, Edobor wanted to go home to his family and to his cozy bed. He picked up his jacket and hurried towards the door, suddenly realizing how hungry and tired he was.

*****

Westland was about to leave the office when the call came. This call would be one of the many calls he had received within the past twenty-four hours. The calls were coming from all over as the plot to dethrone the Libyan strongman gathered momentum. Already, some of his men in Libya had kick-started activities, with protests erupting in virtually all the major cities against Muammar al Gaddafi.

Westland retrieved the phone and knew immediately that the call was a local one, judging from the ringing tone. He had been so busy with his Libyan assignment that he had unconsciously, pushed his other assignments aside. He pressed the answer button.

"I now have the image." A familiar voice announced.

"Perfect." Westland's response was flat but not cold.

"I am sending it across to you right now. I will keep you informed of any further developments."

"Appreciate that." Westland said. He meant it.

Westland ended the call. A beep indicated to him that a message had come through. He opened the message to see the image of a man staring at him. He studied the image.

He was certain that the image staring at him was not exactly the image of his hitman. He looked again, this time more closely. Somehow, a similarity does exist. The disguise was good, but he was still worried about the facial, and its details.

He decided immediately to forward the image to the individual captured. He needed to get his reaction to this new development.

When his phone started ringing a few minutes later, he knew right away who the caller was.

“Your reaction,” Westland demanded without hesitation.

“Nice try, boss. This is not me. He’s one of my many selves.”

“I hope so. This one was close, too close if you ask me.”

“Pure coincidence, boss.”

“Do you have any idea how coincidences such as this, could very easily lead to trouble?” Westland was doing his best not to scream.

“I understand what you mean, boss.”

“Just remember that a cleanup may be inevitable if there’s a threat of any kind.”

“Noted, boss.” The voice on the other end said, flatly.

Westland cut the call. He put the phone away and looked up, staring absent-mindedly at the ceiling. After a couple of minutes, he took a deep breath as he reflected on what he’d just said about potential threats and a cleanup. He meant it. He couldn’t tell, as of now, if the individual he had just spoken to was beginning to pose a threat to him or not.

Westland left the office wondering about this.

Chapter Twenty

Dozie looked right through the trio sitting across from him. He wasn't focusing his attention on any one of them. He was so deeply engrossed in whatever it was that was running through his mind, that he failed to realize that a couple of minutes had passed since the trio walked into his office.

"Sir," Smith said firmly. "You said the meeting was urgent."

Dozie cleared his throat, then shot a quick glance at Smith. He leaned forward, lifting his left eyebrow.

"I was wondering if any one of you was the mole," Dozie said. He shook his head slowly, then continued, "I am now thinking I should rule out the three of you, but should I?"

"I can absolutely say, sir, I trust my team members." Ayeni said, calmly.

Dozie regarded Ayeni for a moment, trying to make up his mind whether to accept his assertion. He allowed a faint sparkle to steal across his face, and his lips curved into a smile.

"Trust is good," Dozie said, impressed.

Bucknor lifted her head slightly to observe Dozie. She knew Dozie by reputation, a veteran, whose ability to crack a seemingly tough case was legendary. She wondered if the police commissioner had something to do with this meeting and was trying to mobilize some extra resources.

"Consider me a part of the team from this moment onwards," Dozie announced, gazing at Bucknor. "Though as an extra resource person."

"What, if I may ask, is your job specification, sir?" Bucknor asked, aware that Dozie was refusing to shift his gaze away from her.

"My primary assignment is to fish out the mole. Nothing more and nothing less, at least for now."

"This's a welcomed development, sir," Bucknor said, dutifully. "This would allow us to concentrate one hundred percent on our assignment."

"I have gone through the file relating to this investigation, and I am building a theory on how to fish out the mole," Dozie said calmly, his lips curving into a smile once more.

Ayeni nodded his head but didn't say anything. He knew Dozie firsthand from years back. He was not a man to throw words around lightly. If Dozie said he was building a theory, that was enough as far as Ayeni was concerned. It was only a matter of time before the mole was smoked out, with Dozie hot on his trail.

"Banji," Dozie's voice was piercing. "Is something bothering you?"

Smith sat upright. "I was just wondering how you intend to trap the mole. Your jurisdiction doesn't cover the DSS, remember?"

"That's one hell of a good question, Banji." Dozie said, nodding his head. "I am having a meeting with Victor immediately after this, to discuss and come to an agreement on how I can expand my reach. I am going to fish out the mole, irrespective of where he might be hiding. I assure you."

The meeting ended when Edobor walked into the room. He nodded to Dozie before going to sit on a padded chair positioned near the window and overlooking the street. He picked up a Newspaper from the small table beside the chair. He opened to the middle page, and stared at the jigsaw puzzle for a few seconds, after which, he started to solve the puzzle. He delights in solving puzzles whenever he has to wait for meetings. It was his way of killing time but, he rarely ever gets to solving any of the puzzles.

He didn't have long to wait.

Dozie got up moments later and started walking towards Edobor, who, attracted by Dozie's footsteps, snapped out of his *"jigsaw puzzle"* solving mood. He got up and advanced to meet Dozie halfway across the room. They shook hands as Ayeni, followed closely by Bucknor, walked out of the office. Smith was the last to leave, staying behind long enough to whisper something to Edobor.

As soon as the two men were alone, Dozie wasted no time in briefing Edobor about the just concluded meeting.

"To be honest, I believe that the mole is from the DSS," Dozie said. He took a deep breath, shaking his head regretfully. "My job is to find out who this person is. I need your support in this area."

"You have my total support. It's time we fish out this individual." Edobor said, his face expressionless. "What do you propose?"

"I see you like to solve puzzles," Dozie said, pointing towards the Newspaper. "I like to solve puzzles too. In this case, I am trying to put myself in the position of the mole. I am trying to figure out the individual before throwing my bait."

Edobor listened. Dozie was being abstract with him. He was careful, trying to perfect his game plan before revealing it. He was going about it the way a skilled craftsman would. He had said he trusted members of the investigative team, and that the leak was not the handiwork of any one of them. Edobor agreed with this conclusion.

"The other people who are in the know, aside from those three and me, are the Commissioner of Police and Deputy Director Davies," Edobor said, trying to sound casual.

"I am aware of that, Victor." Dozie clarified. He regarded Edobor. "I want to assure you that all angles will be covered."

"In that case, let me know when you need my assistance." Edobor rose to his feet.

"Definitely. In fact, sooner than you expect." Dozie got up and shook hands with Edobor.

Dozie walked Edobor to the door, they shook hands once again before Edobor walked out. Dozie turned and started walking back to his desk, he unconsciously picked up the Newspaper Edobor had left on the small table. Then he examined the jigsaw puzzle Edobor had been trying to solve and frowned. He was confident he could crack the puzzle in record time.

He smiled shyly, rubbing his chin. A thought crossed his mind that he was going to solve the puzzle with the mole in record time. The thought was there momentarily before he forced himself back to reality. With reality came the realization that it wasn't going to be as easy a task as he would want. He had no idea whatsoever about the internal workings of the DSS. Besides, he faces the possibility of being stonewalled by DSS officials, once they realize that the mole could be within their ranks.

His grin widened into a smile. He was an old fox and a veteran who had cracked far more difficult cases compared to fishing out a mole. He would set a trap and then bait the mole out of its hiding place. But then again, he realized it wasn't going to be an easy thing to set a trap inside of the DSS, not with the unending rivalry that existed between the DSS and the police.

The smile faded away. He took two steps towards his desk, then stopped abruptly. He hit his forehead repeatedly with the Newspaper he was holding. He had just figured out a way to set his trap.

Victor!

Edobor was going to be his ace card when setting his trap.

This realization that he now holds an ace gave Dozie a great deal of consolation.

*****

They came in three different cars. Smith was the first to arrive, driving his grey-colored Toyota Camry into the parking lot. He scanned the surrounding area before turning off the car engine. He remained seated in his car, the driver's side window slightly down as he waited for the others to arrive. He didn't have long to wait. As he lifted his eyes to glance at the heavy traffic some sixty meters ahead of him, a police car suddenly edged dangerously away from the main traffic in a breath-taking maneuver that caught other motorists by surprise. Cars started skidding in different directions, to pave the way for the police car. Then came the thunderous sound of horns from motorists to register their disapproval.

Smith watched, as the police car drove dangerously towards the shopping mall. The car started to reduce speed as it entered the narrow road leading directly to the mall, until it came to a stop in front of the mall. Smith strained his eyes, trying to get a glimpse of the person driving the police car. It came to him as a rude shock, when he realized that the driver was no other than Detective Bucknor.

Detective Bucknor parked the police car in one of the reserved spaces directly in front of the mall. She knew the space was reserved for one of the managers of the mall but this didn't bother her. The owner of the space will have to find another space while she is there conducting her business. She looked at her side mirrors, then the rearview. She looked across at the main road, the traffic was now flowing steadily again, and nobody seemed to be paying the police car any attention. She came out of the car and instinctively reached for her gun. Satisfied that the gun was within easy reach, she started walking towards the entrance to the mall.

The sound of a car skidding into the parking lot made Bucknor turn around. She recognized the car and the occupant therein. It was Ayeni, in his metallic grey Volvo. She watched Ayeni get out of the car. He waved to her before closing the car door. She lifted her left hand and waved back. Just then, she noticed a figure got out of a car parked four rows from where Ayeni's car was. As the figure started walking towards Ayeni, she saw it was Smith. Ayeni turned his head towards Smith, lifted his hand in salutation, and waited for Smith to come to him. The two men shook hands, and said a few words to each other, before walking over to Bucknor.

Bucknor was leading the two men into the shopping mall as a family with four children came rushing out. The oldest of the kids, who was not more than ten years old, suddenly dashed towards Bucknor. She came to a stop in front of Bucknor, then pushed a phone into her hand.

"A family picture, please!" The kid screamed excitedly.

Bucknor never had the chance to react as the kid rushed back to join her family, grinning from ear to ear. Seeing this, Smith, followed closely by Ayeni, stepped away from Bucknor. The two of them entered the mall and waited by the glass door. They watched as the family of six began to adjust and readjust themselves in readiness for the family pictures.

Bucknor forced a smile, as the youngest of the kids, who was around four years of age, kept changing positions and assuming different poses in a bid to be the star of the pictures. She took a couple of pictures before handing the phone back to the kid.

She waited, arms folded, as the kid strolled through the photos with her mother.

"Hope the pictures are nice?" Bucknor asked when the kid finally turned her eyes away from the photos.

"Great pictures! Thanks so much, ma'am." The kid said happily.

Bucknor nodded her head, then walked over to join her teammates.

When Bucknor introduced herself to one of the ladies at the counter, she reacted as if she had been expecting her. She signaled to a colleague who was standing some distance away, hands folded and observing shoppers as they walked in and out of the mall. The colleague, a tall but painfully thin lady, approached Bucknor, smiling broadly and exposing a set of even white teeth.

A few minutes later, Bucknor and her colleagues were led into a back office where a massively built man in his mid-thirties was waiting to receive them.

"My name is Jeffrey Balogun, and I am the manager here." The man said, extending his massive hand for a handshake.

"I am Detective Bucknor! These are my colleagues, Superintendent Lekan and Banji of the DSS."

"You were the one I spoke with on the phone," Balogun said.

Bucknor nodded her head. The man gestured for them to sit down. He lowered his bulk on a chair that appeared to have been specially designed to take his weight. He looked momentarily at Bucknor, then rubbed his hands together.

"We have cameras covering certain areas, like I mentioned to you on the phone, but we also have areas that are out of camera coverage."

"I want to assume that the parking lot around here is for customers to the mall, right?" Smith queried.

"That's right. You see, parking fees apply to the CCTV coverage areas." Balogun explained, slightly moving his heavy bulk to face Smith. "And there are areas where customers can park their cars free of charge. In such areas, cars are parked at the owners' risk. This means that we are not liable should anything happen to cars parked in those areas."

"I see." Bucknor wasn't too surprised. She had visited the mall many times but had never felt the need to pay for parking. She imagined that only folks with expensive cars would pay for parking in a shopping mall.

"The person you are interested in, could you describe to me where the individual parked his car?" Balogun asked, eager to assist.

"It was the cars parked at the owners' risk section," Bucknor replied flatly.

Balogun watched as Bucknor's face dropped in obvious disappointment.

"I am afraid that we can't help you very much," Balogun said, sympathetically.

"Are you saying there is no way some of your cameras would capture cars driving in and out of the free parking areas?" Ayeni asked, in his cop voice.

Balogun was unruffled. He was used to handling unsatisfied customers from time to time. It was his job to handle them and diffuse tension. He could tell that Ayeni was becoming aggravated, as were the other two.

"The free parking areas have their own entrance gates. Now, the camera would pick up the customer the moment he stepped out of the parking area. We can check the cameras; it's possible that the individual of interest came in to make some purchases. Then, of course, we will have him on camera."

"I don't think so." Bucknor was hardly audible. She was thinking of the night of the chanced encounter. She didn't think the man would be careless enough to risk being caught on camera.

"Since we are already here, we may as well take a look at the CCTV footage of the area bordering the free parking space. We might get lucky." Smith said.

"I agree with you, Banji. Let's do it." Ayeni said.

"What time frame are we looking at?" Balogun asked, not moving from his seat.

"In the evening, between four and nine," Smith replied. He turned to Bucknor, who nodded her head in agreement.

Balogun reached for his phone and dialed a number. He waited a few seconds before the person at the receiving end responded.

"The time frame is between 16:00 and 19:00 hrs."

Balogun tucked the phone away. He gazed at Bucknor, who stared back blankly. He quickly shifted his eyes to Smith.

"The technical supervisor is on his way. He should be able to assist you in whatever way you want." Balogun shifted his gaze once more to rest on Bucknor.

"Thanks for your time," Bucknor said. She was about to stand up when the door swung open. She turned her head towards the door as a tall man in his mid-thirties walked in.

The man stood directly in front of the door even as the door closed noiselessly behind him. Balogun got to his feet and moved to stand beside the man.

"This is Kunle Bankole, the technical supervisor. He will take you to our viewing room. Like I said, he's in a position to help you find anything captured on camera."

Bankole bowed slightly. He turned and pulled the door open, allowing the trio to pass through before quietly closing the door behind him. He then stepped ahead of them, to lead them to the viewing station.

*****

The viewing room was large and situated on the ground floor of the shopping mall. It has eight large TV screens strategically attached to the wall. Six of the TV screens were positioned in such a way as to allow for total coverage of the different floors in the mall. The remaining two were the ones monitoring the areas surrounding the mall, including the parking areas.

When Bankole walked into the viewing room with the team, the eight personnel who were sitting in front of the TV screens didn't even bother to turn around. They had their eyes glued to the screens, afraid to miss out on activities playing across the screens.

"This is the viewing room, from where we have our eyes on activities within our premises," Bankole said. He pointed to two of the screens that were positioned away from the others. "These two are the ones that are of interest to your investigation."

Smith listened, but his mind was on the guys sitting in front of the screens. These guys, he reckoned, must have the toughest job in the world. He couldn't imagine himself trading his job for all the money in the world, with any of these guys.

"Which of these two is the one covering our main area of interest?" Ayeni asked.

"That would be the TV right over there." Bankole walked over and placed a hand on the TV. "You will have to give me the exact date you are interested in. I only have a time frame as of now."

"Perhaps, we could start by taking a walk to the exact area, where our subject of interest was observed," Smith suggested.

Bucknor stared at Smith, bewildered. She couldn't understand why Smith would make such a suggestion, not when they were already in the viewing room. She had zeroed her mind down to view the footage, not to take a walk anywhere. The earlier they start, the quicker they will be over with it.

"By going to the parking area, Bankole would be able to tell us right away, if the camera has coverage up to that point or not." Smith said quickly, aware that Bucknor was about to oppose his suggestion.

"I agree with you, sir," Bankole said calmly. "That should be the best place to start. Then, I can offer my advice based on the assessment. This would also save us plenty of time.

"That makes sense." Ayeni concurred.

"Shall we, then?" Bankole said, pointing towards the door.

Bankole was hoping, against all odds, that he wouldn't have to spend the remaining part of his day, sandwiched between the two men on his one side and the hard-faced lady detective on his other side, staring at TV footage. He dreaded the prospect.

*****

The visit to the parking area was short and decisive. As Bucknor, who was leading the group, reached a certain parameter, Bankole stopped her.

"Ma'am!" Bankole exclaimed. "The areas from this point onwards are out of our coverage area."

Bucknor turned to face him. "We will proceed as planned to the parking lot. We'll talk when we get there!"

"The car park in question is still some distance ahead. I do not see any reason for us to proceed from here." Bankole countered.

"We will proceed as planned," Bucknor said calmly. She gave Bankole one hard look before walking away.

"If you say so, ma'am," Bankole murmured to himself.

He looked from Ayeni to Smith, wishing one of them would try and talk some sense into Bucknor. Realizing that no help was going to come from either one of them, Bankole shrugged and started walking behind Bucknor towards the parking lot.

Once inside the parking lot, Bucknor pointed out where the suspect's car was parked on the day of the encounter. Bankole was by now convinced that they were engaged in a wild goose chase. He shook his head slowly and deliberately until he was sure he had the attention of Bucknor.

"Like I said earlier, our camera's coverage does not extend to this area."

"That's too bad." Bucknor said sarcastically. She could not help but notice the frustration in Bankole's voice. She started to walk away from the group. Smith and Ayeni exchanged glances.

Bucknor walked some distance away from the group to stand beside a billboard, motionless. She gazed at the spot where the suspect had parked his car on the day of the encounter. Then, as if in a trance, she began to slowly walk towards the spot. On reaching the spot, she stopped and turned around.

Smith and Ayeni watched in silence. Bankole watched but was showing no interest in whatever Bucknor was doing. He was convinced they were out here, wasting precious time.

Moments later, Bucknor appeared to have regained herself. She lifted her head, a forced smile on her face. Then, she started walking back towards the group.

"Is everything okay?" Smith asked, as Bucknor rejoined the group.

"Yeah," Bucknor replied. "I just wanted to relive the event of that day."

Smith smiled a knowing smile but said nothing. There was nothing to say. It was, after all, her experience.

"There's nothing here for us," Ayeni said calmly. "Let's get the hell out of here."

Bankole, who had been standing some distance away from the group, moved closer. He stopped an arm's length away from Smith. He looked over at Bucknor, who stared back at him, expressionlessly. He could feel her eyes burning down on him. He felt hated but couldn't understand why. Was it because of what he said? Or was it a case of transferred aggression? Whichever was the case, he realized that he needed to get away from Detective Bucknor and her condescending look.

"My job was to show you the CCTV footage. I am wondering if there's still a need for that?"

"There's no need for that now." Ayeni answered promptly.

"There's no need." Smith reechoed

"I agree with you guys. Let's get out of here." Bucknor said. She pushed past the men but not without giving Bankole one final look. She started walking back towards the mall and to the police car.

Bankole led Smith and Ayeni out of the parking lot back to the shopping mall. They walked all the way back, in silence.

"I have to get back to the office now," Bankole said as they approached the mall.

"Thanks a lot for your time," Smith said. He extended his hand for a handshake.

Ayeni nodded his head in appreciation, then reached out and shook hands with Bankole.

"Feel free to come around if anything crops up." Bankole said, before walking hurriedly away to disappear into the mall.

Bucknor, who was standing by the police car, watched as Smith and Ayeni walked towards her. She felt slightly embarrassed that she had walked out on her teammates. She comforted herself by blaming it on emotion. They would understand, surely.

"It was a good idea to have visited this place. Now, we can safely erase from our minds, the notion that this place holds some vital clues to solving this case." Ayeni said. He locked eyes with Bucknor.

"That's right. Frankly speaking, I suggest we go back to the office and look the case over." Smith said.

"That's exactly what we should do. Now, let's move it." Bucknor said, forcing a smile.

Bucknor entered the car, and started the engine as Smith, followed by Ayeni, walked away to their cars.

They were not to notice a figure seated in a car, parked adjacent to the police car. He was holding a newspaper with which he concealed a portion of his face. He watched as both Smith and Ayeni drove out of the parking lot. It wasn't until the police car started navigating its way out of the parking lot that the man dropped the newspaper. He started his car and waited.

The police car drove out of the parking lot, followed closely by two other cars. Then, a third car emerged, driving purposefully behind the two cars tailing the police car. No one paid any attention to this third car, not even Detective Bucknor, at first.

Bucknor kept to the pace of traffic like every other motorist. She was trying not to draw a great deal of response from motorists. The motorists responded, though. The moment they noticed the police car, the initial response was to unconsciously check to see if they were breaking any traffic rules and thereafter, drive normally, afraid to make even the slightest traffic mistake. Many road users in Lagos appreciate it when a police presence creates these kinds of rare "good" behaviors. It allows for an easy flow of traffic.

Bucknor was slowly turning her head from left to right as she drove, giving the impression that she was scanning the traffic and looking to catch traffic offenders. It was something she enjoyed doing, guaranteed to generate the needed reaction always. She glanced at her rearview. There was a line of cars driving slowly behind her. Then, she refocused her attention back to the cars immediately behind the police car. She was taken aback when she realized that the three cars behind her were the exact same cars that had followed her out of the mall. She looked to see who was driving the nearest car to her, a silver-colored Mercedes convertible; it was an average-aged woman, fair, and wearing a pair of sunglasses. She swung the police car just a hair to her left, in an attempt to get a better look at the other two cars. The second car was driven by an elderly woman with a much younger lady sitting in the passenger's seat. The third car was directly behind the second car, making it impossible for Bucknor to get a glimpse of the person driving the car. This, in itself, was worrisome.

Bucknor looked ahead. She was approaching an intersection some seventy-five meters away. She made up her mind to turn right onto a road where the traffic was light. She wasn't going to make use of the indicator as she wanted some elements of surprise. She was determined to get a better view of the third car and the person behind the wheel.

The police car got to the intersection and without warning, the car did a right turn. The cars closest to the police car stopped abruptly to pave the way for the police car. The moment the police car started to make the turn, the car directly behind accelerated rapidly towards the police car and started doing the exact same maneuver, seizing the opportunity created by the police car to get out of the slow-moving traffic.

Bucknor was certain that she had gotten a good description of the car by the time she completed the maneuver. It was impossible, however, to get a clear picture of the occupant of the car as her view was obstructed by a mini truck speeding away from the line of cars. There was nothing she could do about that. She drove on.

Then Bucknor heard the sound as some cars blasted their horns behind her. She glanced at the rearview just in time to see a car rapidly making a right turn. It was the third car. It was the car she was interested in. The car had waited until the police car had completed its turn before making a move. Drivers in Lagos are famous for trying to get away from police patrol cars, not in following them, Bucknor thought.

She made up her mind there and then, to pull the car over at the earliest opportunity she gets. She could pull any car over for a search for whatever reason, if need be. In this case, however, she had a genuine reason to do so, reckless driving. She would use the opportunity to ID the driver and see how it goes from there. She started to look for a convenient spot in which to pull the car over.

Chapter Twenty-One

Some one hundred meters away from the intersection, was a sign indicating that an AP gas station was a hundred meters ahead. Bucknor saw the sign and decided to make her move the moment she got to the gas station. She glanced at the rearview mirror once more; the car was still some distance away and maintaining a constant speed. A white Cherokee Jeep was driving behind Bucknor and doing everything possible, to keep a safe distance between it and the police car in front. Bucknor suddenly stepped on the accelerator, making the police car surge forward rapidly. As expected, the Cherokee Jeep maintained its steady speed, making the gap between it and the police car widen even more.

Bucknor got to the gas station and stopped the car by the roadside with the engine still running. She hurriedly stepped out of the car to scan the surroundings. She noticed a gas truck parked inside the filling station, a few meters from where she was standing and discharging its contents. She turned her attention back to the road.

The Cherokee Jeep, which was now a short distance away from the police car, suddenly reduced speed further as Bucknor stepped forward, positioning herself to face the oncoming traffic. She could see clearly now the car behind the Jeep. It was a grey colored Toyota Verso. She braced herself, judging the distance between her and the oncoming Jeep.

As the Jeep approached the police car and with the driver getting ready to stop, Bucknor surprisingly waved the car to proceed. In total disbelief, the driver dutifully continued driving, maintaining a constant speed, clinching tightly to the steering wheel and looking straight ahead.

The Toyota Verso continued driving at a steady speed, towards the stationary police car. Bucknor suddenly lifted her right hand above her head in a stop sign. The Toyota Verso began to reduce speed as the car headed slowly but surely towards Bucknor.

The car was a couple of meters from the police car when it stopped. Then it happened.

One moment, Bucknor was walking towards the car, her hand on her undrawn gun; the next moment, the door to the Toyota Verso flung open. A man emerged from the car and almost instantaneously fired a shot at Bucknor. Instinctively, Bucknor threw herself sideways, falling on top of the bonnet of the police car before rolling over to the other side.

Stepping away from the still-opened car door, the man took a few steps towards the police car and fired more rounds in the direction where Bucknor had landed. The man walked quickly over to the police car, expecting to see Bucknor on the ground, dead or dying. But Bucknor was not on the ground, dead or dying. There was bloodstain on the side of the police car, on the ground and zigzagging away from the police car. He lifted his head just in time to see Bucknor limping away towards the gas station. He raised his gun and aimed.

As if on instinct, Bucknor fell to the ground, face down, as the man fired some rounds at her. The man then stepped away from the police car, in an attempt to get a better angle. At that same instance, Bucknor turned sharply and fired some shots towards the direction where the man had been standing when he fired his last rounds. They were good shots. The bullets hit the police car a few inches from where the gunman had been standing. But none of the bullets had the man's name written on it. Standing away from the police car, the gunman fired more shots towards Bucknor, before quickly walking back to his car.

The road was now completely deserted of human traffic as motorists had abandoned their cars and fled on foot, far away from the scene of the gunfight. The gunman got into his car calmly as if he had nothing in the world to worry about. He could hear the sound of sirens a long distance away. The police were on their way.

He engaged gear and drove away, but not without turning his head to take one final look at the place where he had seen Bucknor fall. It occurred to him that Bucknor was dead or dying.

*****

The first police car arrived at the scene exactly nine minutes after the shooting. It has taken nine minutes of threats and more threats against motorists, all of whom were trying desperately to get away

275

from the crime scene. As the police car navigated its way through the traffic, the one thought on the minds of the two police officers in the car, was to get to the scene of the shooting on time to save their colleague. However, seeing the police patrol car parked by the roadside and riddled with bullets, the thought of saving the occupant of the car quickly evaporated.

The officer in the passenger's seat was halfway out of the car before the police car came to a halt. Gun in hand, he raced to the bullet-ridden police car. He circled the car, and seeing the blood stain on the car, he frantically called out to his partner. The second officer came rushing to join his partner. He also saw the blood stain and, at the same time, noticed that the car engine was still running. He reached forward and turned off the car engine, leaving the key in the ignition hole. He ran his eyes through the interior of the car but there was no blood stain on the inside of the car. He signaled to his partner to come towards him.

As the cops were busy talking to each other, three men suddenly emerged from behind the gas truck. On seeing the cops, they started screaming on top of their voices and waving their hands at the officers. The officers were puzzled.

"Over here! The policewoman is here. She is bleeding profusely!" One of the men screamed.

Without hesitation, the two police officers raced towards the men. They could hear behind them, the skidding sound of more police patrol cars arriving.

They reached the gas truck, and the men frantically pointed them to where Bucknor laid, in a pool of her own blood. Looking at one of the huge back tires of the truck, which was stained with blood, the officers realized right away that Bucknor was alive because she had used the tire as a shield. Her eyes were closed, and she was holding tightly to the lower part of her stomach, from where blood was gushing out from a bullet wound. She was gnashing her teeth in agony.

One of the two police officers quickly returned his gun to its holster and fell to his knees besides Bucknor. The other officer stood guard, gun in hand and ready to engage.

"Stay with me!" The officer on his knee shouted in anguish. He felt for a pulse and nodded to his partner.

The other officer stepped back. He brought out his radio and was about to start relaying messages to the control center, when a sudden sound of commotion made him turn around. Racing towards his position were a couple of policemen, guns drawn and accompanied by a pair of paramedics. Seeing this, the officer stepped further backwards to give room for the new arrivals, as he began to relay messages to the control center. His partner joined him just as he was concluding his report. He looked him over, then raised an eyebrow.

"How bad is she, Fred?"

"Pretty bad. The paramedics are on her case now. Hope she pulls through."

"Hope so, too. Let's go have a little chat with those three guys. They must have seen something."

The two officers strolled casually to where a group of people were standing and watching the events unfold. Seeing the cops walking towards them, a man stepped forward. He was soon joined by two others. They were the men who had earlier alerted the cops to where Bucknor lay.

"Gentlemen, we appreciate the speed at which you contacted the police after the shooting. Thank you." Officer Fred said.

The men appeared stunned to hear a policeman in uniform thanking them. The reverse was usually the case. They began to talk.

"It was after the shooting had stopped that I mobilized my colleagues here to go and check on the policewoman." One of the men who introduced himself as Abdul explained.

"That's right, and I called 911 immediately to report the attack."

"And what's your name?" Fred asked

"My name is James. The policewoman parked her car by the roadside and stopped a car. The shooter was a man. He came out of the car and without warning, started shooting at her. I was working on this truck when it started. I ran as fast as I could to safety."

Police officer Tunde Akin, who had been busy taking notes, paused. He looked at Fred and then at his notebook, before asking.

"What type of car was the shooter driving?"

"I think it was a Toyota Verso, grey colored."

"Did any of you get a description of the man?" Fred asked, looking from one man to the other.

"All I can say is that the man is of average height. Nothing more." Abdul replied.

The other two nodded in unison.

Officer Akin took down the personal details of each of the three men before letting them go. He watched in appreciation as the three men wandered away to rejoin the group of on-lookers. It occurred to him that the quick actions of the three individuals most likely saved the life of one of their own. He pocketed his notebook as Fred pointed towards their patrol car. Both officers turned and began walking back to their patrol car. The crime scene was now a beehive of police activities.

Police Superintendent Ayeni arrived at the scene just as Officer Akin was about to enter the driver's side of the patrol car. Fred, who was already seated in the passenger's seat, observed Ayeni from the sideview mirror. He watched as four police officers led Ayeni towards the place where Bucknor was recovered.

Akin entered the car and looked over at Fred, who shrugged his shoulders. As first responders, they both knew they were in for a very long day. It wasn't as if they were complaining. It was all in a day's job, sometimes. However, the uncertainty that comes with such a long day was the scary part for most police officers. Officer Akin was not immune to this, neither was Fred.

*****

It was some minutes past two o'clock in the afternoon when Dozie ended his meeting with the pair of Smith and Ayeni. It had come to him as a rude shock when he heard of the shooting of Detective Bucknor. This was one shooting no one had seen coming. It was as unexpected as a heavy rainfall on a hot, sunny day.

He had listened as Smith recounted their activities at the mall up to the time of their departure. He had listened attentively, occasionally taking notes, after exchanging glances with Edobor who was also present at the meeting. Ayeni sat with his arms folded across his chest and let Smith do the talking. He noticed that Smith was a better storyteller than he could ever hope to be.

"There was absolutely nothing in and around the mall, to suggest that such an attack was imminent," Ayeni added as soon as Smith concluded his narratives.

"Absolutely nothing." Smith reiterated.

Dozie had looked from one man to the other before putting away his notepad. He trusted these two men and had no reason to doubt their account of the event. His mind was racing as he shifted his attention to Edobor.

"You heard them. This attack was totally unexpected." He cleared his throat. "And unacceptable."

"I don't think the shooting was a coincidence. The shooter must have followed Detective Bucknor from the shopping mall. This is the only logical explanation." Edobor said, an edge to his voice. Dozie looked at him sharply.

"This brings me to the question of how the shooter got to know, that the team will be visiting the shopping mall on that day and time?"

"It beats me," Edobor replied, almost automatically.

"This is something we have to figure out and quickly, too," Dozie said, his face wooden. He sensed Edobor was pondering what he was pondering. He decided to deviate for the moment.

"What are the doctors telling us? Is she going to pull through?" He asked.

"The report is that she's going to make it. It was a lucky escape, according to the report." Ayeni replied eagerly.

The news gave Edobor some level of comfort. He had expected the worst, considering the details he had gathered on the attack. He took a deep breath as it dawned on him that Detective Bucknor was officially off the case. He had liked and respected her for her doggedness and eyes for details. Unfortunately, she was now out of the game. Her shooter must be found as quickly as possible and made to face the full wrath of the law.

"It's comforting to hear that she's going to pull through," Edobor said, relief written all over his voice. "I am scheduled to meet with the deputy director in an hour's time for a briefing."

"I shall be meeting the police commissioner at about the same time." Dozie got to his feet, an indication that the meeting was over. He poked a finger first at Smith, then at Ayeni.

"The two of you were partners to Detective Bucknor. It's your duty to protect her while she's incapacitated. Go to the hospital, make sure she's secured, 24/7."

Smith turned his head towards Edobor, and their eyes locked. Edobor nodded his head in approval to Smith's unvoiced question. Ayeni observed them, and seeing Edobor nodding his head, he got to his feet. Smith followed suit. The two of them walked quietly out of the office.

As soon as the door was closed behind them, Dozie walked over to the chair that Smith had just vacated. He adjusted the chair so that it was now directly facing Edobor; then he sat down.

"I think I have a plan." He announced.

"A plan?" Edobor asked; he raised an eyebrow.

"Yes. A plan that is very likely going to lead us to the mole."

"Am listening."

"My plan is for us to move Detective Bucknor to a different hospital," Dozie explained, a sadistic smile crossing his lips. "Then move her same day to a third hospital."

Dozie waited for Edobor to process the information. Then, he waited for a reaction. Edobor pondered for a while.

"What, if I may ask, is the essence of moving her from one hospital to the other?"

"The essence is to smoke out the mole," Dozie replied, his face deadpan. "As soon as we move her from the present hospital, I will notify you, and you, my friend, will notify the deputy director. I want us to try and rule him out as a possible source of the leak."

"Are you asking me to set a trap for my immediate boss?" Edobor asked, almost jumping out of his seat

"I am not asking you to do any such thing. I am only putting measures in place to help us rule out the deputy director. Wouldn't you want to rule him out?"

Edobor was silent. He couldn't bring himself to imagine Deputy Director Davies as a possible source of the leak. It was simply inconceivable. And here was Dozie, making suggestions that appeared to insinuate just that. This idea was absurd as far as Edobor was concerned.

"I am only agreeing to this absurdity because I want to prove you wrong on this one," Edobor said, flatly.

"I want to assume that the deputy director has a personal secretary?" Dozie asked, careful with his choice of words.

"He has a secretary and a very efficient one at that," Edobor replied, impatiently.

"In my racket, I have seen powerful people in authority divulge top secrets to their secretaries. I have also seen secretaries pass such secrets to a third party for personal gain. Such secretaries think they will never get caught, and frankly, many don't. But every now and then, a few of the unlucky ones get caught."

Edobor knew exactly what Dozie was talking about, but it was hard to imagine this happening with the deputy director. The proposal itself was pregnant with trouble. It could backfire and cost him dearly. However, if this was the only way to clear the deputy director of any wrongdoings, so be it.

"You let me know as soon as you move her, and I will notify the deputy director. Then we see how it plays out."

"I will notify you with the details as soon as she's moved," Dozie said. He sensed the discomfort in Edobor as he got to his feet.

"I will be waiting."

"I am sorry that we've to do it this way, Victor," Dozie said almost apologetically. "We need to do everything we can to get this killer out of circulation, before he kills again."

"I appreciate that fact, Mark. Just keep me posted."

Dozie walked Edobor quietly to the door. He extended his hand for a handshake. Edobor grabbed his hand firmly. Dozie opened the door to let Edobor walk through. He returned to his seat and immediately reached for the telephone.

"Get a car waiting for me in ten minutes." He said to the receiver and hung up.

He waited for three more minutes before storming out of his office. From now on, he told himself, he was taking charge of the operation.

*****

Just about the same time that Detective Bucknor was being driven in an ambulance to the hospital, the secured mobile phone in Westland's drawer began to ring. Westland shifted his eyes from the huge map of Libya that was spread out on his desk; he got up reluctantly and went to retrieve the phone. He checked to see who was calling and grimaced. It was Mr. Red.

Westland picked up the call and noticed that his hands were beginning to sweat. He hated it when his hands sweat in such a way but there was nothing he could do about it.

"Updates?" Mr. Red asked authoritatively.

"Nothing of significance, sir," Westland replied, respectfully.

"How's that?"

"At the moment, everything is under control. It's quiet from their end."

"The investigation is ongoing."

Westland couldn't tell, as usual, if this was a question or a statement. He assumed it to be a question, so he answered.

"The investigation is ongoing but at a slow pace. I am on top of the game and ready to check mate their every move, sir."

There was silence. Westland waited. He knew the caller was still on the phone. He couldn't imagine a scenario where he was to disconnect the phone while Mr. Red was still on the line. He waited for what seemed like an eternity.

"I thought there was another copy of the dossier."

"Nothing yet on that, sir. It would appear as if there's nothing of such."

"You can never be sure."

"True, sir. As of now, nothing of such."

"Make sure you get it, if it surfaces."

"Yes, sir."

"Talk to me as soon as there's an update."

Westland held the phone to his ears until he was certain Mr. Red had disconnected the call. He returned the phone to its holding place before wiping his sweating hands. He was certain there weren't any updates since he hadn't heard from his source. The Libyan project was now his top priority, and the logistics were taking much of his time. He now has sufficient men on the ground to start an uprising in Libya the moment the CIA director gives the go-ahead.

His mind drifted to the dossier. Was there another copy somewhere? He doubted it, but like his handler had said, one can never be sure. He was tempted to put a call across to his source but stopped himself. His source was reliable and would notify him of even the slightest development when it occurred.

Westwood shifted his focus back to the map on his desk and started to study it once more. His eyes were fixed on Benghazi. It was a good place to start the uprising. He took a pencil and drew a circle around Benghazi.

Then he wrote the word "Settled" across the circle.

Benghazi would be the place where the fight to topple Col. Muammar al Gaddafi would begin. He took a deep breath, then stared off into space. He imagined himself in Libya, in a war situation as the rebels advance towards Tripoli.

He reckoned it was going to be the "mother of all wars." He smiled sadistically to himself as he reaffirmed, in his mind, that the only agreeable outcome from this war in Libya, was the destruction of Gaddafi and his army, by whatever means necessary.

Chapter Twenty-Two

The First Monumental Hospital, situated at the center of Lagos, was an elitist hospital. The majority of people patronizing the hospital were people with loads of money to throw around, to avail themselves of the first-class services the hospital provides. The hospital was built on a vast acre of land and modelled in such a way as to make the surrounding area as serene as possible. Trees and exotic flowers were strategically planted all around the hospital, with the flowers adding an extra layer of beauty to the surroundings with their beautiful colors, almost all year round.

It was this hospital that Detective Bucknor was taken to immediately after the attack.

The moment it was confirmed that Bucknor was in the hospital, heavily armed policemen stormed the hospital and completely took over the place, to the shock and disbelief of the medical staff. It was only when Bucknor was rushed into the theater room that the resident doctor decided to assert her authority.

Having carved out a no-go area for the police, Dr. Ann-Marie Adedayo immediately stationed some hospital security personnel around the marked parameters. Satisfied that the police had understood her directives and had positioned themselves well outside the no-go zone, the doctor rushed into the theater room.

It wasn't until six hours later that Dr. Adedayo emerged from the theater room. She walked hurriedly past the security barricade, her face devoid of any emotion, with two junior doctors tailing after her. Sensing that their presence was generating a negative reaction, some of the policemen had moved to an adjacent corridor while others stood guard outside to enjoy the fresh air, filled with flower scent.

When Dr. Adedayo walked into the air-conditioned office, the atmosphere immediately became tense. The police naturally wanted news about one of their own, but the medical team was not too pleased with the invasion of their premises by the police. Hence the tension.

"I apologize for the seemingly take-over of your premises by our men," Dozie said, as soon as the doctors walked in.

"I have seen worse cases." Dr. Adedayo muttered.

Dozie smiled as he regarded Dr. Adedayo. She was in her mid-forties, tall and slim, with an attractive oblong face that had probably won a beauty contest in her younger days. He examined her face for any sign of wrinkles but ended up noticing her full lips and a pair of bright, sharp eyes. The other two doctors, a male and a female, each wearing a pair of heavily thickened glasses, did not interest Dozie. So, he ignored them.

"What's the situation with the detective? Is she going to pull through?"

"She's in a stable condition. She was as lucky as she could be. The bullets miraculously missed all the vital organs." Dr. Adedayo said, her oblong face showed no emotion.

Dozie glanced at Ayeni who was sitting on his left-hand side, then quickly at Smith to his right. He nodded his head at the doctor, allowing a smile to cross his face.

"If she's stable like you said, then how soon can we move her away from here?" Dozie asked.

Dr. Adedayo stared quizzically at Dozie. She was horrified by Dozie's question. How could anyone mistake the fact that she said a patient was in a stable condition to mean that the patient was ready to be moved? Then, she remembered that she was dealing with a cop. She took a deep breath. Cops! She shook her head sadly.

"Her being stable doesn't mean she's ready to be moved anywhere. We still have to keep her under close observation for the time being."

"We are thinking of moving her to another hospital, for security reasons," Dozie said, calmly.

"What do you mean by security reasons? Can't the police provide her with the needed security here?"

"It can be arranged, but we were thinking of moving her to another hospital," Dozie replied.

"She's my patient, and I will not sign her discharge paper until I and my colleagues here, are one hundred percent certain that she's out of danger, okay." Dr. Adedayo said emphatically.

"That's okay with me. I will have to talk to my superiors about this latest development."

"Do that, please."

"For now, we're going to beef up security around here for her protection."

Dozie realized that aside from forcefully taking Bucknor from the hospital, there was no way this oblong-faced doctor, gazing unflinchingly at him, was going to sign a discharge paper. He was wise enough to know when he was bested.

"The security details will start with you getting your armed men out of here. We don't want the kind of publicity their presence here is generating."

"I assure you that we will keep our security presence as low-keyed as possible," Dozie assured.

"Great. That will make the lives of everyone here easier." Dr. Adedayo said as she dragged her chair backward. She stood up, and Dozie hurriedly got to his feet, too.

"Thank you so much for your time," Dozie said, extending his hand.

They shook hands. The two junior doctors got up, but didn't think it wise to shake hands with Dozie. They hovered around Dr. Adedayo, the way a chick would a mother hen.

"We've some other patients to attend to, starting in about ten minutes. Let me know when you have made the security arrangement. It might also interest you to know that the patient has been moved to Room 502." Dr. Adedayo said.

She hurried out of the office, followed rapidly by her two junior colleagues.

Dozie walked out of the doctor's office accompanied by the pair of Smith and Ayeni. His mind was racing. Dr. Adedayo had created an obstacle to his plan of moving Bucknor to a different hospital. How was he going to set his trap if he couldn't move Bucknor? He had to quickly come up with a plan B. The plan B should take into consideration that all the actions envisaged will take place at the First Monumental Hospital. It was doable, he assured himself. All that was needed was a little bit of creativity. Being creative was not something strange to Dozie, as his ability to come up with such creative ideas was the reason he was still holding his top job, and he knew it. He started walking very fast towards his car, as he gave his mind to the problem.

*****

It was midday when the phone rang. Westland raised an eyebrow before walking briskly to where the phone was kept. It has been a busy day for him. The situation in Libya was becoming chaotic, with different tribes fighting each other, trying to become the dominant force in the region, in order to attract the patronage of the United States.

Westland had reluctantly dispatched Tommy Anderson to Libya earlier than scheduled, to begin the coordination of the units that will be under the direct command of the US and NATO covert operations. He was getting regular feedback and was worried that some NATO members were starting to re-access the situation and having second thoughts about going ahead with the original plan. This was unacceptable to him. He knew he had to act fast before the plan to overthrow al Gaddafi was sabotaged.

He picked up the phone, pressed it against his left ear and listened.

"Updates." A familiar voice announced.

"Listening."

"There was an attack on Detective Bucknor in broad daylight."

"And?"

"She was shot. She's in the hospital as we speak. Her situation is critical, but she's alive."

Westland took a deep breath. He was startled, not because of the attack but by the fact that the detective was still alive. What happened to the notion that "anything worth doing at all, was worth doing well?" He asked himself.

"Her current location?"

"First Monumental Hospital undergoing surgery. She could be moved to a different location immediately after the surgery."

"Keep me posted. I need minute-by-minute updates on this one."

"Understood"

Westland disconnected the call. A certain anger filled his gut. He never ordered the hit. But if the hit was carried out for whatever reason, then it ought to be successful. This was not looking good. Shooting a police officer, especially a woman, was something that could generate unnecessary attention. Goddamn it! He felt his fist tighten around the phone, he turned his focus to the phone, staring at it for a couple of seconds, before dialing a number.

As soon as the person at the receiving end answered the call, Westland said,

"The attack was unsuccessful. She's alive!"

Silence.

"Why would you carry out such an attack on a busy street in broad daylight? Have you gone nuts?"

"I had no choice, boss. It happened suddenly."

"I wouldn't want to use the word slip, but you are beginning to slip, big time!"

"She should be dead, boss."

"But she's not! As we speak, she's at First Monumental Hospital undergoing surgery."

"She has to die, boss."

"Agreed, but it's not going to be an easy task. The cops would be all over the place providing security for her."

"That makes it easier for me to get to her, boss."

"I will give you the room number and the security details as soon as I have them."

"I will be waiting, boss."

"This is your last chance. If you fail, there's no telling what the consequence is going to be, for you!"

"Failure is not an option, boss. I assure you…"

Westland disconnected the call and dropped the phone angrily at its holding place. He looked around the office, a certain anger threatening to overpower him. He tried and succeeded in getting a grip on himself.

Then, he came to a reluctant conclusion. Failure this time around will lead to an invitation, then a bullet to the head for his hitman. Case closed.

His mind made up; Westland began to breathe more evenly once again.

*****

The police sergeant quickly opened the door as Dozie came charging towards the car. He saluted briskly as his eyes shifted towards Ayeni, who was a short distance away from Dozie. The movement of the sergeant's eyes made Dozie turn around.

295

Consumed in his own thoughts, Dozie had completely forgotten all about Smith and Ayeni. The two had followed him all the way without saying a word.

"The two of you will have to stay with her 24/7." Dozie barked. "Make sure no one gets to her except the medical staff."

The two men nodded without saying a word. There was nothing to be said. Dozie felt sorry for them. Bucknor was their partner, and they somewhat felt responsible for her plight. It wasn't their fault, but it was going to be an uphill task to convince them otherwise, for now.

"Any of you think the doctor's refusal to allow us to move Bucknor was wrong?" Dozie asked.

"Her decision is in good fate. She can't be moved in her present condition." Ayeni replied.

"She's in capable hands, sir," Smith said, slowly nodding his head.

"The idea of moving her was for her security. We know now that we can't move her." Dozie bit his lower lip. "Like I said, make sure no one gets to her except the medical staff."

Dozie dismissed them with a wave of his hand. He watched motionlessly, as both men walked silently back to the hospital, to resume their duty in Room 502. Once they were out of sight, Dozie reached for his phone and dialed Edobor. He needed to give him the update.

The phone had barely started ringing when it was answered. Edobor had, without doubt, been expecting the call.

"Victor," Edobor said calmly.

"I am still at the hospital premises. The doctor isn't sold on the idea of moving Bucknor."

"I suspected that. We can make them release her to us if it's absolutely necessary." Edobor said.

"That we can do. However, she's in capable hands; I suggest we let her be."

"Agreed. What's the next line of action?"

"She's in Room 502. When you brief the deputy director, take time to emphasis the room number. I will take it from there."

"Take it from there? What do you mean? Are you being vague with me?"

"Relax. I am working out something. I will let you know when everything is in place. Trust me."

"Just make sure you know what you are doing. We must be careful to avoid any unpleasant backlash."

"Trust me, mate. I got this under control."

"I am meeting the deputy director in about forty-five minutes. I will get back to you after the meeting." Edobor said flatly.

"Talk to you later," Dozie said.

Dozie disconnected the call. He took a deep breath, then turned and started walking away from the car, back to the hospital.

He needed to speak to Doctor Adedayo, fast. He has about forty-five minutes to put his plan B into action.

*****

Doctor Adedayo hurried along the corridor. She was about to step into an office when she heard someone call out her name. She turned to see Dozie jogging towards her. She frowned.

"We need to talk; it's urgent," Dozie said, ignoring the obvious frown on the doctor's face.

The doctor looked him over, trying to make up her mind if it was worthwhile, to honor Dozie with her time.

"How urgent?"

"Very urgent. It's about Bucknor and room 502. Change of plan." Dozie whispered.

Doctor Adedayo pointed him to an adjacent office. They walked in together. Dozie was relieved that the two junior doctors, with their ever-piercing eyes, were not around this time. He was almost grateful for this.

"We need to move the patient from room 502 immediately," Dozie said pleadingly.

"Why so?"

"For security reasons. You are obviously not willing to sign her discharge papers." Dozie said. He had deliberately added the last sentence to put the doctor on the defensive.

"I won't." The doctor said firmly.

"Then we have to move her to another room."

"That can be arranged." Doctor Adedayo said.

"Good. We will move her to a new room but keep Room 502." Dozie was gambling.

"That I cannot promise. What's the essence, if I may ask?"

"We don't know if the shooter will make another attempt on her life. The plan is to move her to this other room, then set a trap for the shooter using Room 502."

"You want to set a trap using a hospital?" Doctor Adedayo asked, alarmed.

"We are not using the hospital to set a trap. It may be nothing, or it may be something. We just want to be certain."

"I will have to discuss this with management. I am not in a position to make that decision."

"That I understand," Dozie said.

Dozie watched as the doctor hurried out of the room. He wondered if there was ever a moment when Dr. Adedayo was not in a hurry.

*****

Doctor Adedayo returned quicker than Dozie had anticipated. She walked into the room accompanied by an older man in his late fifties who was a shade shorter than the doctor. The man was immaculately dressed in his sky blue, well-tailored suit with a pair of brown shoes to match. He looked priestly in his completely grey hair, penetrating eyes and clean-shaven face. His slightly protruding stomach was a testimony that he was not one, to shy away from a bottle of beer every now and then.

The distinguished way the man carried himself, left little doubt in the mind of Dozie that the man was the bearer of whatever decision the management had reached. He braced himself to receive the news and to put up a counter, if necessary.

"My name is Adewale Cole. I am the Chief Medical Director here." He extended his hands as he reached Dozie.

"Special agent Mark Dozie. A pleasure to meet you."

"I am here to inform you that your request has been granted. Bucknor is going to be with us for a while. Within the period of her stay here, Room 502 and Room 706 will be at your disposal."

"That's great." It had turned out to be easier than Dozie had anticipated.

"If there's any other thing you need, please liaise with Doctor Adedayo. She's been given the power to work with your team."

"I appreciate that. Thanks." Dozie said gratefully.

"A final thing, though." Chief Medical Director Cole said, his eyes penetrating Dozie's. "Keep my people out of your line of fire. Do I have that guarantee from you?"

"I give you my assurance, one hundred percent," Dozie said without hesitation. He knew it was the responsibility of the police to keep the staff and patients safe, while his plan was in motion.

The Chief Medical Director nodded his head, then walked out of the office without saying another word.

"I will need you to help arrange Room 502 to make it look as if Bucknor was still there, receiving treatment," Dozie said to Doctor Adedayo as soon as they were alone.

Doctor Adedayo frowned.

"We are trying to set a trap, here," Dozie informed her. "While she's in Room 706 receiving treatment, you will continue in Room 502 as though she was there. We are trying to see if a move will be made on Room 502."

"Hope you are aware that this operation is going to cost you a whole lot of money?" The doctor asked, genuinely concerned.

"I am not the one footing the bill. The police authority is more than capable of footing it." Dozie said, a ghost of a smile moving his lips.

"I will see to it." Doctor Adedayo said quietly.

"As I promised, we are drawing down on police presence on the premises. We will station two policemen at the entrance of Room 502 and another two at Room 706. Hope that makes you sleep easier?"

"You do your thing, let me do my thing." Doctor Adedayo replied. Her gaze shifted to the door. "I have to leave you now."

"Should I expect that you would have perfected things in, say, about thirty minutes?" Dozie was pushing his luck.

"I would say, in about twenty minutes if you will come with me and help out."

Dozie was glad for the invite. He eagerly followed Doctor Adedayo, the way a sheep would a shepherd.

*****

Westland heard the buzz. He had been expecting that sound. He got up and hurried to retrieve the phone. It was a message. He opened the phone and read,

"Room 502. First Monumental Hospital. Police presence minimum."

Westland picked up another phone and dialed.

"Boss."

"Room 502. Police presence minimum. Keep your eyes opened for any sign of trouble."

"Yes, boss."

Westland felt a surge of anger willing up inside of him once more as he disconnected the call. He had given this individual a final opportunity to rectify his error. If he fails, he dies. It was as simple as that.

Chapter Twenty-Three

Malik Nasiru had led a life of crime. He was the youngest of six children, born to a truck driver father and a mother who was a full-time housewife. Though the family had lived a simple and uninspiring life, Malik was determined; from an early age, to change course and to grab from life all the good things that life has to offer. At age thirteen, he had succeeded in organizing a group of schoolboys, from virtually every class in the school, into an army of thieves. Their mission was to steal items from their classmates, then hand over the stolen items to Malik, whose job it was, to sell the items and thereafter, share the proceeds accordingly.

The boys trusted Malik, and he, in turn, trusted the boys to keep the flow of stolen items steady. The rule was simple among the thieves- *"steal as many items as you can, but make sure to bring every single item to Malik for onward transmission to the buyers."* This rule was never broken except on one occasion, when two of Malik's classmates felt the need to break away to form an army of their own.

Malik had gotten wind of their decision and had tried unsuccessfully, to reason with the boys on the need to have a re-think. It had ended in a stalemate. One strong boy against two. Malik had watched as the two boys teamed up and began a series of activities, aimed at ousting him from his position as the "king" of thieves. Malik had watched from a distance. And Malik had plotted their downfall.

A few weeks later, the principal of the school had his Nokia phone stolen. A search was quickly conducted, and surprisingly, the phone was recovered in the locker of one of the two boys. The chap was subsequently expelled from the school. The other boy knew exactly what had happened. Malik had staged it all, leading to the fall of his comrade. A lesson was learnt, *"don't mess with Malik"*. The remaining chap had become an outcast and no longer welcomed by the army of thieves. His popularity quickly nosedived. Malik had won, and his "kingship" regained.

At age eighteen, Malik had shot and critically injured a cop during a bank robbery gone wrong. The robbery was supposed to be an easy enough job, for a four-man gang led by Malik. The plan was to attack a branch of the Oceanic International Bank located some ten miles from Benin City. Malik had spent a week casing the Bank before making his move. Within the one-week period, Malik was convinced he had collected all the necessary information to make the job an easy one. All he needed thereafter, was a getaway car with a good driver, a gunman to hold the three security men hostage and a fourth man to enter the Banking Hall with him. In his plan, the operation shouldn't last more than ten minutes. A quick get-in, then grab as much money as is readily available and disappear. A piece of cake it should be, "all things being equal". No one mentioned to

Malik, however, that in a real-life situation, all things are not usually equal.

On the day of the robbery, Malik had ensured that his plan was followed to the letter. No deviation whatsoever, and it had worked. Malik had entered the Bank wearing a mask and brandishing a semi-automatic rifle. He had been accompanied by Frank Osita, who was armed with a large hunting knife. Once inside, Malik quickly made an announcement.

"Nobody's going to get hurt if you do as I say. The money is not yours, so don't be a hero and get yourself killed."

The threat in every word was easy to decipher. So, when Malik ordered everyone to lie face down, everyone obeyed. Frank led the Bank manager and one of the cashiers to the safe room and forced them to fill two large sacks with money. Thereafter, Frank ordered the two hostages to carry the sacks of money. He silently led them out of the Bank to the getaway car. Once the money was safely in the boot of the car, Frank led the two men back to the Bank. He gave a signal to Malik before calmly returning to the car to wait.

Moments later, the car horn beeped twice. It was the signal indicating that it was time to make themselves scarce. Malik walked out of the Bank and headed straight to the getaway car. When he reached the security gate, he nodded to Emeka-the gunman holding the security men, then glanced at his wristwatch. It was the signal to Emeka that the mission was complete.

Malik reached the getaway car, he turned to observe Emeka, who was walking hurriedly towards the car. Then, out of the corner of his eyes, Malik saw a cop suddenly emerging from around the corner. He froze as Emeka quickly flattened the semi-automatic rifle along his right side to shield it from the roving eyes of the cop. Malik watched, his heart threatening to burst at any moment. Suddenly, the cop shifted his attention from Emeka to Malik and the getaway car. He frowned, then changed direction, to start walking towards the car.

Emeka got to the car and made to open the door. Malik whispered something to him about the cop. He turned slowly to observe the cop, who was still some distance away but whose hand was now hovering around the gun in his holster. As soon as Emeka turned, the cop, by some instinct, suddenly realized that something was not right. The people in the car in front of him were up to no good. The cop, who was either very brave or utterly stupid, kept walking towards the car. Then it happened.

Malik lifted the semi-automatic rifle and fired several rounds towards the cop, hitting him multiple times. The cop fell to the ground, his gun barely out of the holster. The driver of the getaway car engaged gear and drove quickly away, leaving behind a dying cop.

*****

That night, Malik met for a final time with his cohorts, to notify them that he was skipping town. He advised them to do likewise. He had not reckoned with a cop suddenly showing up uninvited, during the robbery. This he had not factored into his plan. He had had to improvise by shooting the cop. Now, the heat was on, and every policeman in town was out looking for them, with one thing on their minds, vengeance.

"The police are all over the place hunting for us." He had informed them. "I am getting out of town and won't be coming back for a long time. I suggest you do the same. Getting caught is not an option for me."

The next morning, Malik had said goodbye to his mother, assuring her that he was leaving home to seek a better life for himself elsewhere. The mother was shocked but said nothing. There was no need to say anything, not when Malik had made up his mind to leave. She knew her son too well to suspect that he was fleeing from something, but she played dumb, preferring not to ask questions. So, Malik left, never to return, not even when he got words a few years later that his father had died.

Malik arrived in Lagos the next day with plenty of cash. He had asked around and was quickly able to move into a two-room apartment somewhere in the Ikeja area of Lagos. He bought himself a second-hand Honda Accord car a couple of days later and was set to begin a new life in Lagos. He had decided from the beginning that he wasn't going to work for anybody, preferring instead to register his car with an Uber company as a driver. He was happy with the job and the flexibility that comes with it, giving him plenty of extra time for extra activities. His definition of extra activities was largely centered on living the fast life and making extra cash whenever the opportunity presented itself.

It was on a rainy Friday night when Malik, who was now twenty-six years old, had an encounter that altered his life forever. He had just left the club around midnight and was driving home from Victoria Island when he noticed a white man, standing alone by the roadside. The man was carrying a briefcase and smoking a cigarette in the rain. Malik decided there and then that he wanted the briefcase and whatever else the man was carrying. He drove towards the man, who, seeing a car driving towards him, began to flag down the car.

Malik parked the car right in front of the man and watched as the man climbed into the car. The man, who appeared drunk, mumbled.

"Kofo Abayomi Street."

"Where in Kofo Abayomi Street?" Malik had asked.

"Just drive. I will let you know when we get there."

Malik drove for about ten minutes before turning away from the main road into a side road. He drove along the road for a few more minutes, then stopped the car suddenly. He quickly got out of the car and jerked the back door open before the man knew what was happening. The man lifted his head lazily to see a gun pointing directly at his face. He swallowed hard.

"Get out of the car now, or you die!" Malik ordered.

The man-made to exit the car, his right hand holding firmly to his briefcase.

"Leave the briefcase in the car!" Malik barked.

The man swallowed again before letting go of the briefcase.

Malik stepped back to create room for the man to climb out of the car, the gun still pointed at the man. It was a mistake. The man reacted so fast that Malik never saw it coming. The left leg was out of the car and positioned firmly on the ground, but unknown to Malik, the right leg would be his nemesis. As the man wrestled his right leg out of the car, the leg, as if by its own volution, suddenly shot out to deliver a powerful blow to Malik's groin. The kick sent Malik flying violently backwards, to crash into a concrete wall acting as a barricade. The pain was so great that Malik completely forgot that he had a gun in his hand. The man approached him calmly and yanked the gun out of his hand. Malik lay on the ground, drifting between conscious and unconsciousness. The man could have easily taken his life, but he didn't. The man drove the car with Malik in the back seat, his hands and legs tied together with belts, to his residence.

When Malik eventually recovered sufficiently enough later that day, he found himself tied to a bed. He was confused. He was even more confused to see a white man standing and hovering over him, with a cup of coffee in his hand. The man's name was Tommy Anderson, and it was he who recruited Malik Nasiru as a hitman for Raymond Westland. It was him that Malik trusted with all his heart.

Room 502 was a beehive of activities, with Doctor Ann-Marie Adedayo and her team constantly in and out of the room. The two hard-faced cops stationed outside the room had to routinely step aside to give way for the medical personnel. It was an easy enough job for the cops except for the long, boring hours of keeping watch and expecting something unusual to happen. The tough-looking cops were not complaining, though. It was all about one of their own, and they were here to keep her safe. This was not unusual. What would be unusual, however, would be a killer attempting to gain access to Room 502. So, the cops kept their eyes open, scanning the vicinity for any sign of an intruder and trouble.

Far away from Room 502 and towards the end of the long corridor, Doctor Jim Oseni was leaning against the wall and reading through one of the two files in his hand. He was deeply engrossed and seemingly oblivious to the happenings around him. While doctors, accompanied by nurses, were rushing to and from all around him, Doctor Oseni remained unmoved, buried in his own world. But in this world of his, his mind was focused on Room 502, watching and observing patiently like a vulture.

When he was ready, Doctor Oseni suddenly came alive. He turned and walked briskly towards a nurse who was walking hurriedly down the corridor. The nurse was busy talking on the phone and smiling excitedly at whatever the person on the other end was saying to her. The doctor came to a stop in front of the nurse.

Startled, the nurse lifted her head to stare momentarily at the doctor, then quickly ended the call. She somehow got the impression that the doctor had walked up to her, because she was making a personal call, during work hours.

"I am sorry, sir." She said apologetically. "It was an urgent personal call."

Doctor Oseni couldn't care less. He regarded her the way a predator would a prey.

"Listen," he said in a low voice. "I have a patient to attend to in Room 502, and I want you to accompany me, as the nurse to the patient."

The nurse immediately started to protest. She was on duty and assigned to another doctor. She wasn't going to allow some doctor to commandeer her without going through the proper procedure.

"I am sorry I can't do that. I am sure a nurse is already assigned to you. Go to the reception and ask for the nurse."

The nurse started to turn away, but Doctor Oseni blocked her way. He slightly flipped open his white doctor's suit to reveal two guns, tucked into both sides of his waist. The nurse stared at the guns in disbelief. She opened her mouth to say something, but the power of speech had left her.

"Listen to me carefully." Doctor Oseni said. "You will go with me to Room 502 as the nurse assigned to me. Two cops are stationed at the entrance, and we will go past them without any drama from you. If you try any tricks, I will kill you and the two cops. Do you understand?"

The nurse nodded her head quickly. Her heart was racing so fast she thought she was going to have a heart attack.

"Get hold of yourself, nurse." Doctor Oseni inclined his head sideways to read the name tag on her chest. "Remember this nurse, Shade, your only chance of getting out of this alive is if you follow my instructions."

The doctor gently tapped Nurse Shade on the shoulder, then adjusted his suit to conceal the guns. He smiled at the nurse and turned his attention towards Room 502. He could see the two cops indulging themselves in small talk. He began to walk calmly alongside Nurse Shade towards Room 502.

*****

As was the usual routine with the cops standing guard outside Room 502, they immediately stepped aside to pave the way for Doctor Oseni, accompanied by nurse Shade, who smiled at the cops as she walked past them. Once inside, the nurse who was now shaking uncontrollably, moved to a corner of the room. She tried but couldn't take her eyes away from the doctor. She watched, eyes almost propping out of their sockets, as the doctor pulled out a gun.

The sight of the gun made the nurse's legs buckle with fear. She fell to her knees with such force that the doctor turned momentarily to stare at her. Then he turned his attention back to the job at hand by reaching into the large inner pocket of his suit to bring out a silencer. He stood motionless and quickly fitted the silencer to the gun. Once done, he took two quick steps forward, lifted the gun and fired three shots in quick succession at the image on the bed. There were no sounds. The silencer saw to that.

The doctor turned around and regarded Nurse Shade. She was still on her knees, her head touching the floor, in a prayer posture. He was about to turn the gun on her when something made him to stop. He turned around once more towards the bed, his instinct warning him that something wasn't right. He walked quickly to the bed and pulled the white sheet off the patient on the bed. This was when he got the shock of his life. A full-sized human doll, looking almost human, was laying on the bed, eyes wide open and staring at the ceiling above. He was momentarily confused. He groped around the bed for blood, but there was none. Was this a trap of some sort? Was he in the wrong room? His mind started to race. He took a deep breath to calm himself, trying to get his thoughts back. It worked.

The first thing that came to Doctor Oseni's mind after getting his thoughts together was to get out of Room 502, as quickly as possible. Then he remembered Nurse Shade and was glad he hadn't been hasty in killing her. He pulled the bed sheet over the doll and turned to the nurse. She was now in a sitting position, wide eyes and staring distantly at him. She was in shock. He knew exactly how to handle it. He would go over and slap her out of it.

The doctor had only taken three steps towards the nurse, when the door to Room 502 busted open. Smith rushed in, dashing to the right, while Ayeni, following closely behind, dashed to the left, guns drawn. The scene was as if it had been rehearsed. The doctor managed to fire two shots before his body was ridden with bullets coming from multiple directions. The impact of the shots lifted him up and deposited him violently on the bed, alongside the doll. He was dead, long before he hit the bed.

The rapid sound of gunfire jolted the nurse out of shock. She clapped both hands around her ears and began to scream.

*****

Victor Edobor's mind was racing as he pondered over the incident at the hospital. He was now convinced, without any iota of doubt, that the leak was coming from the deputy director's office. It beats him. He could not bring himself to imagine that the deputy director could be sabotaging a mission that he, himself, had personally commissioned. There must be another explanation. The prospect of having to confront the deputy director with his suspicion was not something Edobor was looking forward to. Damn it!

By the time Dozie walked into his office, Edobor had already made up his mind on his next line of action. He would bypass the deputy director and go straight to the DG to make his suspicion known. It would then be left to the Director General to decide on the next line of action.

"I think I know who the mole is," Dozie said as he strolled into Edobor's office.

He paused, allowing Edobor to process the information. Edobor shrugged and said nothing. He pointed Dozie to a seat.

"By all indications, Jessica is the mole," Dozie said in a whisper as he lowered his tank of a body on the chair. "I came with a warrant allowing you to bug her phone."

Edobor was startled. Jessica? She was a strong possibility. That explains it all. Edobor smiled meaninglessly at Dozie.

Dozie was taken aback by Edobor's reaction. He raised an eyebrow, confused as to what was going on in Edobor's mind.

"I will bet my pension that Jessica is the mole. The question now is, who she's working for?"

"You are probably wondering about my reaction to your statement," Edobor said, the smile fading away from his face. "It's because I never factored Jessica into my equation."

"Well, now you know. However, this is not something we can prove at the moment. We need solid evidence." Dozie dropped a signed warrant on the table; he pushed it across to Edobor.

Edobor looked at the warrant distantly. Dozie was really moving fast, not minding whose ox is gored.

"You are asking me to spy on one of our own?" Edobor asked, disbelief written on his face.

"I am asking you to help catch a traitor," Dozie replied. "If she's a spy, then she isn't fit to work in your organization."

Edobor considered Dozie's argument briefly, then took a deep breath. Dozie was right. It was totally unacceptable for anyone to work with the DSS and yet, spy on the organization. He wondered if he was being lackadaisical because the matter now concerned Jessica. Did he not conclude some moments ago that he was ready to take the matter before the DG?

"I will arrange it with the technical guys immediately after this meeting." Edobor eyed the warrant suspiciously.

"Make sure to get that done, before you inform the deputy director about the incident at the hospital."

"Why is that necessary?" Edobor asked, puzzled.

"My calculation is that Jessica will make a call to her contact about the incidence. If she does, then we catch her red-handed, simple." Dozie replied calmly.

"I was told that the dead man's real name is Malik Nasiru!" Edobor said. He looked at the report Smith had submitted to him for confirmation. "And he was Doctor Jim Oseni when he came calling at the hospital."

"That's right," Dozie said. He pointed to the warrant in front of Edobor. "The next line of action is for us to catch Jessica red-handed, after which my job here is done."

"I won't be needing the warrant, Dozie," Edobor said flatly. "We have our way of going about it."

*****

Shola Davies listened and would not interrupt until Edobor was through with his report. The report, as far as the deputy director could tell, was detailed enough. He was not to know, however, that Jessica had been considered as the likely mole. Edobor had deliberately withheld that part of the report from him.

"I am wondering how the assassin got information that Bucknor was in Room 502," Davies said.

"We are working on figuring that out, sir," Edobor responded.

The deputy director nodded slowly. He was relieved that the assassin had been neutralized, but there were still plenty of unanswered questions.

"Nice thing that the team decided to move Bucknor to a different room at the last minute."

"I told them the same thing, sir," Edobor said.

"Do we have any clue as to who the mole is?" Davies asked.

"We are working on it, sir."

The door opened noiselessly, and Jessica walked in. She went straight to the deputy director and handed him a note. She took two steps back and waited. The deputy director read the note.

"I will see him in five minutes."

Jessica nodded and walked out of the office. Edobor thought he caught a glimpse of the deputy director's eyes following Jessica as she cat-walked out of the office, but he wasn't certain.

He was, however, certain of one thing, the mole was about to be fished out. The thought gave him no comfort. The negative fallouts of it would be catastrophic.

*****

Jessica laid naked on the floor beside Davies. The deputy director started talking about the various meetings he had attended during the day. Jessica listened, gently stroking Davies's chest. The details of the meetings were boring to her, but she listened anyway. It wasn't until Davies got around to the reason for Edobor's short visit that Jessica became actively interested. She listened attentively, as Davies furnished her with details concerning Malik Nasiru's failed attempt to assassinate Bucknor.

"And where is Malik Nasiru now?" Jessica had asked nonchalantly.

"Dead! He was shot and killed by our men."

Had Davies been observant enough, he would have noticed that Jessica stiffened the moment he mentioned that Malik had been killed. Jessica listened for several more minutes as Davies continued to talk. She was no longer interested in what he was saying. She gently detached herself from Davies and reached for her clothes. She was fully dressed by the time Davies picked himself up from the floor.

Davies noticed the change in the atmosphere. It was purely his fault. He shouldn't have mentioned the fact that Malik had been killed. Violence of any kind has a way of affecting women. This has affected Jessica's mood somehow. He pulled Jessica over and kissed her. She pulled herself away gently, forcing a smile. Davies blamed himself.

*****

Jessica returned to her office and closed the door behind her. She stood motionless and processed the information she had just received. Then, the usual guilt she felt every time she had sex with Davies came. She closed her eyes and tried to erase the memory from her mind, but she couldn't. The thought of her dutiful husband implanted itself in her mind. She shook her head to try and clear it.

Then she remembered that she needed to make a call before leaving the office. She picked up her phone and dialed a number. The person at the other end answered immediately.

"The name of your man is Malik Nasiru, and he's dead. He went to the hospital to take care of business. He had a shoot-out with the men stationed there and was killed."

"Understood," Westland said coldly.

"What's the next line of action?" Jessica asked.

“Nothing for now. Just sit tight. I may be leaving Nigeria any moment from now for Libya on an assignment. I don’t know if I will be coming back soon, but I will see to it that you are well taken care of.”

“You know how to reach me, if you need me.”

“Sure. And thanks for everything.” Westland said.

“Thank you, too.”

Jessica disconnected the call. Then she picked up her handbag and her set of keys. She suddenly felt relieved as she walked out of the door.

She had no way of knowing, however, that this call to Raymond Westland had sealed her fate.

Chapter Twenty-Four

Janet Anthony had not checked her mail since the death of her husband. The motivation to sit in front of a computer, a thing she would normally do first thing in the morning, just wasn't there. She was aware that she most certainly had unread emails piled up, but she reckoned that the vast majority would comprise of condolence messages. She was still trying to get over the death of Anthony, and reading condolence messages wasn't going to help her achieve that goal. This singular factor has been the driving force behind her unwillingness to sit down in front of a computer to start reading through emails. This was, until today.

Janet sat in front of the computer stationed in a corner in the living room, fidgeting. She wasn't sure if she really wanted to use the computer or not. She sat in front of the computer for a while, not able to make up her mind, staring zombie-like at the screen, unmotivated. She closed her eyes, trying to summon some inner strength. When she opened her eyes, she pulled the keyboard towards her. Then, she logged in.

The bright light coming from the computer blinded her momentarily, making her pull back her head. She used her hand to shield her eyes. Gradually, she lowered her hand as her eyes became accustomed to the light. She stared at the desktop and was surprised at the many documents that were saved on it. She made a mental note to delete some of the documents at the earliest opportunity and to store some others away in files.

She clicked on Yahoo Messenger, wondering if she still recalled her password. On the first try, her Yahoo page opened. She almost smiled. Her mind was, after all, still intact.

Janet stared at the volume of unread messages, not sure which mail to open first. She continued to gaze at the messages, her mind refusing to focus. She was about to turn off the computer when it occurred to her. The last time she checked her email was the morning that Anthony was murdered. The logical thing to do, she reasoned, was to start checking from that day. She reached for the mouse and started strolling lazily, until she got to the day that was of interest to her. She started to move her eyes quickly through the messages, taking notes of the sender and message title.

It wasn't long before she spotted something that almost stopped her heartbeat. The second to the last mail that came in on that day was from Anthony. She stared at the message title, "My Ace Card." Strange title for a message, she thought to herself. She knew as a fact that Anthony was in the habit of sending important documents to her mail, for easy recovery in the future. She checked the exact time the message was received: 3.56 P.M. It was around the time Anthony was scheduled to meet Smith. And this was shortly before Anthony was killed. With a shaking hand, Janet focused the cursor on the message, allowing it to rest on it for a while before clicking. She opened her mouth in total disbelief as she read the message.

"I have a copy of the dossier in a USB format. It contains all the details needed to expose the fraud. Unscrew the wall clock and retrieve it should anything happen to me. You will know who to give it to."

She read and re-read the message several times, then turned sideways to glance at the wall clock. She shook her head slowly and started to laugh hysterically. Anthony's sense of humor was amazing, even in death. She laughed a bit more. Now, she has an Ace card. Her late husband had seen to that. Energized, she got up and walked briskly to the wall clock.

*****

Smith walked out of the meeting with Janet, feeling like the luckiest man alive. In his possession was the dossier in a USB format, the same dossier that had cost Anthony his life.

Smith couldn't immediately believe his ears when he got the call from Janet.

"Get here as fast as you can, Banji. I got the Ace card we have been looking for." Janet had informed him.

"I am on my way, ma'am." Smith had said after his initial shock.

Smith had driven the way he had never driven before to Janet's residence. The moment he stepped into the living room, he was immediately taken in by the transformation he saw in Janet compared to the last time they met.

"Boy, am I glad to see you. Have a seat." Janet had said, pointing him to a chair.

"The pleasure is on me, ma'am."

"I have some tea, and I insist you have a cup." Janet had said to Smith, who was glad to accept the offer.

Over a cup of tea, Smith had listened as Janet had narrated the events leading to the discovering of the USB. She had laughed all the way while she talked, amazement written all over her eyes. Smith sipped his tea, occasionally laughing along.

"Here, this is my Ace card." Janet had said after telling her story. She offered Smith the USB stick as if she was offering him a trophy.

Smith collected the USB, closing his hand around it. He nodded to Janet in appreciation.

"Would I be right to assume that you have made a copy for yourself?" Smith asked, respectfully.

"You may assume that I am able to take care of my interest," Janet replied, smiling broadly.

Smith smiled, too. He was glad to finally have the dossier in his possession. Janet deserved the right to keep a copy, if only as a souvenir. After all, her husband had paid the ultimate price for what is now freely handed over to him. Besides, Smith believed deep in his heart that Anthony would have wanted Janet to keep a copy, just in case.

"Thank you very much, ma'am; I really appreciate this. Smith said. He took a deep breath. "Once again, I am sorry for your loss."

"Just go do your job, Banji. And thank you for your doggedness. I will be watching the TV to hear some good news."

*****

There were seven men in this elaborately furnished room at the Aso Rock Villa, Abuja. Six of them sat in seats arranged around a large semi-circle table, while the seventh man sat on a single chair, positioned slightly away from the group of six. He was a bespectacled smallish man, who was doing all within his power to stay unnoticed. Directly in front of them was a single seat reserved for the big guy, the President of the Federal Republic of Nigeria. The men sat still, expecting the President to walk through any of the four bullet-proof doors at any moment.

They didn't have long to wait. One of the four doors suddenly opened, unannounced. A Secret Service agent held the door open, as the President walked through it into the room. The men hurriedly got to their feet. The President walked over to the single seat, refusing to pay any attention to the men until he got to his seat. Then he lifted his head and nodded to the men, before sitting down. The other men waited until the president was comfortably seated before they, almost in unison, did the same.

The President looked directly at the Director General of the DSS, Hamzat Abubakar, who got up and introduced both Victor

Edobor and Banji Smith to the President. When the President's eyes came to rest on Police Commissioner Micheal Armani, he also stood up and introduced special agent Mark Dozie and Police Superintendent Lekan Ayeni to the President.

"I have read the report." The President began. "I spent the night reading and familiarizing myself with the details."

The President gazed at Abubakar intensely, then shifted his gaze to Deputy Director Davies. His attention then shifted from Davies to the set of pens arranged horizontally in front of him. He selected a red pen, reached for a notepad and began to scrabble something on it. After a moment, he stopped writing. Then he picked up the notepad and stared purposefully at it, the movement of his eyes showing he was reading whatever it was, he had written.

"Where is Jessica?" The President asked, his eyes still on the notepad.

"She'd been arrested and undergoing interrogation," Abubakar replied.

"I see."

The President looked up, his face hardened, and his eyes became ice cold. He looked utterly ruthless. He zoomed his eyes on Abubakar, pinning the icy eyes on him and leaving the Director General feeling very uncomfortable.

"I want to assume that Deputy Director Davies is here to personally hand in his resignation letter."

Abubakar wanted to shift his eyes away from that of the President but couldn't. It was as if those icy eyes of the President had hypnotized him.

"You will be right to assume that sir." Abubakar conceded in an unsettling voice.

The President again turned his attention to his notepad. He started his scrabble once again. He was still writing as Abubakar stood up and personally escorted Davies out of the meeting to hand in his resignation letter. He stopped writing the moment Abubakar re-entered the room.

"I want Jessica prosecuted to the full extent of the law." The President ordered.

"She will be charged within the next few days, sir," Abubakar assured.

The President turned his attention to Police Commissioner Armani. The police boss quickly adjusted himself to sit upright, chest out.

"What is the situation with Detective Bucknor?"

"She will pull through, sir," Armani replied. He felt himself sweating as the President's eyes pierced through him.

The President consulted his notepad, then lifted his head to gaze at Armani once more.

"Every member of the investigative team is to be promoted to the next rank with immediate effect. That includes you, Commissioner."

Police Commissioner Armani got up and briskly saluted the president. The others, except for Abubakar, did the same. They weren't expecting the President to be this magnanimous. They were overwhelmed. Each man was trying his best not to show any kind of emotion. That would come later, much later, away from the President and away from the Aso Rock villa. Now, it was all about remaining focused and giving one hundred percent attention to the President.

"This Raymond Westland of a man. He's the one responsible for it all, the deaths and Bucknor." The President said calmly. "He must be made to pay the price, a high one at that, for his actions."

"Mr. President, sir. The hawks in Washington, D.C., will do everything in their power to protect him. He acts on their behalf." Abubakar said, almost pleadingly.

"I am aware of that. I want you to liaise with Internal Affairs and declare him persona non grata. Then give him 24 hours to leave the country."

"From intelligence gathered, sir, Raymond is about now boarding a plane out of Nigeria on his way to Libya."

"Then let's damage his image as much as we can. Let's make it difficult for him to get a smooth landing in Libya."

"I will put resources in motion to that effect, sir," Abubakar said.

"Raymond Westland is never again welcome to Nigeria, understood?"

"Yes, sir," Abubakar replied.

The President consulted his notepad one final time. He shook his head slowly, his face showing nothing but contempt. He dropped the notepad noiselessly on the desk, then pushed it slowly away, to the far-left corner of the desk.

"Dick Charles is one of the most corrupt politicians in all of modern history." The visibly upset President said. "It's hard to believe that an individual could be this corrupt. His crime against Nigeria stinks to the high heavens. He was the mastermind of all the financial crimes committed against Nigeria, using Halliburton. Sadly, he escaped justice even in the US using his political leverage."

The men present said nothing. They have all seen the report and knew the extent of Dick Charles' involvement in the Halliburton scam in Nigeria.

"Dick Charles will pay a price, no matter what." The President continued. "To this end, you are to look for businesses connected to him one way or another, here in Nigeria. Compile the list and submit it to me as soon as possible. This government will nationalize such businesses."

The President turned towards Nuru Ibrahim, the Economic and Financial Crimes Commission's boss, who was sitting away from the group. The EFCC boss quickly adjusted his glasses to focus on the President. Everyone in the room followed the President's gaze to stare at Nuru Ibrahim. They had completely forgotten that the EFCC boss was present at the meeting. He had, true to his nature, listened to all that had transpired without making himself visible.

"You are to begin the arrest and prosecution of all those mentioned in this file, immediately. Leave no stone unturned. We owe this much to Anthony and to the nation."

"Right away, sir." The EFCC boss affirmed.

The President rose to his feet. "Well done, gentlemen. All of you." He walked over and shook hands with each of the men present.

Then the President started walking away towards the exit door, which was held open by a Secret Service agent. Suddenly, he stopped. He turned around to face the men who were still standing and waiting for the president to exit the room.

"I have two letters for Janet, Anthony's wife. A condolence letter and a letter of appreciation." The President said. He looked across at Smith. "Banji, I want you to personally deliver these letters to her. Her husband Anthony was a patriot. He did noble, and the nation own him and his family a debt of gratitude."

That said, the President reached into the left breast pocket of his suit and brought out the letters. Smith quickly stepped forward. The

President handed over the letters to Smith, who saluted briskly. The President took a final look at the others, nodded, then turned and walked through the open door into another room, to preside over another meeting.

*****

In a dimly lit living room, in his vast mansion located in Wyoming, Michigan, Dick Charles, cap in hand, was watching the news from the large Smart TV hanging on the wall directly facing him. The news headlines were confirming developments that his contacts in Nigeria had already hinted him about. The Economic and Financial Crimes Commission (EFCC) was getting ready to indict him on bribery and corruption charges.

He couldn't understand how his network of powerful politicians and businessmen in Nigeria, could allow the situation to degenerate to such an extent.

"Damn Raymond!" he screamed.

Raymond Westland had assured him that everything was under control. Had Raymond downplayed the situation? He didn't think so. Raymond wouldn't dare. He was smart and knew the consequences of undermining him. Then, what could have possibly happened?

He forced his eyes away from the TV screen and was about to turn it off, when the News anchor's words literarily forced his attention back to the screen.

"The President of Nigeria has announced that businesses and properties confirmed to have been linked to Halliburton will be forfeited to the Nigerian State, and all individuals involved in the financial crimes, both Nigerians and foreigners, will pay a heavy price ..."

"Son of a bitch!" Charles screamed and tossed the hat out of his hand. He got to his feet and began pacing up and down the vast living room. Finally, he picked up the remote control and turned off the TV.

The living room was now as quiet as a graveyard. Charles could hear his own heartbeat. The unfortunate situation in Nigeria and its trickledown effects around his world, was totally unacceptable to Charles. The situation must be remedied fast. And someone, as usual, must pay a price for this.

He walked to the large mahogany table in the middle of the room to pick up his mobile phone. He dialed a number, but the person at the receiving end didn't answer immediately. He waited impatiently for a while, then dialed again. This time, he was in luck.

"Are you watching the News and seeing what I am seeing?" He asked, trying to sound patient.

"Absolutely, sir. I am monitoring the situation." The rich baritone voice of Mike O'Brien replied.

"Goddamn it, Mike! Goddamn it to hell! This is nothing but bullshit and is threatening to become an embarrassment." Charles screamed down the line.

"I will do all within my power to minimize the damage, sir."

"You will have to do more than that, Mike. Put pressure on that son-of-a-bitch calling himself the President of Nigeria."

"We are putting machinery in place for that, sir."

"Don't forget Mike, there's always a price tag. Look for the bastard's price tag and apply it. The son-of-a-bitch is talking of confiscating businesses and properties; that is unacceptable."

"Sir," Mike O'Brien said calmly but firmly. "My task is to minimize the damage to you personally and not to businesses and properties within the borders of Nigeria."

Charles thought he dictated a note of irritation in Mike O'Brien's voice. He ignored it.

"That I understand, but we can't just allow that bastard to start running wild as he deems fit."

"I will keep that in mind, sir."

"I will appreciate that," Charles said, then ended the call.

Deep in thought, Charles walked to the in-built bar situated at the entrance to the living room to fetch a bottle of whiskey. Realizing that he was still clinging tightly to the mobile phone, he proceeded to drop it into his trouser pocket, before pouring himself a glass of whiskey.

He drank down half the swallow in one gulp. The whiskey burnt down his throat so hard that he gasped for breath. He shook his head vigorously as the burning sensation in his throat and chest area slowly subsided.

Charles walked slowly back to sit in front of the TV. He took another sip from the whiskey but this time, he felt no burning sensation. He remembered how powerful he once was, even before he became Vice President of the United States. Back then, he could, with just a phone call, make any problem go away. But those days were long gone. He was getting old and was no longer as powerful as he once was. The Democrats were now in charge and running the country, the way they deemed fit.

He knew he was still untouchable, but his reputation could be at stalk if nothing is done, to checkmate this problem stemming from Nigeria and Halliburton. As a company, Halliburton was no longer operational, so why wouldn't those fools in Nigeria let the sleeping dog lie? He couldn't count on total protection from the Democrats even though he had looked out for many of them in the past. Goddamn it!

His mind drifted to Raymond Westland who was now out of his reach, free from his control. He shook his head regretfully as he realized that his control over Westland and all the others was based on the extent of leverage he had in Washington. It dawned on him also that his leverage was now becoming a burden rather than an asset around Washington, D.C.

His mind drifted to his daughter Isabela, who was running for a senatorial position. He reflected for a while, then stared at the liquid content in the glass. He drank down all his swallow. This time, he felt the burning sensation once more. He gnashed his teeth as he came to a decision.

He was going to pull all his resources together to help his daughter Isabela win the election into the US Senate. This was the only way to protect himself and his legacy, when his own flesh and blood was out there in the senate, looking out for his well-being.

Having reached that decision, he felt a certain feeling of relief overpower him. He dropped the now-empty glass on the table closest to him and started to imagine a future with Isabela as a Senator. He dozed off with this thought in mind.